The Drowning of
Alison Alyward

The Drowning of Alison Alyward

A Mark Dangerfield Detective Novel

Genevieve Lyons

Five Star
Unity, Maine

This novel is a work of fiction. Names, characters, places, and incidents are either the product of the author's imagination, or, if real, used fictitiously.

Five Star First Edition Mystery Series.

First Edition, Second Printing

Published in 2001 in conjunction with Tekno Books and Ed Gorman.

Set in 11 pt. Plantin.

Printed in the United States on permanent paper.

Library of Congress Cataloging-in-Publication Data

Lyons, Genevieve.
    The drowning of Alison Alyward : a Mark Dangerfield detective novel / by Genevieve Lyons.
        p. cm. — (Five Star first edition mystery series)
    ISBN 0-7862-2999-3 (hc : alk. paper)
    1. Antiquarian booksellers—Fiction.   2. London (England)—Fiction.   I. Title.   II. Series.
PR6062.Y627 D76 2001
823′.914—dc21   2001018148

This book is for Maria and Oliver and, as ever, Michele.

CHAPTER 1

She lay face down in the water, floating effortlessly, moving gently to and fro with slow, sculptured grace, and she was dead, dead, dead. Like Ophelia, drowned.

Ophelia had drifted gracefully, hands folded: 'Her clothes spread wide; And mermaid like, awhile they bore her up . . .'

Not Alison. Alison did not stare tranquilly on the world, did not gaze serenely up at the clouds, looking at the blue and beautiful world. Her head was turned from life, face bloated, trailing weeds between her swollen fingers. She was staring wide-eyed at the muddy bottom of the reedy river and fishes darted in and out of her open mouth.

The verdict was death from drowning, a fact that was obvious. The question was how? Why? Was it an accident? Had she committed suicide? Or was it foul play? The police followed every avenue of enquiry, then closed their books on the affair and decided on accidental, though how anyone could fall into a river so shallow and marsh-edged, was, they agreed, a mystery. The suggestion in the press and among friends was that Alison Alyward had committed suicide.

In the heart of the peaceful Berkshire countryside such violence was unexpected and it seemed strange. Alison Alyward had taken her own life while spring came over the land, while birds sang and daffodils spread carpets of gold, and the primrose sun washed the world in gladness. The beautiful, the seductive, the alluring Alison Alyward had committed suicide, or had had a near-impossible accident. The marks on her throat were probably caused by the undergrowth found plaited around her neck. So the pathologist testified. After all, they had to cut her body free from the weeds that bound her, anchoring her beneath the willow tree. That last she did have in common with Ophelia.

There had been no trace of drugs in her body.

When Wendy Cadbury asked me to lunch at Mosimanns she talked about Alison Alyward almost exclusively, but I couldn't think what she was getting at. She did not come to the point until the meal was nearly finished. Over the delicious Roulade of Smoked Salmon with quark and chive mousse, followed by poached fillet of beef with horseradish vinaigrette, then Snow Eggs with caramel cobwebs, I waited patiently for her to tell me why she really wanted to see me.

I had never lunched with Wendy before. She was an acquaintance, a friend of my mother and I was at a loss as to the purpose of my being asked by her to this wonderful Club Restaurant. However I was happy to accept and I enjoyed the lunch enormously. The food was delicious and Wendy had a brittle wit and she put herself out to be amusing, making me throw back my head and laugh at her diverting repartee. Until, at last, over coffee, she came to the point. She brought up the tragic death of her young friend once more.

"I liked Alison a lot," she said, quite unnecessarily. I knew they had been close and the way she had spoken of Alison over lunch left no room for doubt. "And I don't believe her death was either accidental or suicide. It's tosh, Mark. Alison never did anything by accident." Wendy paused and stirred her coffee. "I want you to find out who killed her," she added casually.

I choked and spluttered, a sliver of the almond *petit four* sticking in my throat.

"I heard how brilliant you were over that affair in Greece last year," she continued airily.

I had stumbled inadvertently upon a murder on a Greek island the previous summer and had sat back and watched events develop, and being uninvolved, came up with a solution. Through that I had achieved a notoriety that I had done little to deserve. I forebore, however, to contradict Lady Cadbury. "I have plenty of money, as you know," she said, her shrewd eyes flickering across my face. "I'm prepared to pay you well for your services."

"You want me to investigate?" I still could not believe my ears. That anyone in her right mind would seriously employ me to investigate a murder on so slight a recommendation amazed me.

"Well you see, Mark, it's like this. The police have run out of steam. They are unwilling or unable to proceed further. You cannot imagine the seedy alcoholic PIs I've interviewed. They are either crass or muscle men. You, dear boy, are a gentleman. You'll do it discreetly. You won't be horribly out of place in Mayfair or Belgravia, and I'm afraid most of the men I saw would be. They would obtrude most inappropriately in the circles Alison frequented. You, dear boy, will fit in beautifully. No one will suspect what you are doing. It's all quite perfect. Besides, your mother is a friend of mine," she said as if this clinched the matter. "A hundred dollars a day and expenses," she said, smiling mockingly at me.

"Is this a joke?" I asked, suddenly suspicious.

She shook her head. She was middle-aged, attractive, thin as a beanpole. My mother said that Wendy Cadbury had manufactured herself. She was a Nancy Reagan clone. She toted a Yorkie called Babs who wore Tartan bows and she smoked a lot and consequently smelled of tobacco with a little Chanel No.15 mixed in. Her eyebrows were plucked to a fine line. Her clothes were St. Laurent. She had done everything she could, via surgery—collagen, laser and cosmetics—to procure an even, symmetrical facade. Face, figure, features were all tidy. Nothing flamboyant, nothing too large or too small. Teeth crowned. A medium nose and eyes, face smoothed out, expressionless. Face and figure sexless. She was a skinny clotheshorse who I found very unfeminine.

My mother said it was very sad that Americans like her wanted to eradicate their past from their faces. Looking at them, she said, you felt they had no experience, that there was nothing, absolutely nothing behind the perfected mask. They ran backwards to youth, unable to understand that it cannot be caught, that time flows onwards, not in reverse.

I just found her sexless. She had been married at least three times, maybe more, Mother was not sure. Her first husband was an Englishman, a sportsman, irresistible and feckless, he was also a gambler. While they were still married Wendy had fallen for a poet, also English, also feckless. It seemed she couldn't resist irresponsible charmers. He had swept her off her feet while he was on a lecture tour of America and she was home on a visit. He had emptied her bank account and ran off eventually with a philosophy student from Columbia. He had become, he said, fed up with Wendy's frantic promotion of him and his work. He actually did not *care* about success, a tendency of his that Americans found hard to understand. He held the idea that poets should become successful and famous *after* their deaths, and was quietly confident that immortality was in store for him, eventually, but after his demise. This did not suit Wendy at all. She had seen herself as the mistress of a *Salon a la Madame Recamier*, the centre of a fashionable, artistic group, the leading light at parties frequented by Truman Capote (still alive then) and Gore Vidal, David Hockney and Tennessee Williams (also alive). She was sadly let down by a husband who sat in pubs (or the nearest American equivalent) all day, and quoted Blake and Milton to adoring students. She was a snob. But then, so was my mother.

So, once again she found herself with debts that would have made Kashoggy blanch and, Mother said, she had then disappeared off to Europe. There was no obvious way that Wendy could make a living enabling her to function at the level she aspired to, so she looked around for someone who could procure it for her.

Mother said she had been very attractive before her tinkering days had smoothed her out into bland prettified and petrified middle age. She had had children, Mother said, but she had put them into schools while she lived in Europe. They stayed there when she came back and began to scour London society for a suitable husband.

She had discovered Lord Cadbury and with admirable tenacity, pursued him relentlessly, snaffled him and married him. He was, I believe, as surprised as the rest of England to find himself hooked. A bachelor, not at all gay, enjoying his freedom with an unlimited supply of dollybirds at his beck and call, he had to give up his pleasant way of life and knuckle down to being Wendy's husband. This all happened in the sixties, and the poor man found himself, without knowing how it had happened, run to ground, trapped and caught by a determined American. Wendy usually got what she wanted. He had never really recovered.

"But he seems to adore her, Mark," Mother had said to me on more than one occasion having seen the Cadburys at Ascot, Henley or Glynebourne. "Mind you, darling, he doesn't accompany her to Annabels or Tramp. That would be going too far for Archie. But it doesn't stop her. I believe she's been seen in Stringfellows! Lord, will the woman never act her age? She goes with her son, for God's sake."

Be that as it may, Wendy lived 'high off the hog' as her countrymen would say. She lunched at Harry's Bar and the Connaught, gave frequent parties at which all the *glitterati* were happy to be seen. She wore Valentino and St. Laurent, her shoes were Ferragamo and Frisson, and she packed them in Louis Vuitton. She bought her cashmere in the Burlington Arcade, her furs at Fendi, and she enjoyed it all to the hilt. She always seemed a little anxious, though. She was so afraid she might miss something, some event she *should* have been to and had declined. At a first night at the Haymarket she wondered what was happening at Covent Garden. Had Placido Domingo sung after all? When she dined with the Bluffields in Cheyne Row, she could not help speculating on what kind of party she was missing at the Lenuins in Chester Square and whether Salman Rushdie had been smuggled in and would be there and she would miss the event and would regret it all her life. Wendy was always physically in one place whilst mentally in another.

But she was kind, loyal and generous. She was good to her friends and she took friendship seriously. Thus her concern about Alison Alyward. "Just see a few people," she said, "Ask a few questions, Mark. Find out what her 'set' was up to. It can't hurt. It's all too . . ." she waved her hand, long built-up nails painted cerise, stabbing the air like butterflies. "Too . . . tidy. It's all been tidied out of the way. *She* has been tidied out of the way. She was here one minute, the next . . . gone. The whole of London seems to have forgotten her. She is cast off, like a product that has passed its sell-by date. It's unseemly, really, how quickly one is forgotten." She stared over my shoulder into the middle distance, lost in her own thoughts.

"Tell me what you know," I said, but she answered my question with one of her own.

"Did you know Alison?" As I nodded she added, "Of course you did. It would have been impossible for you not to. What I meant was, how well?"

"Not very well I'm afraid. I saw Alison around," I answered. I thought about her for a moment, the Alison I knew, seen across a room, laughing. Leaving a party on the arm of the escort of the moment, a banner of bright hair, a trail of Lanvin 'Joy', and a sudden dimming of light at her exit. I remembered her incredible face; those Slavic cheekbones, golden skin, taut across the small straight nose and jaws; the feathered definition of eyebrows, fine as the stroke of a Japanese pen; the large sensuous mouth, American teeth; the mane of fair hair, highlighted in the fashion of the moment with shards of pure sunshine. Add to that endless legs and a dazzling smile and you have Alison Alyward. She was not a girl one overlooked, yet what Wendy said was true: society had forgotten her already.

I had never spoken to her. She was so outside my orbit, so unattainable that it had never even occurred to me that our paths would cross in any way other than the most perfunctory way. The men she dated were either old and rich or impossibly handsome, and she was the kind of girl who reduced me to a stammering idiot in seconds.

And now I was being asked to investigate (unofficially of course) her death.

"She was not popular," Wendy was saying. "Beautiful women rarely are. Too much jealousy involved. She made other women feel inadequate. Just by looking as she did. Men too. Great beauty intimidates most men, takes their confidence away. So Alison was not universally liked."

"But that would hardly constitute a motive for murder."

She raised her coffee cup to her lips, made a face and lowered it, turning for a waiter who hurried to her side. "Cold," she said. "Please bring me some more," she asked. She sounded imperious, yet gracious. She loved playing the Queen Mum. She quite overlooked the fact that it was her own fault the coffee was cold.

"Oh?" she said looking at me intently. "So, you think murder?"

I shook my head. "Oh, come on Wendy, if it wasn't natural it was unnatural. Murder is what you are implying."

"I suppose I am," she smiled. "I liked her very much, you see. She decorated life. And she never tried to flirt with Archie."

Archie was Lord Cadbury, and I would be amazed by the foolhardiness of any female who tried anything with a man as heavily guarded by his wife as Archie Cadbury. Wrestling a python would be easier.

"Let me tell you about Alison," she continued, leaning across the table. "She was lonely. Can you believe that? A girl as dazzling as Alison, lonely?" She looked at me incredulously. "It's difficult to believe, isn't it?"

I did not reply, merely nodded my head in agreement. In my experience beautiful women are invariably lonely. There is an invisible wall around them that prevents normal relationships and they are trapped inside it. How was the great beauty to believe she was truly loved for herself alone and not simply for the way she looked? How could you divide the two?

"Alison talked to me," Wendy was saying, "but she never really told me anything. And I'm not at all sure that everything in her life was, as the lawyers say, above reproach."

"Where do you suggest I begin?" I asked.

"My dear boy, that's what I'm paying you for."

I was flustered, unsure of myself suddenly. "No . . . I did

14

not mean . . . Could you give me a list of her friends. That's what I meant."

"Well, as I said, Mark, I hardly knew who her friends were. She was quite secretive." She took out a mini-notebook in a gold Gerrard folder, flicked open the clasp, lifted the pen from the spine and thought a moment. "There were, of course, the Fab Four." As my brows shot up she added, "Her set. That's what they were called. Let's see. Revel Blake. You know him surely?"

I knew him. Sponger, gambler, irresponsible, but madly good-looking favourite of the debs, yes, I was on nodding terms with Revel. I had also been at college with him. It was an acquaintance I did not wish to further. "She adored him," Wendy continued. "Talia Morgan was her best friend . . . in so far as these girls *have* best friends. Alison shared an apartment with Talia. In Wilton Crescent. That's all I know really. She knew *everyone*, but," she shrugged, writing down the names and addresses, "I thought her a rather solitary girl. When she came down to Arlie Hall," (this was Wendy's house in Berkshire) "we used to go for long walks. She would link her arm in mine and say nothing at all. They were very pleasant, those walks."

She squinted up at me through her cigarette smoke. "You know, Mark, the more I think about it, the surer I become that *something*, something happened to . . . I don't know, *change* her. There was something, those last weeks . . ." her voice trailed away.

I interrupted her reverie. "Did she have any family?"

"An aunt brought her up. Alison never talked about her. She didn't seem to include her in her life."

"Anything else?"

"Just that," Wendy hesitated, then looked at me like a bird, head on one side, "Well, Mark, *I'm* sure Alison was a lovely person. It's just that, so much mud was thrown after she died, and, for her sake I want it all cleared up."

I stared at the portraits around the paneled walls. It was a restful place. A group of businessmen came in. One bowed to me and I bowed back.

Wendy did not notice. "Here are the expenses for your first week," she said, "You'll find it quite adequate." She laughed. "I refuse to push envelopes stuffed with money across the table as they do in films. So you'll have to make do with a cheque."

"That's perfectly all right," I said, accepting it. I felt a twinge as I did. I was not at all sure I was capable of helping her and I felt a qualm taking money from her before I had accomplished anything. However I reminded myself that it was the done thing and, after all, I was giving her my time. At this thought I pulled an inward face at myself. It was a very pleasant way of giving anyone your time, lunch in Mosimanns.

She did not look at the bill and I did not look at the cheque. I was dying to peek, but I restrained myself. She threw an American Express card on the salver on top of the bill, and when the writer returned with the little form for her to sign, I could have sworn she never even glanced at it.

I rose and followed her out into the primrose sunshine. She turned and gripped my arm. Her eyes were pleading. "Clear it all up, Mark," she said. "I find I can't rest with questions buzzing in my head. Clear it all up, there's a dear boy."

Then pulling her jacket down at the back, she turned. A black limousine with a uniformed chauffeur was waiting for her at the kerb. She pattered over to it on her high heels, got in, waved an elegant hand as she disappeared inside. The chauffeur slammed the door, got in, started the engine and the car slipped away soundlessly.

I could at last look at the cheque, which I still held in my hand. The amount it was made out for was staggering. Either Wendy Cadbury had a blinding faith in me, or she was stark mad.

CHAPTER 2

I stood for a moment in the sunlit street. Hyde Park Corner was to my right. Knightsbridge to my left. The traffic snaked from Kensington and Old Brompton Road, and from Park Lane down Piccadilly and towards Victoria. I was not sure where I wanted to go next. I had no other appointments that day and I wanted to think. I also wanted to tell someone, to get someone else's reaction. I was not sure yet what to think of the proposition, whether to laugh or to seriously imagine I was capable of detection. Perhaps the Villa Blanc had been a fluke after all.

I thought of my mother and, mind made up, strolled in a leisurely fashion to the bus stop, and caught a number nine to High Street Kensington.

I gazed out at the carpets of crocus around the base of the chestnut trees and the golden waving masses of daffodils as the bus edged its slow passage along beside the park. There were blossoms everywhere.

I got out at the Commonwealth Institute and crossed the road to the Holland Park entrance. A few drunks lay flat out like dead things on the grass. Uniformed nannies pushed baby carriages briskly along and a couple of French women, trim in tennis whites, legs tanned, hair short and squeaky-clean, gossiped, hands, shoulders and arms active as they crossed to the courts on my left. Their voices sounded staccato and sexy to me. There were a couple of colourful punks sitting on a bench, hair Mohican, clothes Oxfam out of

Kensington Market. They were rolling cigarettes and looked half-asleep to me. A few matrons walked their dogs, waiting patiently at every tree until their canine masters were ready to leave off sniffing and peeing and recommence the walk they were clearly in command of.

Holland Park is the most secretive and mysterious of the London parks. Dense foliage shrouds it in green gloom, and rabbits and squirrels are the territorial landowners. You get out of their way. The peacocks strut and scream and the sun is held prisoner.

I walked briskly now, enjoying myself and trying to sort out what I knew.

When I reached the other side of the park I walked down to Holland Park Avenue and crossed to Landsdown Road which commenced right beside the tube station and is a delightful residential road, lovingly tended terraced houses on both sides with apron gardens in front.

My mother lives in the second block down from the station. There is an old chestnut tree beside the gate. Its roots have almost pushed the railings over and the bowl of the tree, like a huge Spanish onion, protrudes from the ground. Its base that day was surrounded by crocus, yellow, purple and white, peeping from between the clefts in the ash-gray, gnarled and twining roots. There was a cherry tree in bloom halfway up the garden scattering confetti looms on the green patch of lawn. Spring in London, I thought, is entrancing. Perhaps it is everywhere.

Stoury answered the bell. A stout porridge-skinned Scotswoman, my mother's housekeeper, I had known her forever.

"She's workin'," Stoury said severely, trying to hide her pleasure. She adored my mother but it went against her character to show happiness or joy, and she hid such emotions under a prickly exterior. I hugged her, kissed her cheek and ignored her hostile manner knowing what lay beneath.

"No, I'm not working, Stoury," my mother's voice sang out, "That you, Mark? I'm in the sitting room. Come in darling, do. How nice to see you." My mother was stretched on the deep, comfortable sofa, a bowl of daffodils on the low table beside her, another behind her and another in the wind embrasure.

"I am just about to order some tea. Will you join me Mark?" she asked.

I nodded and she told Stoury to bring afternoon tea for two. I sat.

"So, what's up?" Mother asked.

The room is cosy and cluttered. Magazines on the table in front of the sofa: *Tatler*, *Vogue* and *Harper's*, *Time* and *Newsweek*, *What's On* and the *Independent*. An empty silver cigarette box and a heavy crystal ashtray containing a couple of biros (Mother leaves biros about everywhere), a chocolate wrapper and some rubber bands were pushed aside when the tea arrived on a silver tray.

"Mother, remember last year? The Greek thing?"

She nodded.

"You were very bright about that," she said. "As I remember."

"Well, I don't know. Thing is, Wendy Cadbury . . ."

"Wendy?"

"Yes, Mother. Wendy has asked me quite seriously to look into Alison Alyward's death, which she thinks is, *was*, murder. I don't . . ."

"Murder? I thought she committed suicide."

"That's what Wendy wants me to find out. Whether it was. Or not."

"Then you must, dear," she said absently. "Tell me

20

more," she said and lifted the heavy silver teapot. She poured us tea.

"Wendy is sure Alison did not drown herself. She is also sure that it was not an accident. To quote her, 'Alison never did anything accidentally.'"

"No," my mother agreed, "She was a very contrived young lady. She and that little threesome, Revel Blake, Talia Morgan and Jason Bestwick hung out together. People used to call them the Fab Four." She looked at me quizzically, "You know, like the Beatles in the Sixties."

"I *do* know, Mother," I said. "Yes, Wendy mentioned something about that," I said, and added, "So she's prepared to pay me to . . . look into it."

She stared at me, riveted.

"How much?" Her china-blue eyes were avid with curiosity.

I showed her the cheque. She whistled, her face comically impressed.

"But, Mother, it's a bit much. I'm not at all sure I'm worth all this money, and I'm not sure either that I can deliver."

"Nonsense, Mark. You were always like that. You don't think you can do something, then you manage it brilliantly. Remember R.E? And all those Copts and Gnostics and Orthodox, God knows how you did it. To this day . . ." She brought herself up short. "But to the point. Of course you can. At least you can try. She's paying for your time, right? And you can't afford to turn down that much money, can you?" Mother sipped her tea, "It's nice of Wendy though," she remarked, "to look into Alison's death. I wonder how many people have such a friend?"

"Lots, I should think," I ventured.

"Of Alison's type? I doubt it."

"Of Alison's type? What do you mean?"

"Alison, and remember I hardly knew her, Alison was invited places, all the right places because she was beautiful. People liked to be *seen* with her, but not many of them *liked* her. I don't think she had much confidence in herself. Not really. Oh, she looked as if she knew why she was invited where she was invited. She couldn't understand her own popularity, couldn't see what people saw in her. She spent her time wondering why she caused such excitement, such a stir. We are never beautiful in our own eyes. We see the flaws. She kept expecting to be found out, unmasked. But I'll tell you something, Mark; she was looking for something more than the other three of her rackety friends. She knew there was more to life than the eternal round of pointless parties they went to. I've often surprised Alison looking preoccupied and troubled. She was searching for something. Who knows what? And now she's dead, poor love, and it's too late. She'll never find whatever it was now."

Mother looked at me sadly. The soft skin puckered in the first tissue paper creases of middle age on the curve of her neck.

"But, as I say, I did not know her well. I just watch. Observe. Those are my impressions." My mother reflected a moment. "But you know, Mark, the last time I saw Alison she looked different. Something had changed, cleared for her. Her face was wiped clean of that look of provocative sexuality it usually wore. She looked younger somehow. Full of purpose. I don't know what. But it was lovely to see."

I listened intently to what she said. I trusted my mother's judgment. She had an uncanny way of sensing what went on inside people. She used to say that no one could tell what passions seethed beneath the calm exterior of the people one met socially, but if one were receptive enough, one could *sense* them.

22

"Jealousy *smells* different to fear, and hatred to envy," she used to say.

"Listen Mark," she continued, "George Barrington is giving a bash tonight. Why don't you join us? The Fab Three will be there and you can assess to your heart's content. You are good at that."

"I'm having dinner with Mandy," I said. I hadn't asked her yet, but I was fairly certain she would say yes.

"Have dinner, then bring her along. I'll square it with George. Do you know Barclay Norman?" I shook my head. "Well," she went on, "he was with Alison the last time I saw her, about a week before her death. They laughed a lot I remember, and Revel Blake sulked. Barclay will probably be there tonight. I can introduce him if you'd like to meet him. Unless you know him already?"

"No, Mother. And I'm very grateful."

My mother is a writer. She writes romantic novels. However, she is the most down-to-earth person I have ever met.

My father died of cancer when I was twelve years old and we both miss him sorely. He was a lovely man: decent, honourable, imbued with old-fashioned virtues. I might have found this irksome if he had lived on until my late adolescence, but, as it is, I remember him as a gentle, reasonable man who always had time for me.

However he left Mother very short of cash. She was in exactly the same position as Wendy Cadbury, but whereas Wendy looked desperately around for someone to sort things out for her, Mother fell back on her own resources. She had the house, of course, and the car and my father had left her some gilt-edged securities, but they gave her barely enough to cover expenses, and my mother is definitely a frill's person, someone who likes the icing on her cake. She is generous and extravagant. She loves spending money. She liked to live a social life.

Something had to be done if she wanted to continue living in the style to which she was used, so she started writing, on the theory that if Barbara Cartland could do it so could she. No one was more surprised when her books were not only published but sold extremely well and made her more than enough money to live exactly as she wished.

"Well," I said now, "I'll certainly want to question everybody. However, let me start with you. Did you know Alison's family?"

She shook her head. "She didn't have one. An aunt brought her up, I believe."

"So she spent her life in the country?"

"As far as I know. Then she came to London and caught on."

I nodded. That had been my impression too, but I did not want to take my impressions as gospel.

"One last thing, Mother. If Wendy is right and Alison was murdered can you think of any reason anyone would have to kill her?"

"Hundreds," my mother said crisply. "She was beautiful and amoral. Anyone like that creates danger. Jealousy. Envy. Hatred. Revenge. Deadly Sins. Deadly reasons for murder. Alison stirred up passions all the time. She enjoyed doing it. Except for that last time. As I told you, she had changed."

She frowned. Her eyes are very shrewd. "You like doing this, don't you?" It was not really a question. "You like probing."

"Yes. I love it," I replied.

"What's going to happen to the shop?" She raised her hand and wagged a finger at me. "And don't tell me! Don't tell me, Mandy'll do it for you?"

"Hopefully." I laughed.

"She'll do it. Mandy'll do anything for you. She'd die for you." She said it lightly.

"Well," I said, rising, "I hope it doesn't come to that."

With hindsight they were prophetic words.

"I'll hope to see you both this evening then," she said.

I kissed her and left.

CHAPTER 3

I grabbed a cab at Holland Park Avenue and it took me down
Earls Court Road to Worlds End then up the Kings Road to the
shop.

It is a neat building on the Kings Road; Dangerfield
Books, with ye olde fashioned frontage, bow-windowed,
wood surround and full of both rare and new books. I love
books. I fell in love with them when my father opened a
leather-bound volume of *Treasure Island* on my fifth birthday
and began to read it to me. I didn't understand a word but I
had begun a love affair that has endured. I have loved books
from that first moment when I breathed in their heady scent,
the mixture of leather, print and paper. I have been so permanently enamoured of the feel and smell and contents of books
that I chose to make them a full occupation. They became my
business.

Mandy Richardson looked up as I entered. A plain girl
with an amazingly interesting face, she can beguile me into
preferring her to the greatest beauty. Her face is a perfect
heart. Ivory skin sprinkled with freckles across cheek tops and
a nose, which is small and retrousee. Her mouth is wide, generous and humourous and her eyes full of hazel lights, little
dots that seem to sparkle and gleam and dance. She wears her
brown hair pulled back in a ponytail, but curls and tendrils
escape across her face and caress her ears and the nape of her
neck.

Mandy is an art historian doing her Ph.D. working for me whenever she can, and while she is doing her thesis on the Camden Group. She loves the Stones, shares my passion for books and is as crazy about opera as my mother and according to the latter is in love with me. Her greeting when I entered was, however, anything but friendly.

"Where the hell have you been, Mark?" she asked, eyes flashing. I forgot to say that those dazzling lights could turn quite quickly to angry sparks and spitting flames. "You said you'd be back after lunch and it's nearly five-thirty now. I know your lunches are long, but this is ridiculous."

"I'll pay you double for the extra two-and-a-half hours," I said, taking the wind out of her sails. The size of Wendy's cheque made me feel generous. However, she was not so easily mollified.

"The money's not the point," she said, "It's . . ."

"I thought it was," I replied primly.

"Don't be facetious," she snapped. "The point is, you should have phoned. Where were you?"

"With Wendy Cadbury."

"She pretty?"

I laughed. "God, no. She's fifty, if she's a day. Fifty pretending to be thirty-something."

"Oh I see," Mandy said in a subdued voice.

"She wants me to investigate Alison Alyward's death."

This stopped Mandy in her tracks. "Greece?" she asked, round-eyed.

"Ummm. I went to Mother to sound out the idea. That's what kept me."

"What did your mother think?" Mandy and Mother got on very well together, too well I sometimes thought.

"She was encouraging."

"So you're going to take it on?"

27

I nodded, paused and looked at her and saw her eyes questioning me. "If you'll do the shop?"

"Oh Lord," she cried, looking up to heaven.

"At double your usual salary," I said rapidly. I would be lost without her.

She capitulated. "Okay," she said, then, "Can I help?"

"If I need help, I'll call on you, Mandy, never fear."

"Truly?" She was excited. I nodded again.

"Did you know her?" I asked.

She knew who I meant. She shook her head. "No. I've seen her in the gossip columns. Nigel Dempster. She's always in *Hello*. But I do know her flatmate, the girl she shared with—Talia Morgan."

"Do you?" I was surprised. Mandy didn't hang out with the fashionable set.

She smiled. "Sure. We were at school together. We sometimes have supper together."

"Could you arrange to do that tomorrow night? With me along?"

"Sure," she said, looking delighted. "I'll set it up."

At that moment the doorbell tinged and Davina Ravenscroft came into the shop. Tall, elegant Lady Ravenscroft was a collector of rare script.

"Good day, Mark." She smiled at me. "Anything new come in?"

"I'm afraid not, Davina," I said, "but I'll let you know when anything interesting does."

I could see her uniformed chauffeur standing at attention outside at the curb and beside the Rolls. It was her husband, Lord Ravenscroft, whose money was "new"—as my mother, ever snobbishly, put it—who insisted on such ostentation.

Davina smiled, a gentle resigned smile that she wore permanently, thanked me and left.

I went upstairs. I live over the shop. The flat had been cleaned that morning and smells of Mr. Sheen, lemon-scented, greeted me. A permanently angry Liverpudlian called Margaret 'does' for me. Her inner rage ensures a high degree of polish everywhere and a spotless flat. Windows, beds, floors, the kitchen, the bath, the lavatory, nothing escapes her furious hand. She pummels, polishes, shines and washes with murderous energy.

Quantities of books from downstairs have spilled up here. They are on bookshelves, on tables, on the floor, everywhere.

I pulled off my clothes, hung up my jacket and trousers and showered. I finished with an ice-cold deluge that made me gasp and wakened me up a bit. I toweled myself dry, put on a formal suit, a silk tie and when I was dressed I ran down into the shop again.

"Mandy, angel . . ."

"Oh God, what do you want now?"

"I forgot—"

"I know you did. Obviously. What?"

"Will you dine with me this evening?"

"I thought you'd already asked me. I thought that was the plan." Her voice was suspicious.

"Yes, well, there's something else. Mother suggested we go to a party at George Barrington's tonight. A lot of Alison's friends will be there. Okay?"

She put her hand on her hip and looked at me with amused eyes. "Listen, buster. It's lucky for you that I have a little black St. Laurent number that I got at the sales upstairs."

"I remember when you left it there." I said with a lascivious smile. She threw a book at me and I returned upstairs. I got my keys, checked that I had money and cards—the magic plastic—and hurried out again.

CHAPTER 4

I had decided to pay a visit to Revel Blake. I had to start some-where, and he was a member of the Fab Four, as my mother and Wendy quaintly dubbed them. He lived in a converted riverside warehouse. He was one of the first people who had chosen to live in what was then thought of as a very unfashionable address. This was before the Yuppies had descended on Docklands. I hoped to catch him before he went out for the evening.

I had my Audi parked around the corner. I got in feeling very good, very fresh, full of zest and confidence and I turned the key in the ignition and drove off.

My good humour soon wore off. I had started out too soon and ran smack into the after-work, rush-hour traffic. It was crawling. The air was full of exhaust fumes, honking horns, the anger of drivers who were hardly moving, frantically tense after a hard day's work, motorists furiously blaming each other for the delays, cursing each other through half-open windows, screaming invectives, all going nowhere. I tried to muster some patience but failed dismally. I crossed Chelsea Bridge, inched past Battersea Power Station, Nine Elms Lane, along Albert Embankment, and Blackfriars Bridge and finally, teeth grinding, underarms damp, knuckles white, I reached Revel's ultrasmart address in Southwark around seven o'clock. If it took as long as this on the return journey, Mandy would have a long wait, which would infuriate her, and boded ill for this evening. Oh, hell!

Revel answered the muted bell. We had been at college to-gether and while we were on nodding terms with each other no one would have called us friends. He stood in the door-way, chain on, holding a whiskey in an enormous heavy-bottomed crystal glass. He wore Calvin Klein designer jeans and a linen jacket and his shirt hung out over the jeans in the latest fashion. He had a designer stubble and his eyes were belligerent. A heavy wing of black hair swooped over one side of his face. He was one of those handsome, petulant mothers' boys who never grew up.

"What the hell do you want?" he asked rudely. He sounded a little drunk.

"Let me in, Revel, there's a good chap," I said calmly.

For a moment it seemed as if he would slam the door in my face, then he shrugged. "Oh all right." He unbolted the chain, opened the door and let me pass him into the apart-ment. It was the view that hit me first and it was stunning. It was as if I had stepped into a lighthouse and the panorama of London lay at my feet. The entrance led directly into the liv-ing room which was huge, ultra-modern and whose main fea-ture must be the glass wall that overlooked the city. The lights were coming on and across the river St. Paul's was floodlit now in the dusk. The sun was setting, the water picked up its golden glow, and the buildings and church spires were etched against the sky.

"Wow!" I said.

"You like it?" He sounded moderately pleased.

"It's dramatic . . . stupendous."

"I got it before they ruined the river. Bloody property de-velopers. They've decimated the place. You go down to the Prospect of Whitby. Used to be magic. Watch the river. Have a pint. Trees there. A view. Now they've overbuilt the place. Can't see a thing. Just skyscrapers, and bloody ugly ones."

He looked at me. "Have a drink?"

He moved to a beautiful ebony drinks unit and, picking up a crystal decanter, said, "Whiskey all right?"

"Yes, perfect," I said, looking around. The apartment was dramatically black and white. The walls were bricks painted, it seemed to me with whitewash. The furnishings against this background were sparse but expensive and elegant. A huge black couch, soft leather, faced the wall-to-wall windows and the view. The music centre would not have disgraced Virgin Records. There were a couple of silk Samarkand carpets scattered on the black-stained wooden floor.

He poured me a large drink and refilled his own glass nearly up to the brim. I tried to recollect whether he drank at Oxford or whether he had a reputation as a drinker, and I could not remember. All I could recall about Revel Blake was that he did no work and that the girls adored him. Just that, no more. I racked my brain trying to remember whether he had liked girls but couldn't.

He brought the drinks to a low table and threw himself down on the sofa. I sat, too. The sofa was sectioned. Before us, the river, golden and black, snaked down to London Bridge.

"What do you want?" he asked and laughed. "Old fuddy duddy Mark Dangerfield. Never thought I'd see you here." He peered at me blearily, a sneer on his handsome face, his black eyes glittering dangerously. He had got to that stage in drinking where he wanted to quarrel, to score. "Know what we used to sing about you? In the Blazers?" The Blazers was an exclusive club that I had never been asked to join. "'Oh, Mark Dangerfield, such a serious fellow, Danger is his name, but, he is . . . YELLOW.' Did you know that?"

I kept calm. I smiled and shook my head. "No, I made it my business never to listen to juvenile rubbish. I grew out of that sort of thing when I was nine." I said it lightly.

He looked momentarily discomfited and drank, or rather gulped some Scotch.

"What brings you here?" he asked eventually.

"I'm investigating the murder of Alison Alyward," I answered crisply, watching him. I really did not like his spoiled-brat confidence, his sharp good looks. He relied on his smile for everything; he put no effort into anything except his charm. But he was not smiling now. He choked on his drink.

"Wha . . . ?"

"I wanted to ask you some questions. You were very close to Alison. You and Talia Morgan and Jason Bestwick. Probably you most of all."

"Get out of here." His black eyes were narrowed spitting anger.

"Calm down Blake old boy. I only . . ."

"Get out of here." He was shaking. His face had gone white. He pointed to the door. "Get out."

I had no option but to go. I put down my drink and I left him standing there shaking, looking curiously vulnerable.

"I'll be back," I said and closed the door behind me. My main thought was, why had he not queried the word 'murdered'?

The drive back to the Kings Road was easy. Traffic had thinned and as I sped along I thought about Revels' reaction. Why had he been frightened? Why? He had also been angry. Again, why? It was a peculiar way to behave. His reaction had been excessive, though I had to take into consideration the fact that he had certainly been very close to Alison and that she was dead, violently, which must have been a shock. Also he had been drinking and his reactions would be influenced by his intake of Scotch.

I sped down the Kings Road, drew up alongside the shop and honked the horn. Mandy came out, slammed the shop door behind her, bent down and locked it.

Mandy has sensational legs. She wore a black skirt that barely covered her ass, long sheer black tights, high heels and a beautiful black leather jacket. I gulped, leaned over and opened the Audi door on the passenger side. She jumped in laughing, giving off vibes of vitality that excited me.

"God, Mandy, you look sexy," I said.

"Don't be a chauvinist," she replied haughtily. I told her about Revel and his odd reaction as we drove up the Kings Road to Sloane Street. We had a drink in the tiny bar at Drones in Pont Street while we waited to be seated. Mandy had on a high-necked Edwardian lace blouse under the soft black leather, which I found utterly irresistible, a mixture of the prim and the provocative.

We ate a wonderful pasta, followed by lobster, drank some wine and left around ten.

The party was in full swing when we arrived at George Barrington's house in Eaton Place and the windows were open to the warm night. There were a lot of older men accompanied by beautiful young women. A South African was telling a group that included Jason Bestwick (whom I knew from his appearances in the social columns of the press) that the blacks *liked* their position in the scheme of things and were quite happy where they were. Sanctions were the order of the day.

"They need us as bosses," he said in his hard accented voice. "It's the media. They exaggerate everything. There is very little trouble really. The blacks are comfortable in the townships. They feel ill-at-ease in the more sophisticated surroundings where we live. It's simply rabble rousers like Nelson Mandela that are causing all the trouble, and, thank God, they are few and far between."

Mandy wrinkled her nose in distaste and we moved on. I felt I might lose my temper, wondered if it would matter, decided it might compromise my mother.

At that moment we saw her. She waved and we edged through the crush over to her. But halfway there I felt my arm gripped. I turned. A blonde girl with a hard face who looked as if she had been crying said: "Boring! His wife found out. It's all over the papers, darling. He's been fiddling around with insider trading, or something, and now he's up to his neck in hot soup. Oh Christ, it's awful. I can't show my face outside or I'm mobbed by the bloody media. Why in God's name they have to . . ."

She held onto me as if she was on a ship in a stormy sea, and I was the only thing that was not moving. Mandy giggled. I glared at her. The girl put her hand on my shoulder. "And I wouldn't mind," she whispered theatrically. "Only *she,* his wife, is bedding half the population. But they never say a word about *her* in the tabloids. Never. Only me. I get all the shit."

"It's because you're young and beautiful dear," Mandy said and tried to steer me away, but the blonde peered at me more closely.

"You're not Eliot!" she said angrily. "I don't know you from Adam!" and huffed away.

"That was Gloria Dawn," Mandy informed me. "Film star. All that scandal about sex orgies in Gramercy Castle with Lord Derridan and poor Lady Derridan banished to the castle in Scotland and his nibs dipping into all sorts of dubious share transactions. Wow, darling, these people! How can your mother bear them?"

"She uses them as material for her book, she says," I replied, trying to see Mother. I spied her and moved towards her.

"Mark! Mandy! Oh, how nice." Mother pulled me over to the group of people she was talking to. I saw Talia Morgan talking to a tall, distinguished silver-haired man in evening clothes. A beautiful woman beside him smiled at me and I recognized Lady Ravenscroft at once. She, too, wore evening dress.

"Isn't she beautiful?" my mother asked me, propelling me forward towards the group, "She was the Countess de Montaigne before she married Ravenscroft. He got his title for all the philanthropic work he does. Wonderful man. So generous. So handsome."

"You fancy him, Mother!" I leered at her and she gave a smug smile.

"So what?" she asked. "Sometimes, Mark, you behave as if sex stopped at thirty-five."

"How did he make his money?" Mandy asked.

"Oh, import, export. Things that happen in the docks." Mother waved her hand about. "All sorts of different ways." She obviously hadn't a clue. "And not all of them above-board. But I do like buccaneers, don't you?"

"I'm not sure, Mother. It depends on what they buccaneer about. Coffee? Legit Imports? Okay. Drugs? Guns? Not so sweet."

"Oh no, that's the Arab over there," Mother said with finality. "I'm fairly certain he's not mixed up in drugs, but, having said that, I'm sure he is not pure as the driven snow. But then who is these days?"

"People should be," Mandy said. She did not share my mother's liking for villains.

"You know I don't understand business, darling," my mother said, stating the obvious. "But I think I could safely say that this room is full of scoundrels and con-artists and, at best, men who did a little something shameful on the way up.

36

Only they are so rich no one dares to throw mud."

By this time, in the swirl of people, the mingling and intermingling, we had joined the group. Ravenscroft was saying, ". . . money for the franchise. Eddie has put up twenty million already. He wants to pick up a third of the investment . . ."

Lady Davina looked at me. "How nice to see you, Mark."

Lady Ravenscroft introduced mother and me to the little enclave. Lord Ravenscroft apologised for his formal dress. They had been to the opera, he said. Davina asked me why I looked so cross. Everyone looked at me and I think I blushed.

"I have just heard that idiot over there spouting a lot of insulting rot," I said, pointing to the South African, feeling naive. "He seems to think we are all cretins."

Eyebrows were raised. I had been too vehement. One was not supposed to show one's feelings or express oneself so explicitly in polite society.

However, Lord Ravenscroft smiled. "Oh, Max is a fool!" he said, following my glance. "He likes to change the facts to suit himself. But he's awfully useful for subscriptions." He gave me a charming smile, then moved me a little away from the group. "Wendy Cadbury told me she has asked you to investigate poor Alison Alyward's drowning," he said.

"I thought no one was supposed to know," I remarked, somewhat miffed.

"Oh, you can't keep something like that quiet. People will talk when you start asking questions." I thought of Revel Blake. "Besides, Wendy and I are great friends," he added, then looked at me intently. "If I were you I wouldn't," he said.

"Oh?" I replied, suspicious. "Why?"

He shrugged. "If one turns over enough stones one is bound to find something nasty, don't you think?" He smiled again. "Besides, I'm not sure Wendy's motives are pure. After all, Jason Bestwick is her son."

"I . . . didn't know," I said, feeling like an idiot.

He spread his hands, "Well then . . ." he said, "I may be wrong but I think she is spying on poor Jason. Trying to find out how deep he is in whatever they are in."

"What are they in? And who are *they?*"

"The Fab Four. Well, three now. I don't honestly know. But Wendy is sure they are up to something." He smiled at me again, apologetically. "Wendy is a nosy woman. She is also a hysteric. I'm very fond of her, but you know Americans. Guns under the pillow and a gangster or mugger round every street corner. I've always believed that Americans are paranoid." He shrugged. "Of course you must do as you think best, but remember, this is England."

"Have any treasures coming in this month, Mark?" Davina joined us. She asked me the question as if she had not been in the shop today. She wore her "other world" smile as I called it, and I realized she must have been on something. There was a tiny grain in the cleft of her nostril and she gave a sniff, but it did not move.

"I'm sorry, Davina. There is nothing new," I said.

Her husband took her arm gently. "We must go, dear. We're tired. Goodbye, Mark. Nice to meet you."

And he steered her to the door.

Benjamin Barchester, a Tory M.P. from some, obscure constituency was banging on about the poor 'asking for it.'

"What do you mean when you say 'it'?" Mandy asked innocently.

"All this homelessness. Bloody disgrace. Shouldn't be allowed." His face was brick red.

"What do you think we ought to do?" Mandy asked sweetly.

"It's all the media's fault," he said. That was the third time someone had blamed the media. I sighed.

"Do you mean that they court homelessness and starvation?" Mandy persisted

"Hang on! Steady on, old girl." Benjamin had a glass of champagne in one hand and a cigar in the other.

"It's all the fault of the bloody Social Security. Encourages them. God, I'd love that post."

"Would you privatize it?" Mandy asked, wide-eyed. He glanced at her suspiciously, but she met his gaze with bland innocence.

"Well, not quite that . . . but I'd soon get rid of the spongers."

"A minority surely?" Mandy asked mildly.

"Millions of 'em," he insisted. "Taking the bread out of honest people's mouths."

"Surely not. Hundreds, maybe," Mandy said.

"This government won't be satisfied until we have rid the country of every last scrounger . . ."

"Even if that makes it hard, no, impossible for the genuine to survive?" Mandy asked.

Benjamin blew his smoke into Mandy's hair. "Oh come on, old girl, I don't think so. Besides," he said, chewing the cigar, "it's their own fault . . ."

"Their own fault," Mandy repeated. "How quaintly Victorian you are." She smiled at him and patted his arm. "I'll watch your progress with interest," she said, and he gave her a fatuous smile. "It will be interesting to see what you become when you grow up," she added beatifically, then turned to me.

"Bastard," I whispered as we moved away. Mother had followed us. She had heard the conversation and looked a bit worried.

"You must not *collide* with people, Mark," she said. "Subtlety is better."

"It's wasted on most of the people here."

"Ah, don't say that. Here, come and meet George Barrington. George, darling, my son Mark and Mandy Richardson."

George Barrington is an ex-Wimbledon champion. He is a very handsome man. At the height of his fame and fortune, he bought up half the Costa del Sol, opened innumerable sports-clothes shops and began to manufacture designer sports clothes. He was now a very rich man. He was also charming and good-humoured.

"Are you having a boring time with this lot?" he asked Mandy. "Your mother, Mark, takes the piss and is a wonderful success. There is nothing Tory men like better than strong women who insult them and order them about."

Jerry Taylor, a business tycoon and entrepreneur standing with his back to Mother, heard George and turned. "Oh we're not all as bad as all that. And we're not all Tories. Assan here is certainly not, are you, old fellow?"

The Arab arms dealer smiled his soft smile and bowed.

Jerry grabbed Mother's arm. "Listen," he said, "I have just bought a Renoir at auction at Sothebys. It cost me a fortune, but it's a gem," he said. He was frankly bragging. Full of self-congratulation, he stood there grinning at Mother, a long-legged blonde model hanging on his arm as if she was afraid he might run away.

"I'm not at all fond of Renoir," Mother said mildly, shaking her head.

Jerry's jaw dropped open and he looked at her as if she was insane. Then we could see, in slow motion, a terrible doubt overcome him.

"He *is* one of the greats, though, isn't he?" Jerry asked a trifle anxiously.

"In my opinion he stops just short of that. Veers on the sentimental," Mother said. "Chocolate box sort of thing, but you love that, don't you, Jerry, so what's the problem?" she added, glancing at the blonde, her blue eyes wide and innocent.

"He has a world-wide reputation, Mr. Taylor," Assan said in soothing tones.

"Well, you must understand, for a lad from the back streets of Glasgow," Jerry's Scottish accent suddenly came into evidence, "to own a Renoir, well, ye have ta admit it's amazing."

"It is indeed," my mother affirmed. "I suppose I was thinking of the connoisseurs, Jerry. Anyhow, I hear you are heavily tipped for next year's Honours list."

Jerry Taylor turned a delighted pink and Mandy pulled my sleeve.

"Mother, Mandy and I want to go," I said and the others turned away. "I'm getting very uncomfortable, Mother dear."

"Darling, you are a stick-in-the-mud. I'm having a very amusing time. You must not take things so personally. We do, after all, live in a democracy." She looked around. "And I'm afraid Barclay Norman hasn't arrived. You'll miss him."

The Arab turned me around. Literally. "You are a detective, are you not, Mr. Dangerfield?"

I nodded.

"It is a dangerous thing to be?"

"No more dangerous than arms dealing, Mr. Assan," I replied.

"I would have thought, someone like you, it's, how you say, tacky? Yes? I think people do not like to have people like you poking about in their affairs?"

"Well, Mr. Assan, if they have nothing to hide . . ."

"Is there a man in the world who can claim that, Mr. Dangerfield? If you know him, I wish you'd introduce me to him." He laughed and turned away.

I grabbed Mandy's arm. "Let's go, Mandy. Just let's go."

All in all it had been an interesting, if aggravating, evening and I wondered if I had learned anything new or helpful, or not.

I drove Mandy home, then turned in. I put my arms behind my head in bed and thought about Alison and the people she mixed with, but before I could work anything out I fell fast asleep.

CHAPTER 5

When I woke up the next morning the sun was shining, the Kings Road was humming with life and activity and I could hear Mandy's voice below and the ting of the shop doorbell. I reflected complacently how lucky I was, how agreeable my life was. I had a lot to be grateful for, I loved my girl, my work and my lifestyle was very comfortable and secure. I was safe and cosseted in my little world and it was a very pleasant feeling

I turned on the radio. Brian Hayes on L.B.C. was being rude to some woman who was waffling on about how terrible the youth of today were. I would simply have cut her off. I flipped the switch and got Kylie Minogue, singing, "I should be so lucky," and I thought, yes, dear, you are, winced and flipped again and got some lunatic Hezbullah goon telling me why they should assassinate Salman Rushdie. I turned the radio off.

When I had bathed and dressed I went down to the shop and kissed Mandy good morning.

"Boy, you're in a good humour," she said, smiling at me.

"Did you set up that meeting with Talia?" I asked.

She nodded. "Didn't you see me last night?"

"I wasn't noticing."

"Gosh, you're great at making a girl feel essential."

"You know you are to me." I kissed her again and went next door to Mr. Gupta in the Indian mini-market and bought a paper.

43

I spent the day thinking, figuring out what I knew, asking myself questions, forming opinions. I took Mandy to lunch in L'Express Cafe, sounded out some of my ideas on her, gave her a couple of hours off and looked after the shop.

I had spent the previous week cataloguing recent acquisitions and was in the enviable position of being up-to-date in my work. All that was necessary was to take care of the customers. I enjoyed that.

When Mandy came back to the shop that evening I put on a white T-shirt and dark blue jeans. I pulled on a pair of cream wool socks and brown leather loafers, threw an off-white Professor Higgins woolen cardigan over my shoulders.

"Will I do?" I asked Mandy.

"Oh God, Mark. Talia will expect to go somewhere terribly smart. We can't go anywhere ultra with you dressed like that."

"Well, tough! Why didn't you wear your St. Laurent last night, by the way?"

"I wondered when you'd remark on that. I decided that, with the best will in the world I was not going to kowtow to those people."

"Exactly," I said pointedly. "Precisely."

"I do not like you, Mark, when you go all righteous on me."

"Come on," I said. "Let's go get it over with."

Mandy was wearing a red suit in gored grosgrain. The jacket had a peplum, which bounced over her bum delightfully. "I think you'll like Talia," Mandy said. She looked at me with amused eyes. "She's an old-fashioned girl."

"What's that supposed to mean?"

"Never mind," she laughed. "You'll see."

I saw. Talia Morgan was something else. I had seen her,

sure, the previous night and on many other occasions, but she was a girl you needed to get close to to really appreciate. Her skin was milk-white; it looked soft as creamy ice cream and just as edible. Her eyelashes were thick and curly, her eyes green. She had a long, elegant body, far too skinny for me, and she was stunning. She jumped into the back of the car.

"Where're we going?" she asked, and when she heard she grimaced. We had decided on the local Trattoria, which served excellent homemade pasta with a fresh salad and a good red plonk.

"I thought at least Santini's," she murmured disconsolately.

"Well, this place will have the novelty of the new," I said briskly.

Mandy made a face at me. I wondered again at Mandy's misconception of me. She simply did not believe that I, or any man, could resist someone like Talia. Just because I letched after her body she assumed that I was turned on by any figure that was sexy. And she thought that the more perfect the body the more I desired it. She could not have been more mistaken. Personality was, for me, an essential ingredient. Spoiled brats like Talia left me cold.

Talia was bored and showed it all through the meal and I thought she needed her bottom spanked. Mandy worried in case it was her fault. Talia's large green eyes roamed the little restaurant searching, scouring, and when she did not find one famous face there, they came to rest with contempt on the red-and-white checked tablecloths, candles in Chianti bottles, the garlands of imitation vines and grape bunches that hung from the ceiling.

A lot of London-Italians came here, and the air was thick with voices speaking in their native tongue. People waved hands and laughter was loud and the little place was packed.

Mandy and I adored it. We would have enjoyed ourselves if we had been alone, but Talia spread an awful disease that prevented pleasure.

"Why did you ask me to join you?" she asked eventually when we were drinking coffee. "There must have been a reason. I'm not used to playing gooseberry," she added petulantly.

"I'm looking into . . . er . . ." I thought of Revel's reaction and tried to pick my words carefully. "Into Alison Alyward's death," I said.

She looked up under her impossibly thick black lashes. Her eyes glittered suspiciously. "Why? The verdict was accidental death. The police were satisfied." She was alert now, like a cat who has suddenly scented danger.

I shrugged. "Well, it's just that there were a few odds and ends that needed checking." I was being as delicate as I could possibly be.

She said nothing, just sat there, staring at her clasped hands on the checked tablecloth.

"Was Alison afraid of anything? Anyone?" I asked.

I could see fear stirring deep in those sea-green eyes.

"No," she said, looking down. "No."

"Do you know of anyone who might have wanted to . . . well, get rid of her?"

She shook her head, subdued, yet when I forced her to look at me, I was sure I had hit on a truth. Almost instantly her face closed and a mutinous expression came over it.

I leaned forward. "Talia, listen, would you mind awfully . . ."

"If I saw myself home?" she finished.

"No, no, I'll give you a lift," I said reassuringly, surprised by her insecure reaction. She looked relieved, then I added, "But could I see Alison's room? When I drop you?" She looked alarmed. "Just for a moment. Otherwise perhaps I could call you a taxi?"

The inference that the lift would not be available unless she let me into the flat tipped things in my favour.

"Okay. Okay. Okay," she said impatiently and stood up. "But the police have been over it with a fine-tooth comb."

I got the bill, paid it, and we left. Mandy and Talia were waiting on the pavement.

"This is all very strange," Talia said. She had been thinking. "Why is anyone interested in Alison's drowning now? After all this time?"

I stood beside the car, opening it.

"It's only a month ago," I said.

We all climbed into the Audi. The flat in Wilton Crescent was a lovely, elegant apartment. Alison's room had obviously been partially cleared out. It told me little about her. The closet was still full of her clothes, which I thought was strange.

I went through everything, every drawer and cubby hole, every nook and cranny and found nothing. But women don't usually put things onto dressing tables as men do, emptying everything out at night. I thought of my mother. Things got transferred from handbag to handbag or got left in pockets. I searched a dozen handbags and found nothing.

I then went through her clothes. Coats, suits, fine wool and cashmere, gabardine and suede, and they held a lingering fragrance that must have been hers. But still there was nothing.

Then, in the pocket of a pair of old beige Armani pants, I struck lucky. Two little leather-bound books: an address book and a diary. Small and neat, I had almost overlooked them.

I glanced around the room again. There was a framed

photograph on the bedside table of a bunch of boys and girls in some kind of fancy dress. They all looked drunk to me, and I picked it up and took it outside.

"Who are these people?" I asked. Talia and Mandy were together in the living room, the atmosphere uneasy.

"Us," Talia said. "I've just buzzed Jason and told him to pick me up in half an hour. There's a party at the Gore-Robinsons' I've been invited to and I've got to get dressed. It's formal. I wasn't going to go but . . ." She was dying for us to leave, couldn't get rid of us fast enough.

I was disgusted with her. I resented her refusal to make even a small effort to enjoy herself, if only for the sake of politeness, and I'm afraid my male ego was insulted by her implication that this evening had been a waste of her time.

"I have to change, please excuse me." She was unzipping her black top at the back. The gesture started as automatic, unconscious.

"Who are these people?" I asked again, pointing at the photograph.

"Oh, the gang," she said lightly, "Just me and Revel Blake and Jason and Alison at a fancy-dress."

She had undone the zip to the waist and she held up the front with the flat of her hand.

"Who are they?" I pointed to the other couple that brought the total number of people in the snap to six.

"Oh, that's Bob and Abigale McNaughton," she said, "Just friends. Now I really must . . ."

I put the picture down on a table with the other framed photographs tastefully arranged around a tall crystal bowl of lilies.

Talia turned in the doorway to her room. "Did you find anything?" she asked without interest.

"Yes. These little books. Address and diary," I said and

slipped them into my pocket. She stood transfixed, staring at me in mute horror.

"Give those back!" she demanded.

"No."

"Please. I'll do anything. Please."

"Oh no, Talia. I need them."

She was still holding up her black top with her hand flat on her chest, fingers spread-eagled. The top was slowly drifting down over her arms, leaving her creamy shoulders bare. She began to move towards me, completely ignoring Mandy's presence on the sofa. She moved in slow motion, a sort of erotic undulating movement. Everything about her screamed sex, and eventual nudity. It was as if she had taken the stopper out of a bottle of perfume and the smell that emerged was an aphrodisiac. The change in her startled me, the transition had been swift.

"Gimme, gimme, gimme," she purred.

I stood and stared. She was the snake and I was the rabbit. She curved her shoulders over sinuously, hollowing her chest and moving her pelvis oh so slowly with subtlety. She was biting her bottom lip.

I don't know how I would have acted if Mandy had not been there. There was in her sexy gestures something that demanded response at the basest level and I succumb to temptation easily. But the fact that she was putting on this show with my girlfriend present enraged me, sickened me. Nevertheless I stood like an idiot unable to move, hypnotized. Mandy was staring at Talia and I could feel her anger.

"Give them to me," she said softly. "The books, baby. I want them."

"No," I said firmly.

She gave a shriek and pounced on me, hands curved, nails at the ready, and would have torn me limb from limb, only that I gripped her wrists and threw her bodily onto the sofa. We left immediately.

"Jeez," I said when we reached the car. "What a woman."

"Told you." Mandy slammed the car door and belted herself in.

"What?" I'd lost her. I started the engine.

"That she was . . . that men, you would like her."

"Who?" I was turning the car into Sloane Square.

"Talia, you fool." Her voice was high and tense. I realized she was nearly in tears. We had reached Sloane Square and I drew in to the pavement where I should not be, and stopped the car where I should not stop it.

"What is it?" she asked, looking at me apprehensively. "Why are you looking at me like that?"

"Because I love you," I said. "Don't you understand that, you little fool? I love you."

I looked down into her hurt eyes and kissed her. Nothing Talia could do would ever affect me like the sight of Mandy or Mandy's kiss. I could feel my throat closing and I held her close to me.

Someone knocked on the window. I could hear a Cockney accent yell, "Get a move on mate. Wot you think your doin'? Can't you wait till you get 'ome?"

I paid no attention. I kissed Mandy again.

How to explain that her little button-nose and dusting of freckles across her cheeks took my breath away? That the curve of her ample breasts and the overlapping tooth you could only see when she laughed sent tingles all through my legs? That kissing her, the way she smelled, the taste of her tongue, acted as a trigger and made me ready and willing to ravish her here and now in the car in a way that all Talia Morgan's gyrations could never do. I was aroused in a way that Talia could never arouse me, for my heart was full to the brim with tenderness. Mandy's vulnerability made me ache and I touched her cheek and whispered, "I want you so bad."

"I want you, too," she answered.

Mandy lived in Fulham with her mother. Sometimes she stayed with me. She could have stayed for good but she preferred this arrangement. She liked to feel free, she said. But tonight was going to be one of the nights we spent together.

She insisted on having the last word. She said that Talia, although I did not desire her, had turned me on, triggered the mechanism that made me hot for her, Mandy.

Women are devious.

CHAPTER 6

The following morning Mandy and I slept late. The phone ringing awakened me. It was my mother.

"Did I wake you?" she asked brightly, then said without waiting for a reply, "It *is* eight-thirty."

"Oh, damn!" I said mildly. "So it is. I slept on, Mother. Shall I call you back?"

"No Mark. I've got a dental appointment," she said. "Mandy with you?"

"How did you know?"

"Mark! I'm your mother! You sound smoothed out and benign. Whenever you sound smoothed out and benign at eight-thirty in the morning I know Mandy is with you. Have you a pencil and paper handy?"

"Yes, Mother . . . Why?"

"Just write. It's Alison Alyward's aunt. Mrs. Everton, The Old Forge, Cottesloe. Near Hungerford, Berkshire. Thought I'd let you know. How are you doing?"

"Hopelessly!"

"Don't despair. You'll get there in the end. You always do. Now bye, darling, I'm late already."

Mandy stirred and turned over. Her fine amber-brown hair covered her face in a shimmering veil and her firm, plump breast was half-revealed, rising from the duvet which fell away from her shoulders. I was torn. I wanted to dive into the warm burrow that held her naked body. I wanted to caress

her, which would arouse her and that would mean respond-
ing to her, which would lead to half-an-hour of lovemaking
and intense pleasure, and I could see the morning slip away.
So I quickly averted my eyes from the delights on offer in the
bed, showered and dressed with admirable restraint. I made
some coffee, brought some to Mandy, who, fuzzy with sleep
and almost unbearably seductive, kept trying to wind her
arms around my neck and entice me into her embrace. I refused to be tempted and, wondering where I was getting the
strength from, left her to open the shop and set out for the
country.

The congestion on the road was murder. Hammersmith
was a nightmare. The M4 was chock-a-block with traffic for
Heathrow and it wasn't until I had passed Windsor on my left
that things began to ease up. The fairy-tale castle rose above
the trees, its turrets a magic mirage in the misty morning
awaiting prince on horseback. The fields became greener,
less dust polluted the air; I had reached the country. I wondered what Dickens or Wordsworth would have to say about
the distance one had to travel out of London in order to
breathe clear air.

I reached Hungerford, stopped and parked the car in the
main square. I found a delightful "olde tea shoppe" where
they served their own homemade scones and buns and a wonderfully moist ginger cake. There was homemade jam too and
as I piled it (black current, my favourite) onto the tea cakes (I
had had no breakfast, which probably accounted for my
ill-humour on the motorway), I engaged the middle-aged
lady in a floral overall who served me in conversation.

"It's the best jam ever. It's delicious," I said.

"Oh, thank you, sir." She blushed with pleasure. "Yes, our
customers seem to enjoy it. You can purchase some at the
counter . . . to take away."

"I'll certainly do that." Mandy would love a jar. "Er, do you know a small hamlet hereabouts called Cottesloe?"

"Oh, yes, sir. On the left at the end of the main road as you leave the town. About three miles. Going south."

"I'm looking for The Old Forge."

She had been polishing the thick glass that covered the tabletop and she paused, looking at me in amazement.

"How extraordinary, sir . . . how odd!"

"What?"

"That's where the jam comes from; where we get the jam and some of the cakes. Mrs. Everton. The Old Forge. In Cottesloe." She looked at me as if I was the Second Coming. "Fancy you looking for Mrs. Everton and you eating her jam!" I bought three jars of the jam and paid the bill. The floral-aproned woman stared after me as I left, shaking her head in wonderment. "Fancy," she kept saying, "Just fancy."

I reached the Old Forge as the sun blazed out from behind the veils of clouds that had obscured it all morning. It was surprisingly hot for April. I pulled off my sweater and threw it on the rear seat.

There was a crazy-paving pathway between tall hollyhocks that bordered an old cottage garden. It promised to be a delight in the summer, though at the moment, and perhaps because of the good weather, it looked very pretty.

The bell chimed "Home Sweet Home," and the little woman who answered the doorbell was right out of central casting: a rotund, compact, energetic little body, round-faced, apple-cheeked, faded blue, raisin small eyes twinkled at me in the most friendly way. I couldn't believe my eyes; she was perfect. The good fairy. The Gingerbread Man's wife. She wore a Liberty-print cotton dress and an old-fashioned Mrs. Bridges apron, and her sleeves were rolled up, her plump arms were bare, her hands floury.

"I've been baking," she said, dimpling, eyes smiling, confident, obviously unafraid of strangers. "Come in, come in. You've come at a good time; I'm letting the pastry cool."

I followed her through the cosy little cottage. There were floral prints everywhere. Chintz covers on sagging, but obviously comfy, sofas and chairs. Bowls of flowers were scattered about in windows and on tables. A ginger cat opened one eye as we came into the kitchen. He glanced indifferently at me, then closed it again.

The sun lit the kitchen directly, and that fact added to the heat emanating from the old-fashioned range that roared away in the corner, made the room unbearably hot.

Mrs. Everton opened the door leading to what I saw was the vegetable and fruit garden in the back.

She beamed at me. "There, that's better, isn't it? Now young man what is it you want? Selling something, no doubt. Well, I'm sorry to tell you I'm not in the market for buying."

I shook my head. "No, Mrs. Everton. I've not come to sell you anything. Let me introduce myself. I'm Mark Dangerfield and I've come to find out what you can tell me about Alison Alyward."

She was filling a lined pastry dish with fruit. "Bought stuff," she remarked, nodding contemptuously at the fruit filling. Then she pushed a strand of grey hair off her forehead. She sighed.

"About Alison? Not much really. I brought her up. Her mother was my half-sister. Beautiful woman, Alison took after her. In looks. She married James Alyward. He was handsome too, but a playboy. He was killed at Brands Hatch racing his car. Car racing is such a stupid profession, if you can call it a profession. It's asking for trouble. Irresponsible behaviour with a child to support, don't you think? They were such a frivolous pair, those two. Alison inherited that quality, unfortunately. You know the sort racket around all their lives, build nothing, create nothing, contribute nothing. No husbandry. No diligent provision made for the rainy day, that sort of thing."

She worked busily as she spoke, filling, trimming or rolling out pastry. Popping dishes in the oven, taking others out, the smell was heavenly. She was economical of movement; no gesture was wasted. She did not pause to rest until the clock struck twelve noon, then, suddenly, all motion ceased as if a switch had been thrown.

"Tea," she announced.

The kettle was boiling on the hob. She wet the tea, put two cups and saucers on the table, took down a cookie jar from the dresser and sat down opposite me.

The biscuits were delicious and tasted of cinnamon. The tea was perfect, flavourful, yet not stewed or too strong.

"When James was killed, Alison's mother went to pieces. Poor woman. She was never the stablest of people. Well, to cut a long story short, she dumped Alison on me. My husband had died." She glanced at me sharply. "Oh, of natural causes. Certainly nothing like a racing accident." She pursed her lips in disapproval as if the method of death were important. "He had a heart attack. Ran in the family." This obviously made him respectable. "I was alone and she parked Alison on me without a by your leave and went off to Italy. She married someone important there and she never told him about her past. Not a word."

"You mean her husband doesn't know she was married before? That she had a child?" I sounded incredulous. She gave me a speculative glance.

"Exactly. She had learned by her mistake. She wanted security. But it's hard to fathom, isn't it? People, you will find out young man, are devious and complicated, and I can't say

I like them very much, do I, Tiddles?" she asked the cat.

"How did Alison take all this?" I asked.

"Oh, she never knew. I never told her." I gasped and she held up her hand. "I don't want any criticism from you, Mr. Dangerfield." She took a deep breath with her eyes closed, then said, "Which was better I ask you; tell her her mother and father had died in an accident, which was what I did, or tell her that her mother had dumped her and was now in Italy living like a queen, busily denying her existence? Well, which?" She peered at me assuming that if I was a reasonable man I would of course agree with her. "I like my life neat and tidy. No loose ends," she said firmly. "As you can see, everything in its place and a place for everything. I don't want dramas and moods and grievances building up, emotion and confusion! No, Mr. Dangerfield, it's not my style at all."

"What about Alison?" I asked carefully.

She put her hands on her hips. "I didn't like Alison very much," she said. I kept my face bland, expressionless. "She was messy," she continued reflectively. "Made messes. Both physical and emotional. I'm not at all surprised she committed suicide." She shook her head and clicked her tongue against her teeth. "'Put your things away Alison' I'd say, reasonably, quietly. I never raised my voice to her. 'Tidy up your room.' Tidy up your mind was what I really wanted to say, but she would not have understood. Messy she was right from the start. Took after her mother. Rackety people both. Never listened. I had to discipline her severely."

"How did you do that?"

She smiled at me. "Very effectively, if I do say so myself. I deprived her of things if she didn't behave. I took away her books. I made her sit in the dark cupboard under the stairs. That was very effective. I never struck her," she added virtuously. "Not once did I ever lay a hand on her. No. There are better ways to teach a girl discipline, Mr. Dangerfield."

She had cleared away the cups, teapot and plates and now she washed them thoroughly, dried them carefully, replaced them on the shelf. She obviously loved her possessions. She fondled the china, polished it as if she were about to place it in the window of Gerrard's. In that idyllic kitchen, the cat sleeping in the basket, the old clock ticking, the smell of fruit pies cooking, the pots of jam, copper and steel glinting in the sun, it was like an advertisement for *House and Garden*. I was suddenly acutely uncomfortable.

"Would you like to have lunch?" she asked.

"No, thank you very much." I replied hastily. "I've got to get back . . . the traffic, you know."

She nodded, smiling at me sympathetically. "Yes, it's awful, isn't it?" she said cosily. "I don't know why so many people want to rush about these days. I can hear the planes coming and going, and going all day long. Everyone rushing about all over the planet. What for? I used to say to Alison, 'Look around. Who could ask for anything more than we have here? The prettiest little house in the world. Our lovely garden. Why on earth would we want anything else?' " She sighed and shook her head. "But she went anyway. Out into the hurly-burly, and look what happened to her. Much good it did her.'Auntie's advice is best, Alison' I'd say, but she didn't listen and off she went." She looked at me brightly. "Which was just as well, really. I was quite glad to see the back of her. I wasn't cut out to have children."

Her tone was jolly. I could feel the prickles rise on the back of my neck and a shiver played a scale down my vertebrae. I was halfway home before I shook off the sticky feeling that had caused that shiver. What must it have been like for Alison to have to live with all that sweetness and determination? All that insistence on 'a place for everything and everything in its place'? I wondered how the child had felt when she realized that Auntie didn't like emotion, in fact didn't like her? I wondered how she had felt in the dark cupboard under the stairs. I pondered upon the strangeness of human behaviour, then gave up. I got back to the shop and Mandy as quickly as I could.

CHAPTER 7

I kissed Mandy on my way up to the apartment. The sight of her always gave me pleasure.

"Any business?" I asked.

She nodded, her eyes clear and full of love. I didn't, however, want to get involved in that area just then; one thing would lead to another and the whole afternoon would be written off. I couldn't afford to do that just now.

"A lot," she said, reluctantly bringing her mind back to business. "I made about five hundred pounds for you this morning."

"Great. You're wonderful, Mandy."

"I know," she laughed. "How'd it go?"

"Well, the old lady is a monster. No, really!"

"Do you think she could have murdered her niece? Banged her on the head and drowned her? After all, she was found in that general neighbourhood."

"No. She'd kill with kindness more like. She's one of those sweet old biddies who make you feel guilty because the cushion got squashed when you sat on it. Golly, I'd hate to have had her as a parent."

"Speaking of parents, your mother called. And you'll never guess who else?"

"Who?"

"Revel Blake." My eyebrows shot up.

"I'll phone them both now. I'll be upstairs if you need me.

Are you all right for the moment?"

She flashed me a radiant smile. "Could you bring me a coffee around four?"

"Done," I said. "Have you had lunch?"

She shook her head. "You?"

"No. I'm full of buns and cake and jam. Which reminds me, I brought some homemade stuff for you. It's delicious."

"Mark!" she moaned. "My figure! Jam!"

"You know very well how I feel about your figure," I said severely. "So, perhaps we could have an early bite together after the shop closes?"

She nodded enthusiastically and looked up as a customer came in.

I bounded upstairs. I put the kettle on, made myself a mug of coffee and one for Mandy even though it wasn't four o'clock just yet. I brought hers down to her and got Revel Blake's number from Alison's book. He sounded very contrite.

"I'm sorry, Mark, I behaved in a beastly fashion. I was drunk, you see. Ghastly, isn't it? And er . . . Alison's death still leaves me very raw. Know what I mean?"

"Course, Revel. Think nothing of it. Anyhow . . ." I didn't know what to say next. I could hardly ask, 'Have you got anything to tell me?' like a priest. I waited.

His voice came after a silence, and it seemed far away. "How are you doing with your inquiries? Had any luck? Talia said you were over with her last night. She said something about you finding some diaries or address books?"

He obviously had been in touch with Talia.

"I'm doing fine," I lied. "Yes, I found some books of Alison's. I'm unearthing all sorts of interesting things about her."

"Oh," he said. He sounded nervous. "What, for instance?"

"It seems to me, Revel, that I'm beginning to get to know and understand Alison Alyward."

"Really?" His voice was noncommittal. He paused. I waited. "You're lucky then. No one really knew Alison," he said eventually.

"Well, thanks for phoning, Revel. I just wanted to return your call . . ."

"Well, as a matter of fact, there is, are, one or two things you might be interested in."

"Oh?" I said patiently.

"Can I come round to see you this evening?" he asked, suddenly charming. "It's only fair after all. You drove all the way out to Southwark to see me, and I was beastly to you."

"Look, forget it, Revel, okay? Listen, I'm taking my girl-friend out for an early supper, so there'll be no one at home. So, say you came to see me late? About ten, ten-thirty?"

"Sure. That'd be fine."

I was about to hang up when he said, "Oh, Mark, the address? I don't know where to go! Goddamn, I'm getting senile."

I gave him the address, cut the connection, then dialed my mother.

"How'd it go?" she asked.

I told her about Mrs. Everton.

"She sounds foul," Mother said. "I had a chat with Bessie Margold and she said—"

"Mother, who is Bessie Margold?"

"Oh Mark," she said impatiently, as if I should know, "Elizabeth Margold is my dentist. I told you this morning I was going to the dentist. She's in Devonshire Place. She treats all our friends. Just because you insist on the National Health . . ."

"Mother!"

"Oh, sorry. I got her name from Wendy Cadbury. That's what I wanted to tell you."

"That you have the same dentist as Wendy Cadbury?" I tried not to sound sarcastic.

"Don't be idiotic, Mark. Listen. You mentioned Alison Alyward and Revel Blake? Yes? Well, Talia Morgan was also mentioned? Did anyone talk about Jason Bestwick?"

"Yes, Mother. Lord Ravenscroft told me he was Wendy's son. Why? Is it important?" I couldn't help sounding casual.

"Oh," Mother sounded very let down. "You knew?"

"But that's *all* I know. She, Wendy, may be stringing me along. Mother, but I'm curious, too curious to stop now. It would be like *coitus interruptus.*"

"Mark! Don't be disgusting."

"So, Mother, I know Jason is Wendy's son. Can you add anything else?"

"No." Mother was crestfallen. "He was her son by Paul Bestwick. He was the poet. Did you know that?"

"I figured it out!"

"Oh!"

"You going out tonight, Mother?"

"Mark!" My mother sounded reproachful. "You've forgotten. It's my Garden night. The Major will be here at any moment. Got to fly."

Major Jack Carstairs was my mother's favourite escort. They went once a month to Covent Garden. I had once asked my mother why she did not marry Jack, and she had stared at me and said, "Don't be silly Mark," so I had never asked her again.

I bathed and changed so that Mandy could use the bathroom unhindered when she closed the shop. She kept toiletries in my apartment and also clothes for convenience.

I phoned Clark's on Kensington Church Street for a reservation. It was usually difficult to get a booking, but tonight they had room for us. I sat then, at my desk, and picked up Alison Alyward's twin leather-backed books. She had obviously not followed the Yuppie fashion trend for Filofax. Alison's books were neat, extremely small and the entries were, to say the least, miniscule both in actual writing and in content.

There were quite a few names in the book that I knew and quite a few that I didn't and quite a few that I couldn't decipher. Mrs. Everton was there as Ant. Sal. Revel Blake as Rvl. Blk. and Jason Bestwick similarly shortened. There was an Abgl. McNgtn. and a Mr. Moto. Just that. I scribbled them down in a jotter, working them out, finding it quite interesting. Like doing a crossword.

Then I got to her diary. Here the entries were so cryptic as to be indecipherable. Example: M.10.30. J.L.S. Mang. tnt. Find G.K. Meet. 12.30. Then R. a few times and a question mark. Then S.K. and B. On the day before she died and the entries stopped, there was S.K. and R. and 10.30.

I tried to work it all out, deciphering what I could. Some were easy. The R.B. for instance and the J.B.dn: Jason Bestwick dinner, but the rest was obscure. Some of them could be doctor's or dentist's appointments. I lost track of time, became engrossed, and it wasn't until Mandy put her head around the door that I pulled myself back into the present. I stretched and felt Mandy's arms around me and her soft breasts against my shoulders, her lips on my cheek.

"Time to go, darling," she said and I grabbed her. She evaded me saying, "Later. I'm looking forward to Clark's and I'm not going to be deflected."

We had a marvelous supper in Clark's. They served their wonderful selection of homemade breads: olive, walnut, garlic and tomato. All the food is cooked in fresh herbs. We did not talk much about the case. Did I but know it, it was the last evening I was to spend in sweet ignorant content, cosy and protected in my safe world. The food, the place, Mandy, everything was perfect. Mandy wore a starched white shirt that was far too big for her. The collar was turned up, which made her look like a naughty choirboy. It was tucked into a tan leather miniskirt and her legs were bare. It was a warm night. Her glorious hair was a cloud on the pristine whiteness of her shirt, which was unbuttoned at the neck and revealed the curve of her breast. I knew I would be accused of being sexist if I told her how tantalizing I found this so I said nothing but let my eyes stray to those perfect-shadowed globes every so often. I was content to admire the view in silence.

"I can't understand why you are friendly with that superannuated social-climber," I said.

Mandy shrugged. "We went to school together," she said, "Talia and I. I know her so well that I suspend criticism when I am with her. I suppose I'm tolerant of her bad traits because I'm used to them. It's a habit. We sat together in class and we became friends out of proximity . . . you know?" I nodded and she looked reflective. "I think she likes to go out with me because I confirm for her that she is beautiful. I'm a wonderful audience. She sort of gloats over me." Mandy looked at me over the rim of her wineglass. "No, that's bitchy and I don't mean to be." She frowned. "But, you see, she's so slim and gorgeous and I'm so fat and ordinary. She makes me feel . . . inferior."

"Mandy, never talk like that again. Ever, do you hear me?"

I was angry. Mandy had nothing to apologise for. It seemed stupid to me that she could be so neurotic about Talia who, after all, and in my opinion, was an animated stick, an extremely pretty stick but still a stick with delusions of grandeur. Also, I felt it a slur on my taste, a blow to my male vanity. I did not deal in second best.

"Mandy, don't be stupid. You're supposed to be clever," I said. "Ask anyone. You have far more to offer than that dim clothes hanger."

"Like what?" she asked dolefully. "My boobs are huge."

"And your waist tiny. Perfect. Your beautiful milk-white, honey-filled—"

"Stop it at once, Mark," she interrupted, looking around and blushing, but smiling now.

"Well, you asked. Girls like Talia are having silicone implants to get to look like you."

We got onto the subject of what she had that Talia hadn't, which we both found arousing and she felt for my foot with hers, which she had slipped out of her shoe. She slid her bare toes up and down my ankles and up my legs. I tried to keep my cool above table, which was difficult. We ate, caressed, enjoyed ourselves in a deeply engrossing, satisfactory way and the time slipped past.

"I'd like to stay with you tonight," Mandy said, confident again.

"But, of course," I said. We had nowhere to go but on. Then a thought struck me, and I looked at my watch.

"Good Lord, it's nearly ten. I told Revel Blake I'd see him at my flat at half-past. We'd best move."

"Do you want to be alone with him?" she asked and I kissed her cheek.

"No. I want to be alone with you. Stick close."

I paid. The car was parked down a side road farther up Kensington Church Street. We walked to where I had left it. The moon shone, there were few people about and the night was balmy.

Something made me jump.

Mandy said, "What is it?" and I realized I didn't know. I

simply felt something was odd, not as it should be in the silent street.

A street lamp had gone out where the road curved past the Carmelite Church. It had left a huge part of the area in shadow and the shadow was moving.

I jumped again and Mandy grabbed my arm and we stood there, stock-still, frozen to the spot. A scurrying, scratching sound, infinitely sinister, hardly audible, was constant in the background, somewhere in the deep darkness.

"You hear?" I whispered. She nodded, holding on to me tightly. I peered into the dense gloom. There seemed to be bags of refuse about and they were moving. Like the sea. Movement, rustling, scraping, as if a thousand rats lurked in the darkness. My heart had jumped into my throat and an uneasy fear clutched my heart. I told myself I was being silly and imaginative and moved nearer. On the ground around the wall of the church and down farther in the doorways of the shops, bundles heaved and moved and squirmed and stirred restlessly and were still.

I could not for a moment believe the evidence of my eyes. I thought it was an optical illusion. Perhaps I would more readily have accepted what I saw if we had turned down an alley, where corrugated iron partitioned wasteland from brick walls decorated with graffiti, and there were no street lamps or smart shops. Perhaps I might have been horrified, yes, but not totally taken aback at the sight of human debris lurking under cardboard boxes and black plastic in Kensington Church Street, for God's sake? Christ!

We stood listening to that eerie sound, then realized how foolish my reaction was. It was the topic of the moment. Everyone spoke of the disgrace of the homeless. You could not open a newspaper or turn on a current-affairs program without someone thundering on about it. I had tut-tutted at what

I had seen on TV and read in the papers, but this was the first time I had been brought face-to-face with it and the actuality was horrifying. To walk down a familiar road, Kensington Church Street, God's sake, I just couldn't get over it. Leaving an expensive restaurant after a delicious meal and finding the doorways and church porches of that comfortable street littered with human outcasts was quite a shock.

"What is it, Mark?" Mandy asked.

"Good God, those are people. Sweet Jesus, Mandy, here? I thought at least they'd be where it's warm; in stations, the underground."

She shook her head. Her voice was sad but resigned. "No. The stations are full. This is the overspill. They are everywhere, Mark. Everywhere."

"I can't believe it. Jeez!"

"Come on, Mark. There's nothing we can do," she said and pulled me away.

As we were turning off Church Street to where I'd left the car, I felt my sleeve pulled. I turned. A young black man stepped back, palms of his hands in the surrender position, as if I might strike him otherwise, and I suppose to show that he had no violent intent. He was approximately nineteen and I could see, over his shoulder, the shop porch he had obviously just quitted. There was a lot of black plastic there and the kind of cardboard boxes you see behind supermarkets. It looked like something out of a nightmare, an abode in hell. There was a girl there. She was sitting up, her back to the wall and I could just decipher her pale child-like face hovering like a small moon in the darkness of the embrasure. The boy had a cocks-comb hair-do and a stubble on the rest of his scalp where the hair had been shaved off. He wore an earring, a tissue-thin circle of some base metal and the earlobe looked swollen and infected. He wore a torn black T-shirt decorated with skulls and chains, and torn blue jeans that were an indeterminate grey colour. He had on a ladies sleeveless old knitted cardigan that had long lost any colour it had had, and black ragged mittens on his hands. I think they may have started out as gloves and ended up frayed and ineffectual as they now were. His hands were filthy and he held an unlit made-up cigarette between his fingers, and I kept imagining it was going to set his mittens on fire. His eyes held the professional beggar's plea. "Please man, spare us the price of a cuppa? Please, the price of a cuppa?"

The old training rose to the fore and I almost responded in the way I had been conditioned to. I almost said, "I don't give money to beggars, they spend it on drink and drugs. Pull up your socks (he wore none) and get on with it!" But the words froze on my lips. Whatever he had done, however to blame he was, no one, no one, deserved this comfortless hell. An underlying intelligence in the boy's eyes as he watched me told me he knew what I was thinking. I pulled out a fiver from my pocket and gave it to him. It didn't make me feel any better at all. The boy tried to hide his surprise but failed. He looked moderately pleased if a little suspicious. He turned back towards the porch.

"I say, just a minute."

I didn't know what prompted me. The boy looked at me over his shoulder, warily. The girl extricated herself from the pile of rags, stood and came forward. She was very pregnant. She seemed alarmed, afraid I was going to harm her man in some way, giving him her support.

"What's your name?" I asked. He rolled his eyes.

"What's it to you, man? Conditions with the hand-out, eh?" He sounded bitter.

"No. No," I said. "It's all right. I just . . ."

"Wondered what a nice boy like me is doin' in a place like

this?" he grinned sarcastically, showing ivory teeth. "My name is Kelvin an' I come from Liverpool. I came lookin' fer work. But there's none fer the likes of us. Ye have te have an' address fer anythin'. Fer work, fer anythin'. Even the DHSS won't give you nuthin', man, unless you have an address. Jade there," he indicated the waif who had circled us and was now tucked into his arms, her head in the hollow of his shoulder. "Pregnant, won't give her nuthin'. She was sexually abused by her father. She ran away. Well, wouldn't you? That's why we're here." Jade stared at me solemnly. Kelvin shrugged. There was no self-pity there, just bitterness.

"It's okay though. Could be worse. We got some straw from Safeway tonight. Jade's got me. An' there's money to come."

He nodded and turned his back on me. Mandy pulled my arm.

"Come on, Mark. Let's go."

"Yea, you take your woman's advice, get outa here," Kelvin called.

I glanced over my shoulder as we left. The boy had his arm around the girl and they were moving back to the doorway and the cardboard and the plastic and straw that was a luxury. Their home.

I drove home in silence. The traffic was light. People strolled along the pavements. A boy and a girl, hand-in-hand, ran across the street laughing, just as the lights turned to green. I cursed them and Mandy glanced at me. There were people in the glass-fronted coffee shop on the Cromwell Road, chatting, eating, cosy at their tables, bathed in light, smoking cigarettes. Others had spilled out of the pub onto the pavement in the warmth of the evening. They drank their beer and laughed and talked at the top of their voices. Long-legged girls in pocket-handkerchief skirts flirted with young men with their jackets hooked in a finger and held over their shoulders. And all I could think of was how? And why? What kind of a country did we live in that homeless people spilled out of the stations and onto the streets, that youngsters slept in porches? I tried to imagine what it would be like and failed. I banged my fist on the driving wheel and said, "Jeez!" and Mandy sighed.

"Don't take it to heart so, darling," she said.

"Damn it, Mandy, it's obscene," I muttered. "I'm so ashamed, I don't know why."

"You feel guilty. We all do."

"Not enough of us," I replied. "Not nearly enough. Ignorance is no excuse."

She looked at me. "Think you could drop me in Fulham?" she asked and added ruefully, "I know you, Mark, and I think you're in the mood to be alone tonight, darling. Yes?"

I nodded. "Sorry, love."

"I feel the same way. It was a nasty last act." She stared out of the window. I drove the car down Earls Court Road.

"The stores are packed with more food than we can possibly consume, and yet people are hungry. They have to beg for a cuppa. Something is very wrong here, Mandy."

"Oh, Mark, I know. Yet what can we do?"

"We have to change. That's what we have to do. Change."

I dropped her home then drove back to the Kings Road.

There was a light on in the window over the shop. My apartment. What the hell . . . ? My first thought was that Revel Blake had got into the apartment to keep our appointment. I had almost forgotten about it and him. I kicked the wheel of the car, said "damn, damn, damn" before it occurred to me that he couldn't have entered, that no one could without forcing their way in. The security was tight. I had some very valuable books. Banhams had assured me that they had made me impregnable.

The only other person with a key was Mandy and I had just dropped her in Fulham.

I opened the door and the light went out! The pool of orange it had cast on the pavement was cut off suddenly. I stood back from the door in the street and looked up, puzzled, then alarmed.

I went inside. I did not turn on the lights. All was silent but it seemed to me as if someone were there, listening to me in the darkness as I was listening to him. I moved cautiously into the shop, then tripped over what I thought was a pile of books in a place they should not have been. They thudded to the ground making a noise like thunder.

Suddenly the silence was broken. Someone clattered down the stairs from my apartment, pushing past me, and vanishing out into the Kings Road. I was shoved to one side and I fell over the pile of books, crashed down heavily on my hip, scattering volumes everywhere. I was too startled to follow whoever it was, too busy trying to get my balance in the dark. I groped my way to the lights and turned them on. Some of the books in the shop had been pulled from the shelves and lay on the floor, leaves open, spines cracked back.

I went upstairs. My apartment was devastated. I couldn't believe what I saw. Chaos reigned. A typhoon had passed through. I stood looking around me shaking my head. Everything was a mess. Tables were overturned, chairs lay on their sides. My books were strewn everywhere, pages torn, wrenched apart by some callous hand. Drawers had been pulled out, their contents tipped on the floor. My wardrobe was open, suits, trousers in violent disarray, laundered shirts ripped from their packaging, crushed and discarded. I stared at the utter devastation in the living room and bedroom. The kitchen had not been touched.

I phoned the police, then checked everything. A jade Buddah was missing. A rare copy of "Chinese Erotica in the Ming Dynasty" could not be found. And Alison Alyward's diary and address books had gone.

It seemed to me that the Buddah and the book were taken to cover and perhaps make less obvious the theft of the diary and address book.

I did not mention this to the police. What was the point? I did not say anything about Alison Alyward when I reported the theft. I was reticent because I felt the police would find it all terribly amusing and I was in no mood to be ridiculed. In fact I was in a terrible temper. The anger that I had felt in Kensington Church Street, that impotent rage had found a focus. I had been burgled. Invaded.

It was not until after the police had left, promising to return in the morning to dust for fingerprints, and warning me not to touch anything, that I discovered my wallet had been swiped from the back pocket of my trousers. Luckily I had had no credit cards in the wallet. They were in a small leather holder in my inside jacket pocket. The wallet, which had been lifted by Kelvin or, most likely his girlfriend, Jade, had held about twenty-five pounds. I was sick about it though, and I felt betrayed, let down.

I went to bed at last. It was a little before 2.a.m. I tried to sleep but my head was buzzing. Then I remembered Revel Blake. I wondered why he had not turned up.

Then I wondered if perhaps he had.

CHAPTER 8

My sleep was fitful. My brain seemed like a pudding-basin; a mixing bowl full of all sorts of ingredients, mostly nasty. Nightmares were peppered with sexual fantasies figuring Alison Alyward in scarlet satin and a suspender belt. Visions of her in lewd positions intermingled with dreams full of violence. Squirming piles of rat-infested refuse that when I touched them burst apart revealing whole armies of people, diseased, disfigured, bloated, lice-ridden lying in the rotting debris. Vermin abounded in the living darkness and all manner of fearful half-formed things that only manifest themselves in the subconscious appeared to terrify me, trapped as I was in unconscious immobility. These scenes dissolved and changed into a ring of Kelvins and Jades dancing around me, waving my possessions at me, my money, my wallet, Alison's address book and diary.

I awakened early, bathed in sweat. I leaped out of bed, grateful to escape, showered and brewed some coffee. I turned on the radio. Madonna was singing something about being like a virgin, which made me hoot. I felt disillusioned and angry, in a thoroughly bad mood, and I wasn't sorry when the fingerprint blokes arrived at the crack of dawn and started dusting. They were followed by Mandy who blew a fuse when she saw the mess. She nearly gave the game away by asking, in the policeman's hearing, "Mark, do you think this has anything to do with Alison?"

"Who is Alison?"' the Detective, a Sergeant Taylor, asked

casually, but I was not deceived; his eyes were sharp as razors. I parried the question, hustled Mandy out into the hall and down into the shop.

"I don't want them to know about Alison," I said firmly.

"Why ever not?"

"Well, think about it, Mandy. I say, 'I'm investigating the drowning of Alison Alyward.' They say, 'Oh, are you, sir? Has anyone told you that her drowning was thoroughly investigated by us, sir? That there *was* an inquest and that the verdict was suicide or accidental death? Sir? And certainly not murder?' And a lot about 'amateur.' Oh yes, Mandy, I can just hear them."

"Don't be so sarcastic, Mark. My, my, my, but we are in a bad mood this morning." Her voice had become affectionate, and she looked at me with a tender expression in her eyes. Then her expression hardened. "This is the pits," she said, "I'd like to get my knee in the groin of the bastard who did this." She looked very fierce.

"Don't worry, darling," I said, kissing her. "They haven't done too much damage. I'll start putting the books back on their shelves as soon as the police let me. I would have done it last night but I had strict instructions not to move or touch anything."

"Poor love. I'll help you."

"That boy Kelvin or, more likely his girl, Jade, nicked my wallet last night," I told her. "It's disillusioned me. Mankind stinks!"

She shrugged, "What do you expect?" she asked. "Wouldn't you if you were in their position?"

"They'll probably buy drugs with what they took."

She touched my cheek lightly. "Again, wouldn't you? But I agree. It wasn't nice."

She hugged me. We held each other close. She smelled of

Shalimar and shampoo and that private scent that I loved. Eventually she pulled away.

"What are you going to do today?" she asked.

"I need to see Revel Blake," I said. "I don't think he kept his appointment with me last night, and I want to know why not. And if he did, he's the one who created all this mess. Guess what's missing?"

"The diary and the address book?" she asked, breathlessly, eyes wide.

I nodded. "I have some very pertinent questions to ask Mr. Blake. But first we have to do the books."

"Do you remember what was in the books? Alison's?" she asked.

"Yes. You know my photographic memory, sweet. Besides I wrote down the more cryptic bits and pieces in an effort to decipher the messages. They are still in my jotter. Obviously, that I might do so did not occur to whoever took the books."

"I expect they were so chuffed to get them." Mandy smiled.

The police called us to tell us they had finished. I dressed in my beige canvas trousers with an Italian cotton striped shirt and a tan Armani blazer and tan loafers over cashmere socks. I suppose I wanted to impress Revel. I wanted to look cool, calm and collected. Mandy gave me a "Wow!" as I came down. I helped her for a couple of hours. It didn't take as long as I had thought, and I was able to leave while it was still early.

The traffic was even worse than the day before. Exhausts belched foul fumes, and drivers leaned out of windows screaming invectives at each other. They seemed to have lost all their manners and jockeyed for position at each other's expense and to the detriment of the traffic's flow.

I was surprised to find Revel's door open. I pushed it and

it swung wide. I stood listening a moment, then went in. The apartment was deadly silent. I could feel icy shivers up and down my spine as I entered and I tried to put my apprehension down to the fact that I was trespassing. That was enough to rattle any law-abiding citizen, but even as I used the excuse to myself I knew that I was lying. I called his name and my voice echoed, "Revel. Revel." No reply.

There was no heating on and the stone walls gave off a cold chill that made me pull my jacket closer around me. Silence.

There was a sudden bang behind me and I jumped, but it was only the front door slamming.

I stood, irresolute. The river flowed past the windows in indifferent motion. It was grey and the sunlight danced and sparkled on its opaque bosom. There were little boats tootling up and down, and a crowded pleasure boat chugged towards Southwark and people waved. One of the boats hooted. There was the sound of a tap dripping in the apartment, but otherwise it was quiet with a stillness that only unoccupied places have.

I opened the door to my right. It led to a stainless, immaculate kitchen, which looked as if it had never been used. I was terrified to make myself a cup of coffee but felt constrained to explore further. Why was one okay, the other not? I wondered.

I opened the next door, which led to the bedroom, and stepped back in surprise at the sight that met my eyes. The bedroom looked much the same as my flat had looked last night after the burglary.

For a moment I thought it was a natural chaos. Revel was the type who turned untidiness into an endearing virtue. The bed was rumpled, the black-and-white duvet cover was half on, half off the bed. Papers strewn about everywhere. Everything was in confusion. But the disarray was not that of an untidy person, lamps were broken, drawers pulled out, turned over and emptied onto the floor, exactly as they had been at my place. It was an appalling mess, and I was convinced that for some reason not clear to me at that moment, Revel had the same visitor that I had. It meant too that it had not been Revel, and I was glad about that. I had convinced myself that he had been the thief and this proved he was not.

I glanced around, taking it all in, then noticed on a table near the foot of the bed, standing in splendour, my Buddah. Beside it, my book. And beside that, the diary and the address book. My heart sank. It *had* been Revel after all. Then why . . . ? Revel had plundered my flat, taken my things. Then who had plundered his?

The room was *en suite* and as I looked around trying to figure it all out, I saw that there was a door ajar that led to a bathroom. There was a bright light shining there. I could see a *bidet,* the edge of a lavatory. And a bare leg.

My heart missed a beat then recommenced its hammering at twice the normal speed. I walked very hesitantly to the bathroom door and pushed it trying to open it wide enough to enter. Something obstructed its movement and I suddenly knew what it was. Reluctantly, I took a step back and sidled around the door. My eyes were unwilling to look at what was there.

He lay on the floor in the harsh strip lighting, naked and dead. Poor Revel. He looked very graceful, lying there, his body so slim and perfect. His black hair fell across his white cheek, his eyes were wide, but when I pushed back the glossy wing I recoiled from the terrible sight my gesture revealed. Revel's lips were drawn back, his teeth bared in a grimace of agony.

I noticed then that there was a syringe, a small empty

packet, all the paraphernalia of an O.D. And I was sure it wasn't. Revel Blake wasn't the suicide type any more than Alison Alyward had been. I was quite sure he had been murdered, but at that moment I didn't know why.

I decided to leave and I stood up, then paused in mid-movement, all senses alert.

There was someone outside. I heard the sound of soft runners across the floorboards, the sound of sneakers sneaking, the infinitesimal creak of boards. I was frozen, immobile, petrified with fear and revulsion and shock. I heard the front door bang as I came out of the bathroom and saw at the same time that the address book and diary were no longer on the table.

Had the murderer been in the bedroom all the time? Behind a curtain? In the wardrobe? He/She had watched and waited until I had gone into the bathroom. Jeez, it was spooky.

Perhaps Revel Blake *had* O.D.'d and the man (or woman) who had just fled had been as horrified as I to see a body in the bathroom. I just didn't know what to think anymore, and I had the distinct feeling that things were getting out of hand.

I decided to get the hell out of there. There was nothing I could do for Revel and if the police found me there, how could I explain what it was all in aid of? I wasn't sure myself, and some of my actions could be misconstrued. The less I had to do with the police the better.

I left the building and sat a moment trying to steady myself. I was in a state of shock. My head reeled and suddenly, there on the dockside, I leaned over like any drunk, and threw up. My stomach hurt. There was a terrible tearing feeling below my lungs and I stood, helpless, my forehead against the concrete wall. I wiped my mouth with my handkerchief. I felt foul and I took a couple of deep breaths to try to steady myself. What to do now? Where to go next? What to make of it all? I was out of my depth and I knew it. Yet I had to go on. Too much had happened to stop now. I couldn't see Alison Alyward's drowning and Revel Blake's overdosing as accidents and I couldn't allow them to go unpunished.

I took the list of names out of my pocket. Whoever had stolen the diary and address book obviously wanted a name or appointment that they contained. They would not realize that I had copied those names and appointments down. Whoever wanted them so badly had something to hide. What was it? I did not know, but one thing I could be certain of: a name or an appointment in one of those books would give me the answer and I was going to work my way solidly through every one.

Abigale McNaughton headed the list. An appointment with her was mentioned (A.McN. re b.) She was in the address book as Abigale McNaughton (and Tom) and an address in Elgin Crescent. Near Mother.

I drove until I reached a phonebox. My hands were shaking and I was cursed roundly half a dozen times, deservedly, for my appalling driving. I called Mother and told her I would drop in for lunch. I called Mandy and told her what had happened.

"But, Mark, you'll have to report it to the police."

"I'm going to."

"But I thought you said . . ."

"I'm going to do it anonymously. Look, Mandy, it wouldn't help Revel now. And it might hamper me. I intend to get the bastards who did these things. Wendy was right. Something very fishy is going on and I must get to the bottom of it. If I tell the police about it they won't believe me, and I'll get into all sorts of trouble. This will be called an overdose. You mark my words."

I could hear her sigh. "Well, if, you're sure." She sounded doubtful. "Are you here for lunch?" she asked.

"I'm going to Mother's for lunch."

"Okay. Good idea. Perhaps she'll persuade you to behave like a dutiful citizen."

I called the police, said I had reason to believe there was the body of a man in the apartment in Southwark. I gave the address and hung up. They did their best to keep me on the line, but I cut the connection promptly as soon as I had told them where to go.

I still felt very shaky. I got in the car and, trying not to let the traffic get to me, I drove from the city, down the Strand, up Haymarket, down Regent and Oxford Street. The traffic was infinitely better there, and I drove along relieved until I realized why the traffic had eased up. No private cars were allowed. I cursed, was waved to the kerb by a policeman. As I apologised I realized I was barely holding myself together. I decided to have a drink before I went much further.

I stopped at a pub in Westbourne Grove. People were drinking on the pavement, girls and boys curiously alike in torn denims and T-shirts. Some of the girls looked very tasty in jeans, which they had cut off high up the thigh, but I was in no mood to sit and admire the view. I had a brandy then moved on but couldn't help noticing the black plastic bags and rubbish festering everywhere.

The world had changed. I was not sure when exactly it had happened, but I knew it had been brought about by two events: my encounter with Kelvin and Jade and the sub-life of the homeless, and the death of Revel Blake. I had been secure, cocooned in my warm protected world, and I had not had the eyes to see the misery around me. Now I would find it difficult to ignore, impossible not to feel responsible. I would never see the world I lived in through the innocent eyes of ignorance. From now on I would be acutely aware of what was hidden in the corners others did not see, what was going on beneath the glossy surface. And I mourned my lost innocence as I drove further into the mystery. No, I would never be the same again.

CHAPTER 9

Elgin Crescent connects Portobello Road and Clarendon Road in a graceful curve. Abigale McNaughton's house was between Ledbroke Grove and Kensington Park Road.

I ran up the steps and rang the bell. A blonde girl in a navy pleated skirt, a blue-and-white striped shirt, and a navy cashmere pullover thrown carelessly over her shoulders opened the door. She was pretty in a Sloane Ranger way: delicate features, flat blond hair cut in an even shoulder-length bob held back by a navy padded Alice band. She surveyed me with hard blue eyes.

"Abigale McNaughton?"

"Good God, no! Abby is down there." She pointed over the parapet to the basement.

"Oh. Thanks."

She immediately closed the door before I had time to turn away.

"Don't enter any charm school competition—" I muttered, and I could hear the thump-thump of her loafers as she ran up the stairs.

I went down to the basement and rang the bell. The girl who answered could not have differed more from the yuppie lady upstairs. She was what I would have described as Conservative Ethnic, a sort of leftover Seventies flower child, or perhaps, today, she would be called a Greenpeace person. She had lots of pre-Raphaelite hair floating about and she wore no make-up. Her feet were encased in leather monk sandals. Her Dirndl skirt was Laura Ashley and she wore a cotton blouse in an unbecoming shade of yellow. Two round-eyed children stood, one on either side of her, holding her skirt with one hand, a raw carrot in the other.

"Yes?" Her lashes were fawn, her eyes lacked definition and were innocent of mascara.

"Could I speak to you a moment?" I asked.

She looked dubious. "I don't know . . . what about?" She peered at me and the wide-eyed children stared unblinking and solemn.

"Have you got identification?" she asked in a small, apologetic voice. She was so indecisive that if I had been a burglar, a con man or a sex maniac, I would have been inside the house long since. She needed lessons from Miss Sloane upstairs.

"I'm making enquiries about Alison Alyward. She was a friend of yours, I believe?"

Her face cleared as if I had said some magic word and she stood back. "Come in. Come in. A friend of Alison's? Of course I am. Her best. Oh, do come in."

She led me into a living room-cum-kitchen furnished with the best of *Habitat*. There was a clotheshorse laden with drying nappies in the corner. A bunch of dried flowers in a bowl on the table said a lot about her. The stalls were a riot of cheap fresh flowers and these were dusty and tired-looking. The whole place had the appearance of careless housewifery. There were some homemade candles stuck in jam jar, the kind that smelled of India when lit, which in an English kitchen was a bit weird.

Abigale seemed unconscious of her cluttered home. She retrieved some children's toys and books from an easy chair, and, without apologising, asked me to sit down. I liked her better for her lack of pretension. She sat the two children down on the sofa and gave them the toys and books she had taken from the seat of my chair.

I'm not very good about children's ages, not having had any experience with them, but it seemed to me that the boy was about four years of age and the girl, probably three.

Near the window was a carrycot on a steel stand.

"Tea?" she asked.

I nodded. She looked a little shame-faced.

"I don't suppose you like herb teas?" she asked hesitantly.

"As a matter of fact, I do," I said. "What kind have you got?"

She looked relieved and two bright spots of pink flushed her cheeks.

"Oh, all kinds," she said breathlessly, obviously delighted. "Chamomile, Rose-hip, Vervain, Peppermint . . ."

"Chamomile will be fine," I said. She relaxed and went to the kitchen part at the other end of the room. It was a pleasure to watch her make the tea; she did it with a tenderness that was almost Japanese.

Neither of us spoke until the tea was made and served. Then she placed a cup on a little bamboo table near me and sat opposite me, all attention.

"Well? How is Alison? I haven't seen her for . . . oh, ages!"

This was not what I had expected and I was thrown. I stared at her and seeing my expression, she cried, "What is it? What's the matter? Has something happened to her?"

"I thought you knew. Thought you must have known . . ."

"Known what?"

"Must have heard about . . ."

"Heard about . . . something's happened to Alison?"

"Yes, I'm afraid so." I felt very awkward. "She drowned. She is dead, I'm afraid."

"Oh, poor Alison." Was there relief in her somewhere trying to hide behind sorrow?

"I would have thought you would have read about it in the newspapers or seen it on the telly."

"We don't have television," she said primly. "And I don't often read papers. I don't have much time. Besides, we've been in the cottage." Then she sighed and said again, "Poor Alison," and again I sensed a lack of sincerity. She glanced at me and she saw what I was thinking. She gave a little shrug as if to say, "What does it matter" and said, "I never really liked her, I'm sorry to say. I'm sure you'll think me awful." Her eyes were hard and matter-of-fact. "It's no use pretending. She was so selfish, you see. Everything, everyone was for her own personal use. She took; she never gave. She was the kind of person who took it for granted that you wanted her around. It never occurred to her that people existed independently of her, had a life to live when she was not there. I think she thought people froze, were on ice, until she needed them. No. I never really liked her." She looked at me defensively this time. "That doesn't mean I wished her ill," she added hastily. "I hope she didn't suffer . . . ?"

"She drowned," I said.

"Oh, Mr. Dangerfield, what an awful thing. Of course she suffered." She clapped her hand to her cheek. "Oh, Mr. Dangerfield, what on earth will you think of me?"

"It's not important what I think," I said coolly. "But I need to know all about Alison; I want you to tell me what you know."

"But why? What do you want to know for?" She looked uneasily this way and that as if seeking escape. "You said she drowned? Are you a policeman?"

"No. No. I'm not. No, wait. I'm a friend of Lady Cadbury, who was also a friend—"

"Of Alison's, yes. I know. And?" She was wary now, staring at me intently.

"Well, Lady Cadbury is worried that Alison's drowning was not accidental, that something, er, happened."

I did not think I was doing very well and quite expected her to ask me to leave. To my surprise, she nodded.

"Yes. Lady Cadbury is right. Alison would not drown accidentally. She was a terrific swimmer."

"Do you think she would commit suicide?" I asked and Abigale shook her head.

"Never," she said with certainty. "Not Alison. If it's a question of suicide or murder then it'll have to be murder."

"Why do you say that?" I asked. "And by the way, do call me Mark."

"Okay, Mark. And I'm Abigale. Look, I better explain. I've known Alison a long time. She would never do anything that private. There would be an audience. Alison liked attention too much to go drown herself." She wrinkled up her nose. "Besides, Alison was conceited about her looks. Well, maybe that's a little unfair, not so much conceited as proud of the way she looked. She'd never destroy that. No. If she was going to commit suicide she would have taken sleeping pills of some sort and hope to be found in bed looking lovely. Not all bloated by the water, y'know?"

I nodded. "You said you had known her a long time?"

"Yes. We were at school together in Berkshire. The village school. Alison was brought up by her aunt, a Mrs. . . . ."

"Everton. I've seen her, talked to her."

Abigale gave a little snort. "Bet she didn't care too much—about Alison's death, I mean." She didn't seem to expect an answer and continued. "She was always acting kind and sweet, a real Mrs. Tiggiwinkle, but underneath she didn't like children. You could tell. You could see she was restraining herself. She would smack my hand when I tried to grab a cookie hot out of the oven. You know how impatient kids are." She gazed fondly at the two children on the sofa, the girl staring solemnly at the illustrations in a fairy tale book, the boy systematically tearing a comic to pieces. "She'd go to smack me with her teeth clenched, and you could see she really wanted to hurt, you know, strike hard. Only she never did. She controlled herself. Alison said she was like that, always holding back." Abigale was speaking to herself now, remembering. "I met Tom at school. He's my husband. He adored Alison. All the boys did, but they were afraid of her as well. Tom and I were always friends. He went out with Alison but something happened, and he said he never wanted to go out with her again. She was fast, he said. Then our friendship developed and we got married and came to live in London. I lost touch with Alison. I saw her when I went back to Cottesloe to visit my parents, or Tom's. Then she left, too. They said she had come to London. People said Mrs. Everton threw her out when she found out about the baby."

"The baby? You mean . . ."

"Alison had a baby." Abigale's cheeks changed colour. Her face went bright red. "Oh, yes. She got pregnant when she was about eighteen. Down there in Cottesloe. Can you imagine? Old Mrs. Everton was furious. So out Alison went. She had it adopted," she added quickly. "I felt so sorry for her." She glanced at the two children on the sofa, eyes tender. "I don't know how she could bear to part with it. But she did . . ."

"Do you know who the father is?"

Abigale shook her head. "No. No one did. Alison never said. At least I never heard. Never asked." Abigale was looking shifty. "I think that was why she liked coming here—I didn't pry."

A baby began to cry. I had not realized that there was a baby in the carrycot. Abigale picked up a little wrapped bundle. The crying stopped as if a needle had been taken off a record. Abigale stood with the baby against her shoulder, her back against the window. I could see feet passing by outside.

"I'm afraid I haven't been much help," she said and it sounded like dismissal.

"Why did Alison have your name and number in her book?" I asked. "You don't sound as if you saw much of her."

"Oh, yes, we did. Later. It was funny, though. Alison the socialite, the glamorous *femme fatale,* you wouldn't think she'd want to come here. But she called me up one day out of the blue. One day last year. It was cold. Snowing. She asked to come and see me. She seemed very distressed. She never told me why. She just sat there where you are sitting now, swathed in furs, chinchilla, I think." A frown creased her brow. "Poor little animals. She knew how Tom and I felt about fur coats." She glanced at me for understanding. Apparently the fact that I drank herb tea made me a kindred spirit. "I suppose it's a bit loony," she said.

"Your views are quite fashionable today . . . about things like that." I coughed. "And?"

"And? Oh, yes. Well, she sat there and played with the child. Flower." She indicated her daughter on the sofa. "After that, she came often. About once a month. She never talked about her life, but I could see she was unhappy. There was deep despair in her eyes. A kind of hopelessness. She was often jittery. But she never confided in us." This last was said quickly and earnestly. "I gave her all the help I could."

I thought it a strange and contradictory thing to say.

"Was she very much in love with Revel Blake?"

She stared at me incredulously, jaw dropping open. Then she burst out laughing. "Revel? Revel? Revel Blake is gay," she spluttered finally.

"Gay?" It was my turn to be surprised. I had never heard anything like that about him, but then, why should I? I had not been interested in him in college. I hardly knew him.

"But, I thought he was her boyfriend?"

"No. They were just great friends. No doubt about that. They were very close. She often asked him to be her escort. But boyfriend, no, never. I think she had an older man, someone very important. I think she may have used Revel as a cover-up. I don't know. I'm sorry . . ."

The baby began to cry again. Abigale started to sway and pat it on the back. "Now if you don't mind . . ."

She obviously wanted me to go. I stood and she followed me into the hall.

"There *was* someone in her life," she said. "But I don't know who. I've been curious for a long time about who it is . . . was," she said, showing me out. "Like who was the father of her child. But I expect now we'll never know." She sighed.

I hoped desperately that she was wrong.

CHAPTER 10

"I know nothing, Mother. Nothing. I've gone backwards instead of forwards."

I know I sounded impatient. The morning had been a strain, my nerves were taut.

"Nonsense Mark. It's just that at the moment none of it makes sense, but it will, it will."

"I was sure I had the answer. I had a pattern. But it keeps shifting. I feel I have a theory and I am bending the facts to try to fit my theory instead of the other way around."

"What is your theory?" Mother asked.

"Well, Alison was killed and so was Revel because of something they knew that I didn't. I think it's something to do with drugs. It always is. The drug scene is the one sure area of violence. It was something in the diary or address book, a name, a telephone number that gives something away: a source, a connection." I shrugged. "I don't *know*. And Mother, Alison changes daily—no, hourly—from angel to villainess and back again. One moment I'm feeling sorry for her, the next all my sympathy for her vanishes."

"That, Mark, makes her sound human. Most of us are a mixture of the hateful and the lovable."

My mother and I were having coffee in her living room. Lunch had consisted of a delicious cheese soufflé with salad, followed by a bowl of fruit, from which I had taken and consumed a peach, a pear, and a fistful of grapes. We sat talking now, comfortably. She had enjoyed Covent Garden the previous night.

"It was 'Romeo and Juliet.' Wayne Eagling danced a magical Mercutio. It was so good that the Major didn't drop off—not once!"

Then she had asked me about the case, knowing how much I wanted to talk about it.

"I'm beginning to regret ever getting involved with it all," I said.

"Nonsense, Mark. You're being impatient. You know a great deal more now than you did at the beginning. But do be careful. I don't like the sound of what is happening. Revel Blake's fate has made me distinctly apprehensive."

"It *might* have had nothing at all to do with Alison Alyward."

"You don't believe that for a moment, and neither do I." Mother frowned. "It's all connected somehow," she finished lamely.

"But there's no motive, Mother. No one seems to have had a motive for killing her. Or Revel Blake, for that matter . . ."

"You'll find a motive, I'm sure. There are still so many unanswered questions. Like why, if she didn't want the baby, did she have it in the first place?"

"Perhaps she didn't know she was pregnant until it was too late?"

Mother's eyebrows shot up. "In this day and age? A girl like Alison? I doubt it."

"When you say 'a girl like Alison' what do you mean exactly?"

"Worldly-wise, I suppose. She gave the impression of being very sophisticated, very knowledgeable."

"Appearances can be very misleading," I said, and she nodded.

"What next?" she asked.

"Well, this afternoon, I thought I'd visit Jason Bestwick. He's the obvious one to see, the last of the Fab Four, the only one I haven't spoken to. The address is Hampstead. I thought I'd drive up there to see him. I must remember, though, not to mention Revel Blake's death."

"Why ever not?"

"I'm not supposed to know about it, am I?"

"Oh, Mark, I heard it on the news. On the radio minutes before you arrived. I didn't connect it at all with you at that point. And they didn't release a name. But it said that the body of a young man was found dead from what appeared to be a drug overdose in a warehouse apartment in Southwark. That's Revel Blake, right?"

I nodded. "Right."

"You must be careful," she said, seriously for her.

"Oh, Mother, don't be silly. I'm old enough to look after myself," I said briskly, "Besides, that combat course and my judo ought to see me through. Please, Mother, don't worry about me."

"Well, solve it quickly, Mark. For all our sakes."

She was right though; it had become a dangerous business. Whoever it was, whoever killed Alison and Revel, was not playing. They were ruthless people. However, I did have one advantage: I was prepared. I said good-bye to Mother and hoped it would be enough.

The drive from Mother's to Hampstead took me along Westbourne Grove, up Chepstow Road, through Kilburn. As I drove I became aware of the piles of black plastic bags filled with refuse everywhere. Had they always been there? If so, why hadn't I seen them before? It was as if the output of filth that people accumulated had increased and now threatened to split its seams, overspill and drown, or bury us. Has plastic taken over? I wondered. I changed course, unable to bear the festering clutter I saw everywhere. The skyscrapers raped the sky and decimated the horizon. The concrete jungle leading up to Kilburn and all down Adelaide Road had hard edges, no softness anywhere. The only green straggled in a sickly manner.

The trees were isolated. My eyes searched the world for plant life as a thirsty traveller searches for water in the desert. Was I becoming paranoid?

I was unbelievably relieved to reach the sweet greenery of Hampstead. The heath was gentle on the eyes and the air seemed clean and fresh after the fume-laden atmosphere of the city.

I found the house Jason Bestwick lived in, and I parked just around the corner.

He was sitting in the garden at a white wrought-iron table, a Panama hat on his head. He was wearing a blue-and-white striped shirt open at the neck, and unstructured blue gabardine pants. A little tail of brown hair in an elastic band stuck out from under the back of his hat. He was handsome, clean-cut, with brilliant white teeth, tanned skin, and his hand shook. I could not help noticing because he was drinking lager and the glass threatened to spill, so he jerked it to his mouth, drank greedily and returned it to the table with a bang. He was talking into a portable telephone. He squinted up at me when I stopped in front of him.

"Jason Bestwick?" I asked. He covered the mouthpiece.

"Who wants to know?" His voice was arrogant, the expression on his face pugnacious.

"My name is Mark. Mark Dangerfield."

"So? What do you want from me?"

"A few words. May I sit down?"

"No. Not until I know what you want."

"I wanted to ask you a few questions about Alison Alyward."

"What for?" He was really making it difficult. He took a gulp of the lager, lifting the glass carefully, this time trying to steady his hand. "Look, something's come up," he said into the telephone, "I'll get back to you," and he snapped down the collapsible aerial with a flourish and looked at me coolly.

"Well?" he said.

"I'm checking into the death of Alison Alyward, as I said."

"She drowned. They brought in a verdict—"

"I know." I sounded impatient now. "Lady Cadbury hired me to make sure it was the right verdict."

I did not need to bring Wendy's name in, but I couldn't resist the temptation in the face of his rudeness. It made him sit up, alert suddenly.

"Mother?"

"Yes. If your mother is Wendy Cadbury, yes."

"But *why* in God's name?" He sounded exasperated. "Why? What the hell is she up to?"

"She just wants to make sure that Alison didn't meet with foul play. She was very fond of her, you know."

"Oh, balls! Mother has never cared for anyone except herself. She's doing this to get at me."

"Why would she do that?" I asked mildly.

"I don't know. I haven't a clue. But she always wants to know what I'm up to and—"

"With respect, I think that's a bit far-fetched . . ."

"You don't know my mother."

"Oh but I do, Mr. Bestwick. I do know Wendy. And I think that if she wanted to 'get at you' as you put it, she would find an easier way of doing it."

I wanted to ask him what was the matter with him, why his hand shook like an old man's, what made him so angry. His anger simmered beneath the surface all the time we spoke. He looked as if he was spoiling for a fight.

"What are you afraid of?" I asked.

His eyes widened and he looked at me as if I'd threatened him. Then he recovered. No doubt he was worried that I would report unfavourably to his mama. I wondered about that, too; why Wendy Cadbury had not told me about her son.

"Look, you and Alison and Revel Blake and Talia Morgan were friends. Is there anything that you can remember that Alison said to you, anything at all that happened that would lead you to believe she was afraid?"

He shook his head violently to left and right. "No. Absolutely no."

"Did you know she had a child?"

He choked on his beer. He was sweating now, and he took off his hat and fanned himself. It was hot but not that hot. What was worrying him so?

"Look, I didn't know *that* much about Alison . . ." he said, but he sounded doubtful.

"Nonsense. You were buddies." I took a chance. If he went to the police I would be in deep shit. But I somehow didn't think he would. He was not the picture of an honourable man. He stared at me, visibly shaken. "Did you know that Revel Blake has taken an overdose?" I asked. "But I don't think that was how he died. I think he was murdered by the same person or persons that murdered Alison."

If I had wanted to scare him I couldn't have succeeded better, but I had not wanted to frighten him witless, which was what happened.

He gagged, his eyes bulged, his breathing became uneven and harsh.

"Get away." He looked at me as if I was Freddie from "Nightmare on Elm Street." "Get away from me. I have nothing to say to you, nothing." And like a hunted man he rose and literally fled into the house.

They were all afraid. Revel Blake had been extremely nervous. Talia Morgan, under those luscious lashes, was scared. And without doubt, Jason Bestwick was terrified. I felt frustrated and irritated. I had not got any nearer to knowing why.

CHAPTER 11

You expect Soho to be tawdry. The black plastic there is understandable, although as that thought crossed my mind, I shook my head at myself. Why should piles of rubbish be okay in the West End, but not in Kensington or Fulham?

Red, yellow, blue and green neon signs flickered on and off, colouring the faces of the crowds that thronged through the narrow streets. Porn shops everywhere, plain-fronted by law, they nevertheless indicated their purpose clearly. The word 'Adult' was displayed for all to see. The word meant explicit sex. People knew what to expect when they saw 'Adult'. There were less discreet awnings to the strip joints. Clipped behind glass, photographs of girls in various stages of undress, bondage, sexual positions that owed nothing to missionaries, advertised what went on deep down in those sad caverns. Outside, cheerful, gaudily painted Bet Lynches' cracked repartee with bright-eyed boys on the make, their pimps never far away. Black guys in cerise- or silver-padded jackets and gaudy shirts with earrings laden with gold and diamonds, lounged against dark hallways in Wardour and Dean Street. Lager louts linked arms and walked four abreast down the pavement singing, "Here we go, Here we go, Here we go," over and over, loudly and tunelessly, scattering all before them. Formally dressed men and women on their way to the theatres in Shaftsbury Avenue quickly gave way and parted before the louts like the Dead Sea before Moses. Music blared from the sandwich bars. Hawkers plied their wares. Artists painted the sleaze life parading past them. Hookers sat in the tawdry glass-fronted cafes chewing on rubbery sandwiches, drinking coffee from polystyrene beakers, eyes mindlessly casing the crowd, looking for trade. Tramps, bag ladies, whey-faced teenagers, mothers with babies in their arms, begged.

I stepped over the feet of an eighteen-year-old boy. He sat on the pavement, a notice printed in felt-tip on a piece of cardboard: 'HOMELESS, UNEMPLOYED, I DON'T WANT TO BEG BUT I HAVE NO CHOICE. GIVE ME WHAT YOU CAN. IF IT'S A JOB I'LL THANK YOU FOREVER.'

His eyes were bright blue and still held a twinkle of hope. He gave me a smile and a nod as I dropped a pound coin in the upturned lid of a biscuit tin, the contents of which were mainly coppers. I thought of Kelvin and Jade. Little white face like a star in a dark corner.

I had gone down Wardour Street past the film houses and recording studios. Chinese, Italian, French restaurants swallowed up great crowds of chattering people, loud and gaudy as macaws. Delicatessen and specialist shops were, at this time of night, closed. It was nine o'clock on a warm April evening in the year of Our Lord 1989.

I asked the louts standing in doorways, luring the bashful down the stairs to the promise of erotic delights below, "Do you know Mr. Moto?"

The answer, when I got one, was always "No." Sometimes a bouncer glowered at me and did not reply. Sometimes a jaded-looking woman behind a cash desk licked her lips and said, "Come on down, dearie. We got anything you want here."

Sometimes I got no reaction at all.

Up Greek Street. More plastic bags full of refuse; bags advertising Sainsbury's, Argos, Selfridge's, Bejam, Marks & Spencer, even Harrod's elegant green container, all full of rotting food; chicken bones, dirty tissues, MacDonald's red cartons, used Tampax, orange peel, decaying fruit, empty baked bean tins, foil containers empty of their TV dinners. A lot of the stuff was indestructible, imperishable substances. People kicked the bags as they passed by. Dogs nosed around them chewing and scavenging, then peed on them and the bags split, disgorging their festering contents onto the pavement. The bag ladies and the old tramps rummaged for a cigarette butt, a half-eaten hamburger, a morsel from a chicken leg: the crumbs that fell from the rich man's table.

I walked up Dean Street. There was a cacophony of the combined noise of taxis; car doors slamming, disco music blaring, the raucous shouts of drunken yobbos, the high chatter of the pros, the excited greetings of people catching up on their news, the sound of humanity at play.

I realized eventually that I was being followed. I wouldn't have noticed if my tail had been any good, but he was hopeless.

A seedy little man, his clothing was too distinctive for him to be as anonymous as a good tail should be. You could see he had once been dapper. His coat looked about fifth generation via a charity shop, and had once been camel. It was clapped out, pileless on the seams and edges, stained and creased as if it had been used as a blanket. He wore a paisley scarf, brightly coloured, jaunty at his throat. At a distance, if I half closed my eyes, he looked like an old actor in a twenties farce. His hair was dyed, parted at the side, swept tastefully over a bald pate, and slicked back. His nose was a huge cherry world dotted with craters and he had a little toothbrush Hitler moustache and wildly inappropriate National Health false teeth.

He had stuck behind me for at least the last half hour, weaving and dodging, and I saw him first out of the corner of my eye and pretended not to notice him even when he became more and more conspicuous. He had become cocky. I waited until he got quite close, then turned suddenly. He started, jumped at my abruptness. The red and blue lights from a pool parlour shone alternately and his face and his eyes, startled, slid away from mine.

"You're following me," I said. "Why?"

"I'm no—" He was going to deny it, but I took his arm and pulled it behind his back in a hammerlock. No one paid any attention. The crowd swirled around me, people laughing, intent on each other. A taxi mounted the curb, the driver close to us, the headlights catching us in their glare. He shook his fist out of the window almost under my nose at some obstruction that was slowing him down that I could not see. Then he backed the cab and drove away. I think I could have knifed the little man or shot him as I held him and walked away and no one would have taken any notice. I think he thought that too and it made him nervous.

"Okay, okay. I was. I was. Hey! Hey! Leave me alone. Hey! God's sake!"

"Why?"

"Buy me a drink, I tell you," he said, brushing himself down, sounding indignant. "God's Sake! People today!"

I cogitated, decided it would be the quickest way to get to the bottom of the situation, took his arm and led him into The Three Greyhounds.

"I'll have a short," he demanded as I sat him at a small table, its surface awash with beer. The place was crowded. Dense cigarette smoke made it hard to breathe. Someone was singing "My Way" in a tear-filled voice.

"Oh, no," I said. "No short until you tell me why you were

101

following me." I could hardly hear myself over the din. The little man searched my face.

"I heard you ask for a certain gentleman," he said with a canny expression on his face, his eyes darting about uneasily. "An' I know where you can find him."

I had expected him to say someone had paid him to follow me and I had hoped to find out who it was in the certainty that I could then find out what was behind the violence and the murders. I was therefore thrown by the turn of events, but I got his drift. He was just a poor sod of an opportunist.

"Mr. Moto?" I asked.

He looked wildly around. "Shush. For Christ's sake! Jeez, man, you crazy?"

"Oh for God's sake this is not . . ."

"Look, Mister, I din' say nuthin.' See? I don' know you, you don' know me. Now, you pass me a tenner. I buy my own drink."

The shifty eyes skidded around the pub, but we were the only two sitting down and we were surrounded by a wall of bodies, a thick pall of smoke and an unmerciful din.

"That's a very expensive drink," I said.

"It's a expensive time—'spensive decade we live in." He fingered his paisley scarf delicately. His accent was a mixture of Cockney and Maltese or Portuguese.

I held the note in my hand just out of his reach.

"Okay," I said. "Talk."

"Try Mangoes." He reached for the note.

"How do I know you're not just playing me for a nerd?"

"You don'," he said, smiling, and showing the row of uneasy false teeth. "But does it look like I'd try that? You might come back. Find me. Naw, I'm not lyin'. Me no, I don' take such risks. I don' wanna end up, a broken arm mebbe. So I tell the truth."

He palmed the note so swiftly that even if anyone had been watching us, I doubt if they'd have seen him do it.

Then he was gone. One moment he was there, the next swallowed up in the crowd.

I pushed my way out. Neither of us had bought a drink but no one noticed. A tall black hooker buttonholed me as I left the pub.

"Want some pussy, baby? Any way you want it, man." She licked her lips. Her lipstick was mauve and shiny, her tongue bright red. She wore a silver Lurex dress cut down so low you could see her nipples, the skirt riding provocatively up to her ass showing long legs in high-heeled, ankle-strapped shoes. The shoes were red.

"Could you tell me where Mangoes is?" I asked.

The exotic facade vanished, the face became ugly, the lips curled in a snarl. "Fuck off," she hissed, tossed her head and sashayed away.

I asked the first tout I came to where Mangoes was. That was a mistake, his aim was to get me into *his* place.

"Look, be reasonable," he told me. "Mangoes got nuttin' we ain't got. Down 'ere, G'vnor, is ecstasy."

I felt someone tap my shoulder. It was a bobby on the beat.

"You asking for Mangoes, sir?" he said, then added helpfully, "Just keep straight on, turn right at the next traffic lights and you'll see it right in front of you."

"Thank you, Officer," I said, trying not to look guilty.

"Not at all, sir."

He was a bright-eyed, clean-faced, healthy-looking young boy smelling strongly of aftershave. His companion was a slim, tiny girl. She looked very cute in her uniform. I thought there was something vulnerable and hopeful about them, which in this environment made me sad. Which was, I suppose, sentimental of me.

Trying my best to look like a law-abiding citizen, I followed the directions I had been given. They were accurate and I found myself in front of the place. The sign flashed on and off. A girl with a Betty Boop figure was picked out in red-and-blue neon on a sign a floor above me and beside it the name Mangoes. It was exactly the same as most of the other strip joints in the area outside the pictures, the tout, the jaded has-been at the cash desk, wearily filing her nails.

I paid the fortune asked of me, and a man in a dinner jacket and bow tie with an unhealthy grey skin and bags under his eyes led me down to the lowest depths.

The walls that flanked the narrow staircase were lined with red plush and framed pictures of girls with over-sized mammary glands in various poses of what was supposed to be provocative erotica, but was simply crude and gross. The unhealthy-faced usher took me into the auditorium. The air was heavy with Georgio and the smell of sweet perspiration as we passed the stage. A blast of loud bump-and-grind music blasted my ears and I was ushered to a small table in an atmosphere heavy with cigarette smoke and the stale smell of a place that is never aired. The stench mixed with some cheap-smelling air spray made me feel giddy. There were waitresses around, lounging, sitting, indifferent expressions on their faces. They wore black net tights and frilly maid's uniforms and looked creased and used-up. Their eyes were dead, like stones at the bottom of a dark pool.

Men sat at the tables and drank a dubious champagne and gawped.

"You wan' some champagne, dearie?" A dyed blonde leaned over me, skin thick with make-up. She slid her hand down my groin then she stood up and winked at me with a look that promised undreamed-of debauchery.

"It's expected," she said, scarlet lips pouting, trying hard for conspiratorial chumminess, and failing. "I'll get in trouble, duckie, if you don't buy the champers."

It was grotesque.

"All right," I said. She tried to look pleased but only managed to look tired.

The girl on the stage held a whip, which she cracked now and then in a half-hearted sort of manner. She was dressed in leather. Her nipples poked out of a top like a straight jacket designed by Gaultier. She wore hot pants with a zip at the front. The zip was halfway down, or up, depending on the way you looked at it. She cracked the whip listlessly, then put one booted foot on a school chair and suddenly arched her neck and threw her head back till her hair swept the floor. The nipples stood out against the white backdrop. She jerked her head over, seemed to be doing odd things to herself, then slowly began to unbutton the nasty little hooks that held her top together. This went on for some time. I had difficulty keeping my eyes open. My inertia was due, in all fairness, not to the leather-clad chick's ineptitude but to the lack of oxygen in the room and the fact that I had had little sleep the previous night.

The other men, sitting at the tables, sipping their drinks, seemed intent on her every move. One man behind me was breathing heavily. Poor bastard, I thought, there was no joy here.

The champagne came. It was awful. Tasted like mouthwash. I beckoned. The blonde was hovering and her mechanical smile switched on quickly when I managed to catch her eye.

"Yes, sir?" she purred, putting an almighty effort into being nice. My heart bled for her. The energy it must have taken! You could almost feel her exhaustion.

"Could I see Mr. Moto?" I asked politely. Her face paled.

She looked disconcerted.

"I don't know . . . I think maybe . . . I'm not sure, you see . . ."

"Just go and tell him Mark Dangerfield wants a word. Tell him it's about Alison Alyward."

There was another girl dancing now, in the process of revealing herself slowly to the gaping crowd of fish-eyed men that stared at her with slack jaws. She jerked about to some fast rock that pounded with a primitive beat and she looked down at her gyrations as if her body did not belong to her and its amazing contortions had nothing whatsoever to do with her. Every now and then she looked into the blue smoke of the room and pouted her lips and blew a kiss into the dark silence, gave a mechanical smile, then switched it off and returned to the contemplation of her bumping and grinding torso.

The blonde returned with the bouncer. I thought I was going to be thrown out. I stood up. The music became louder, faster. I had a moment of pure panic. The bouncer must have been about six-four in his stocking feet and built like Arnold Schwarzenegger. His neck was as thick as a tree trunk and he had the muscles of a man who spends a lot of time in the gym pumping iron. Above this sat a curiously small head, tiny vacant eyes, a broken nose, dainty mouth and a head that was completely shaved. This was a vain thug programmed to do his master's bidding. There would be no reasoning with this bloke, he would do as he was told and logic would not enter into it.

I braced myself, the music blared, the arc light shone on the bouncer's bald pate. To my surprise, the blonde said, "Bernie will take you upstairs, Mr. Dangerfield. Follow him."

Bernie jerked his head and led me to a door at the back, opposite the entrance and concealed by a beaded curtain.

The bouncer led me up a narrow, linoleum-covered flight of stairs to a landing. He knocked at a door and there was a muffled conversational exchange, then the door opened and the bouncer stood back to let me pass inside.

I found myself in a small office. The room was dark and ill-lit. The walls were covered with pinup posters of a more erotic type than usual. There was a cluttered desk and behind the desk sat a tall, thin albino around thirty years of age. He wore a black jersey polo shirt, a white linen jacket with a black silk handkerchief sticking out of his top pocket. He was quite the dandy but there was something terrifying about him.

His skin was white and fine as tissue paper and stretched over the bones of his face. I could see blue veins like a map of the underground across his forehead and temples. The pinkish eyes he fixed on me were curiously blank, and for a moment I wondered if he were blind.

"Can I help you?" he asked. His voice was high, polite and distant.

"Mr. Moto?"

He did not reply, simply stared at me unblinking. There was something unnerving in his vacant gaze.

"I found your name in a diary and in an address book belonging to Alison Alyward. I'm investigating her death . . ."

"Investigating . . . oh?" Temperately curious. One white eyebrow went up. He clasped soft milk-white hands. His nails were pink and polished.

"Yes," I said. I was trying to dominate. He sat. I stood. He seemed pale and passive and I, coming in from outside, brought energy and a certain vitality with me. I was attacking. He should be on the defensive. But it did not work the way it should. It was as if, like a sponge, he absorbed my strength and left me weak. There was something reptilian about his stillness, something menacing about his soft, controlled voice.

I cleared my throat. "I'm sorry to disturb you," I found myself saying.

He waited, watching me expressionlessly.

"I have been asked to investigate the drowning of Alison Alyward. Your name was in her book, and I'm working my way down the list in the hope that someone knows something that will help me."

"Like what?" he whispered, spreading his hands.

"I don't know," I said. There was a pause and he sighed.

"I don't think I know any Alison Alyward," he said.

It was his first mistake. The denial came too late. He should have said that line a couple of sentences back.

"Then why did she have your name in her book?" I persisted.

He shrugged, then smiled. His smile was terrifying, as if a skull smiled. The teeth were large and he revealed a lot of them in the wide, mirthless grimace.

"I'm sorry I can't help you," he said and stood, indicating our interview was over.

The bouncer had been standing, breathing noisily (he sounded as if he had adenoids) with his back to the door. He gave way for me respectfully as I passed him, and I heard the door close behind me and realized I was alone in the corridor.

I had achieved nothing. Absolutely nothing. I would have believed the albino was telling the truth only for the fact that he had hesitated about knowing Alison Alyward and his name was in her book. If he had given me a plausible explanation as to why it was there, I think I would have accepted it and gone away.

I was alone. It was too good an opportunity. I decided to have a quick look into the other rooms on the corridor, taking a chance that no one would see me. I opened the doors carefully, cautiously, but I soon realized that there was nothing to be found. The rooms were full of theatrical props and scenery of a sort used in sex shows all over the world. Bits and pieces of the strippers' costumes were littered about. They were not in good condition and I assumed that they had been discarded. I picked up a G-string. The lace was torn, the red satin stained. As I dropped it, I heard voices in the hall. I pressed myself against the wall behind the door so as not to be seen from the hall. I had left the door open. There was a tutu on the back of the door. It scratched my nose as I stood there hiding in the darkness, feeling like a small boy.

". . . thought you had sorted out that whole fuckin' business. You want a blowtorch to your balls, Bernie, eh? It'll change your expression for good!"

The voice was Mr. Moto. It was still soft but the silky tone he had used to me had disappeared. It had razors in it now.

My heart was beating uncomfortably hard. I was not used to this sort of thing at all, sneaking about, hiding behind doors with my nose in a net tutu. Also I did not fancy being physically thrown out into Soho by the gorilla. I kept very quiet.

"But I did, G'vnor, honest. I did," the bouncer said, panic in his voice.

"*Get it*. That's what I said, that's what I meant. Get it. It has to be destroyed."

"But I did, G'vnor, Mr. Blake did. 'e got it first. Then I did, after 'e tried to blackmail—"

"Shut your face, Bernie. You are thick as two planks. Leave Mr. Blake out of it. He *is* out of it. Christ's sake!"

"But I did—"

"Then how does it happen that this geezer comes in here askin'? Eh? He says he has the books. Got *my* name, Christ's sake, in the books? How? Just explain. Mebbe I'm

109

stupid or somethin'? Eh?"

"No, G'vnor. No."

"I'm glad you don't think so, Bernie. But explain."

"I dunno. Mebbe he looked at them when they were in his apartment? Before Mr. Blake got them. Mebbe he has a good memory?"

The albino chuckled. He mimicked Bernie, "'Good memory. Good memory.' Fuck off before I break your neck." The menace in the voice was palpable. I heard a door slam and waited but the bouncer did not go downstairs. All was quiet in the corridor outside except for the sound of adenoidal breathing. Bernie was obviously standing outside the door to Moto's office, and I was stuck.

I stood there, trapped. Then, as I wondered what on earth to do, I realized I was not alone. I was staring at someone whose eyes glimmered in the dark.

There was a window in the room and directly outside it the neon sign that I had seen below in the street, 'MANGOES,' flashed, red and blue. The window was open and sitting on the narrow sill, still as a statue was a slim young girl. She must have watched me come into the room, nose around, then hide, and I don't think she could have moved or I would have heard her.

We stared at each other for what seemed like a long time. I opened my mouth but she put her finger to her lips and shook her head. As she was in silhouette, I could not make out her features, but I could follow her gestures. She beckoned to me and I crept over to the window. The street noises rose, I could clearly hear what people below were saying as they walked past. Horns blasted at each other and a radio across the road played Jason Donovan. The Aussies had a lot to answer for! The girl looked at me. I could smell the tobacco on her breath and see the smooth skin across her cheekbones. Across the

110

street a whore sat in the window, like us, on the second floor. She had tangled dark hair and she winked at us. She was close enough.

"This is not a nice place for you to be," the girl beside me whispered. "Not a nice place at all."

She looked very young. She was dressed in all sorts of baubles, bangles and beads. She had a little black bolero embroidered in yellow and russet and edged in tiny gold discs. She wore nothing under it. She had hoops in her ears and her skirt was gathered at the waist and it too was black and trimmed with gold discs. It had little circular mirrors and flowers of red and yellow. Her midriff was bare and on her silver-blond hair she wore a scarf edged with tiny gold coins. She had a multi-coloured fringed shawl around her waist and what could have been a hundred bracelets on each arm, rings on every finger and her feet were bare.

The lights, picking out her features in lurid colour, showed her pretty with large dark eyes.

She contemplated me and there was no fear in her scrutiny. It was a leisurely perusal that embarrassed me and caused me to wonder if perhaps she was older than she appeared in the grotesque light. She was perfectly relaxed and she did not seem at all worried about our concealment in the little room. She smiled at me. "Don't worry. I can handle Bernie," she whispered as if she had read my thoughts. She put her face close to mine, pulling me down by my lapel. "I'll meet you tomorrow morning, 'bout twelve in the Criterion Brasserie in Piccadilly Circus. Okay?"

I nodded.

"Now wait here. I'll chat up Bernie and when you see your opportunity, go."

She pulled up her skirts, revealing long, slim legs, and slid off the windowsill. She pattered across the room on her bare feet and at the door she turned and gave me a little wave.

"Noon," she mouthed, and I nodded again. Then she vanished.

I waited.

"Hi, Bernie. Have they been angry with you? Are you in . . ." I could hardly hear her. There was some muttering, then, " . . . something in my eye. Can you see?" I sneaked my head around the door. Bernie's back was to me, and he leaned over the small girl intent, presumably on her eye.

I slipped down the stairs. The door in front of me was the one I had come through. It led from the auditorium. To my right was a corridor that, I could see, led out into an alley, and if my sense of direction was correct, was the exit at the back of the building. I decided, on impulse, to go that way. It was nearer and I did not want to go through that room again. I was sickened by the degradation on the other side of the beaded curtains, sickened by the depths humanity could slide to. So I turned down the passage that led out the back way.

There was a single naked bulb swinging on its cord from the ceiling, and black and orange linoleum underfoot. The wall was blistered with damp patches and decorated with graffiti. I could see four-letter words scratched there, a couple of ideas new to me, and a heart pierced through with *B loves J* carved in it. It looked incongruously innocent beside an obscene and inventive message to gays. I shivered and took a few steps, then stopped as a door at my left began to move open. I froze, stood stock still, waiting as it opened stealthily.

A boy of about nine stood there and a girl of approximately the same age. They looked at me for a moment, staring at me, unblinking. They did not appear afraid, just curious. The girl smiled at me and the boy pulled her back inside and slammed the door. I did not know what to make of it and I went out into the neon-lit night, grateful to escape.

CHAPTER 12

The Criterion Brasserie is a vast emporium, still beautifully preserved in its art nouveau style. It is a meeting place where they serve coffee, tea, drinks, snacks as well as meals. It is more like an elegant railway station than a café, and it possesses a wonderfully impersonal atmosphere and a marvelous cross section of the public. One can sit here waiting or reading, feeling anonymous and at ease. It is a hustle and bustle place, a place for assignations, and I could imagine spies or illicit lovers meeting here. There is a huge bar at the back where they also serve meals, and the main body of the hall is full of tables and chairs, waiters bustling about, as near to Paris as London is ever likely to be.

I ordered a cappuccino, and sitting at a tiny table for two, opened my paper. The same old things were happening; the Conservatives were blasting Labour and Labour was having a go at the Blues. The Greens were predicting the demise of the world as we knew it, and I wondered idly if that would be such a catastrophe. I reflected sadly that as long as there was a human race there would be greed and greed is corrosive and leads to destruction and/or poverty.

I read on to discover that a couple of old ladies of eighty had been raped and mugged. A vicar was holding secret black masses in a graveyard beside his church and was accused of using human babies for sacrifice. A man had been arrested for exposing himself to some nuns, and there was a chronic shortage of nurses, teachers and social workers . . .

But the city was healthy; so that meant all was okay.

A shadow fell across the paper and my gloomy thoughts were cut off. I looked up and saw her there; fine-blonde fuzz of silvery curls confined by a scarf edged with glittering discs, gypsy skirt, bolero. She wore huge orthopedic black shoes today and thick black tights. I wondered how she could bear to in this heat.

She was prettier than I had realized, and her large eyes were dark as night fringed by lashes that curled both above and below her eyes.

"Sit down." I indicated the chair opposite me, folded my newspaper and stuffed it between my chair and the wall. It held no hope for me, no hope, or laughter, or pleasure at all.

The huge dome-like place was gently shadowed and air conditioners whined hypnotically. A shaft of old-gold sunlight fell across the floor revealing the myriad motes of dust in the air and turning her hair platinum.

As if to echo my despondency she said, "He's going to kill you."

I must have looked startled for she asked then, "Didn't you guess?"

"But why?" I looked at her, dubiously thinking she exaggerated.

She clicked her fingers, waved to a waiter who rushed up to her. "A Coca-Cola with ice," she said and turned back to me. "God, you are stupid. It's not difficult to figure." Her voice was amused. "You see, you're the only one who knows his name was in Alison's books."

"Whose name?"

"Can't tell you," she said, then pressing her lips together like a child, "Won't," she insisted.

"Mr. Moto? Well, he warned me, I suppose, yesterday."

She shook her head impatiently.

"No," she said. "You didn't talk to Mr. Moto yesterday. You talked to Kohl."

"That wasn't Moto?" I couldn't believe it.

"No. It was Sebastian Kohl. The Albino. He's not Mr. Moto."

"So, he was the S.K. in the books, right?"

"Oooo, you *are* smart! Wow, how bright can you get!" She sounded derisive. "You're so smart you're gonna get yourself killed."

In the subdued lighting I couldn't see her face clearly, only her hair shone.

"I'm coming from the outside, remember. I don't know what I'm into," I said in defence.

She was sucking the Coca-Cola through a straw. She rolled her eyes. "Neither do I, sap. No one does. It's all segments. But I know it's dangerous. Tough. Kohl is dangerous. You don't want to mess with Kohl."

"Then why do you stay there?"

"Kohl is my father."

"Oh!"

"Sometimes I worry he's bats. That it might be hereditary, that I might go the same way."

"But he can't be more than thirty years old."

"He's thirty-six, very well-preserved. Like Cliff Richards he doesn't smoke or drink. Doesn't screw. 'Cept he must have once or there wouldn't be me. He's very cold," she said.

"Why are you warning me?"

"Well, *I* think it'd be foolish to try to ice you. *I* think you got friends. Maybe powerful friends, I dunno. Friends who wouldn't give up till they found out who was responsible. And you've no handle, nothing Kohl can grasp and twist you with, not like Alison, Talia, Jason or Revel."

"What do you mean?"

115

"You can't be blackmailed," she said.

"They could?" I asked. She nodded. "How come?" I persisted.

"Drugs," she said simply, wrinkling her nose. "Those four were hooked. All Kohl had to do was dangle a fix in front of any of them or threaten to cut them off and they'd jump through hoops." She frowned. "Except Alison, at the end. That's what worried Kohl. Something happened to Alison, he kept saying. She was growing out of it, getting strong, going to bloody Narcotics Anonymous. You know. He was furious. They all were. They were frightened, too. The thought of Kohl's fury makes me shiver." She undid the fringed shawl at the waist and pulled it up over her shoulders as if to protect herself. She took a last noisy suck on her Coca-Cola.

"Won't you have something else?" I asked. She ignored me.

"Listen, I'm warning you, that's all. If Kohl knew he'd kill me." She shivered. "Be careful," she added.

"What age are you?" I asked, for suddenly she seemed younger than I had thought.

"Sixteen," she said, pulling the shawl off her shoulders and wrapping it around her waist twice and knotting it at the side on her hip.

"Why don't they want anyone to know they were connected with Alison Alyward?" I asked. "Why did they take the books? Was it the drugs? Is that why they killed Revel?"

I realized as I spoke that Bernie must have killed Revel. That Bernie must have been in the flat with me that morning. That Bernie had probably killed Alison.

She shook her head. "No. They could handle that. They have the drug scene sewn up. No, it was Alison. She was getting close to something. That's all I can say. I've said too much already."

"Who is Mr. Moto?"

She didn't answer me. She took my hand. "Listen, get out. Take off somewhere. Abroad, if you can. I'm not kidding. Outa sight, outa mind. Get anonymous. Like, fade. An' later, like sometime in the future, send a message to me by Bernie. Kohl thinks Bernie is totally his man but he ain't. Bernie'd die for me, I mean it. Well?" She leaned over the table and thrust her face near mine. I could smell the cola on her childish breath, see her small white teeth, the soft sheen of her skin.

"Listen honey, you fancy me sometime, you want to party, you got me. You just let me know. I think you're cute, I really do."

"How many videos do you watch?" I asked. "Using that slang, talking like that. I think you should be in school learning to be grown up instead of gabbing about things you don't understand."

I could have bitten my tongue out. I was furious with myself for being so undiplomatic and insensitive.

"Wanna bet? Oh, _I_ understand, mister. It's you who don't. You're way out of your league. You still don't understand, do you? Godamn infant," she said contemptuously. She was angry. She stood up, knocking over her glass. It clattered onto the floor. A couple beside us looked over at us. I felt guilty as if I had been engaged in some illicit act that I was ashamed of.

"Don't go," I said, taking her hand.

"I'm off now," she said furiously, pulling her hand from my grip. "Don't say I didn't warn you."

"What's your name?" I asked, feeling foolish. "I'll get in touch."

The man at the next table glanced at us again.

"Gilda," she called over her shoulder as she left. "Gilda Kohl."

Her body was a silhouette against the sunshine outside in

the street and for a moment she stood there, then her shadow lengthened and she was gone.

I thought how fragile she seemed, so young, so damaged, her moral sense so twisted, yet so curiously honourable. I was glad she was on my side, amazed at the thought that anyone would want to kill someone as unimportant as me, touched by her desire to protect me from harm and disgusted at the pass, albeit verbal, she had made.

I paid the bill and left, went out into the teeming masses in Piccadilly Circus. I walked down Piccadilly on my way to the car park at Hyde Park Corner. My car was still there. I went into Fortnums and bought some handmade Belgian chocolate for Mandy. People pushed and jostled. There were a lot of American tourists afraid they would miss something and when I asked the girl at the counter for Scotch smoked salmon, a woman with Edna Everage glasses, a blue rinse, a fur coat (it was seventy degrees outside), and sneakers leaned over my shoulder.

"Scotch? Is that the whiskey, honey? Why did you order Scotch smoked salmon? Do they cure it in whiskey or something? Is it better than the ordinary stuff? Hey, Buck, you hear him? He's ordering Scotch smoked salmon."

"I heard him, Mamie." A tall silver-haired giant with an amiable face wearing a Burberry hat, raincoat, scarf, all matching plaid hovered beside me, and when I opened my mouth to explain, I felt a searing pain in my right side. I was stuck, mouth open, face frozen, and he stared at me with a puzzled expression on his face. The pain was needle-sharp and excruciating in its intensity. I swerved, pushed out wildly, clutched my side, tearing at the agony.

Mamie was outraged. "Godamn hooligan. Jeez, Buck, this guy pushed me, hard." The amiable voice of the husband came to me and went, came and went, faded in and out as waves of agony broke over me.

"I'm sure he didn't mean to, honey . . . English . . . after all . . ." Then something about, ". . . real gentlemen."

I saw Mamie's face over me, angry and shouting something, then her expression changed and her eyes widened, her mouth opened. I barely heard her voice, shrill with fear. "There's blood, honey . . . he's covered in blood."

I felt everything go black, felt my head hit the floor. How had my head got so near it? I wondered. I saw Mamie's face hover into my glazed vision.

"Should we leave . . . or . . . I'm afraid . . . Let's get outa here . . ." and Buck's infuriatingly calm reply. "No, honey. This is England. Not like New York. They know how to behave here."

Like hell they do, I thought.

Then the reassuring voice of an official. " 'Ere, 'ere, let the poor chap breathe. God Almighty, he's hurt bad. Get an ambulance. Phone for an ambulance . . ."

This time the darkness descended in earnest.

CHAPTER 13

I awakened in my own bed in a fuzzy, numbed but distinctly
good-humoured state. Mandy told me what had happened.
White and shaken, she said I had been taken by ambulance to
casualty. There they had diagnosed and treated me for a severe
knife wound, which had, miraculously, missed my vital organs.
The doctors told her that it was almost unbelievable that I was
not dead for the knife wound was deep and should have been fa-
tal. They had patched me up and sent me home because there
was no bed for me in the hospital.

"No room at the inn," Mandy said. "Jesus would have
been quite at home in England in the eighties."

I said I was happier to be home in my own bed.

"They would have liked to have kept you under observa-
tion, darling," she said, "In case of complications. But they
couldn't. Government cuts to the NHS, they said. So there
you are. There was, according to the doctor, who I must say
seemed run off his feet, an empty ward in the hospital, but no
nurses, and no money to run it. They asked us to let them
know if there was any change in your condition."

I had been mercifully *non compus mentus* throughout the
whole episode and had no memory of it at all. I was full now
of something that helped me feel no pain and, to boot, made
me feel a little drunk.

The police arrived.

"You got enemies?" Detective Sergeant Taylor asked. He

had a Detective Inspector Rawlings with him this time. I shook my head.

"Why do you ask, Officer?" Mandy's voice was smooth as honey.

"Well, you were done over here, couple days ago. Now this." He shrugged as if his observations were self-explanatory.

"We all have enemies, Officer," Mandy said.

"Well, can you give us a list of their names?"

I shook my head.

"One name?"

"If I have enemies, Detective, I don't know who they are. Who he or she is."

Detective Taylor did the talking. Rawlings was watching me. His face was tired, his eyes shrewd. He shook his head. "When you decide to come clean, give me a ring at this number," he said, and handed Mandy a card.

"I'm tired." I looked at Taylor. "Could you leave this until tomorrow? I'm distinctly woozy and I don't want to mislead you." Rawlings snorted and Taylor put his notebook in his pocket and sighed.

"Trail'll be cold by then," he said as if he didn't really care. "Not that it was ever hot exactly. Ah, well, someone, if you don't mind me saying, sir, is after your blood."

"He knows that, Fred; he's well aware of that," Rawlings said dryly and Mandy made a funny little noise, then stood and showed them to the door.

When she came back, I said, "I'm going to sleep now and then I'll sleep some more, and then some more. I'm very, very tired. I am also becoming very, very angry and I need strength to deal with it. The whole thing has gone far enough. How *dare* they . . ." Her face became vague and indistinct and I drifted away.

I slept my seven senses away. I woke in the middle of the night, drank some mineral water, then slid back gratefully into dreamless sleep.

When I again regained consciousness, it was afternoon and Mandy was sitting beside my bed.

"The shop," I said.

"It's Sunday."

I stirred. My body still felt stiff and sore. The painkillers had worn off and my torso throbbed every time I moved.

"Let me get you some soup," Mandy said and left the room.

I tried to think. Sebastian Kohl's expressionless face, cold and deadly, floated in my consciousness. Then it dissolved and became the nymphet face of Gilda warning me, then the sardonic face of Inspector Rawlings, which melted into Bernie's bull-like countenance. Question and answer chased each other through the fog in my mind. Had Gilda knowingly (I thought not) or unknowingly (probably) led the would-be assassin to me? It couldn't have been Bernie in Fortnums; I'd have noticed him. He'd have stuck out like a sore thumb. I tried to remember who had been near me, but the only faces I could remember, except for a rather colourful black guy buying coffee, were the faces of Buck and Mamie. Gilda was right. I was a marked man, or so it appeared. But were they seriously trying to kill me? And if so, for what reason? What was the link between the seedy little strip joint, Sebastian Kohl and Alison Alyward? Was it drugs? Probably. How on earth could I solve this mess? I didn't know. Would I be a marked man for the rest of my life? And who was Mr. Moto? The elusive Mr. Moto? Probably a dealer. The head man. The boss.

I decided that drugs were the likely link and that it seemed probable that Alison had been murdered because she had threatened the syndicate or the cartel in some way. Perhaps she had needed more than they were prepared to give. Perhaps she couldn't pay. Perhaps they wanted her to push and she refused. It could, in that scenario, be a million reasons. Perhaps, as Gilda had said, she had got clean and they believed she would give them away. Grass.

Mandy brought me a steaming bowl of lobster bisque, toast and butter and a glass of Chablis. When I had finished this delicious repast, I asked her to draw the curtains and I took a couple of painkillers, emptied my mind and went asleep again, the sunlight bathing my face in a warm golden glow.

CHAPTER 14

It took longer to recover than I expected. I wanted so badly to be up and out and doing, but my body refused to obey me.

My mother came to see me, but I sent her away. "You're a survivor Mark," she said.

The police came to see me again, asked endless questions and took a statement. Inspector Rawlings did not accompany Detective Taylor, who said he didn't think there was much to gain from talking to me.

" 'E doesn't think much of your evidence, sir," the detective said. "Said to phone him when it gets too much."

"How does he know that—I mean, why should I have to?"

"Don't know, sir. Talks double-Dutch 'e does sometimes, our Inspector."

Then I had a visitor.

It was on the Thursday after my near miss. I was feeling worn out because for the first time I had dressed myself completely. I was sitting in the window watching the people pass by, feeling shaky and irritable, for I was impatient to be well again, when Mandy knocked on the door so I knew she was not alone. I called out and she put her head around.

"Someone to see you," she said, and left me staring at a complete stranger. Mandy was a bit short with me because since the accident—attempted murder, whatever you'd like to call it—I had not been in the mood for love. She said I looked vulnerable lying in bed and it turned her on. I kept telling her that I was in pain. She said every other detective she had ever heard of had managed it. Even after they had sustained far more serious injuries than I had. She mentioned Spencer and Sam Spade. I said they were American and everyone knew about the American libido. Then she mentioned James Bond, the indefatigable, and I yelled that they were all fiction, for Christ's sake, and she left in a huff.

The man who stood before me was a handsome, fortyish American type with a tanned and healthy face, even teeth, bright intelligent eyes. He was well built, athletic and exuded a warmth and straight-forwardness that was very attractive.

He came forward, hand extended. "My name is Barclay Norman," he said. He had an American accent and a contagious grin. He was instantly likable.

He shook my hand with a firm grip. I tried to remember where I had heard the name before but had to give up.

"Your mom said you wanted to see me." He frowned. "Let me see, how did she put it? She said, 'The poor boy is going out of his mind with boredom. Go round. Tell him about Alison.' So I took her advice and here I am."

Then I remembered. The last person Alison had shown an interest in. Her last escort, according to Mother.

"Your mom says you've been in the wars," he said.

"Grab a chair and sit down," I said.

He did just that and sat opposite me in the window looking out, very relaxed, very at ease. His was a comforting presence, something about him encouraged trust. But I was wary. I had learned to be careful. He remained waiting quietly. There was no anxiety in the quiet; in fact I was more at peace than at any time since all this started. At last I broke the silence.

"Tell me about Alison," I asked. "I've heard so many conflicting things."

"They were all probably true, depending on your point of view. People saw her as they wanted her to be and she responded to their vision of her. She was whatever part you cast her in." He looked at me. "How did you see her?"

"I didn't really know her," I said, "I suppose I saw her as beautiful, unattainable, a sort of glittering, out-of-reach goddess. The ideal woman. But not for real."

"Well then, Alison would have divined that, and she would have become that unattainable woman for you. But that was before she changed. Your mother said you were investigating her drowning. I gotta tell you I'm glad. No way did she take her own life. No way. She had everything to live for."

I looked at him quizzically.

"I guess I better explain," he said. He was silent for a while, then he nodded towards the street. "The whole spectrum of society, eh?" he said, and I smiled and nodded. He drew a deep breath. "Alison did not know who she was, what she was, when I met her. You saw her as unattainable, beautiful, and I told you she would have become that for you. If you thought of her as a tomboy, then that's what she would have been. If she impressed you as a whore, or an ice-cold maiden, then that's what she would have become. She was everybody and nobody. She had been on drugs: crack, heroin, smack and amphetamines with her pals, Revel, Talia and Jason. But it was getting out of hand for her. Maybe she didn't have their tolerance. I dunno. Anyhow she had a couple of nasty experiences. I mean, real nasty. Epileptic drug-induced fits. Blood-flecked vomit, green bile, period stopping and she began hallucinating." He looked at my pale face. "Sorry," he said, and continued, "She decided she wanted out. She was very scared. So she checked into a clinic, dried out, then came to us."

"Us?"

126

"Narcotics Anonymous," he said calmly. "You see, the difficulty is not staying off the drugs, but learning to live without them. She had a lousy self-image. She hated herself. Oh, yes, I know it's difficult for you to believe that anyone as beautiful as Alison hated herself so, but it is a common factor among us addicts. We have a program. It works. It rebuilds our personalities, shows us how to live. If we are prepared to go to any lengths to achieve sobriety."

"But that means that you . . ." I could hardly believe what he was telling me.

"I'm an addict, yes." He nodded. "But I haven't used in ten years." He glanced at me. "Don't look so horrified. It is an illness like any other, but it's not catching. Anyhow, as I was saying, Alison came to meetings, immersed herself in the recovery programme and began to live. You have no idea what a wonderful thing it is; to see someone who has been totally dependent on mind-altering substances, regain their sanity, their freedom and discover what a wonderful world it is if looked at through the correct end of the telescope. They blossom and that terrible negativism is replaced by confidence and joy. Alison was radiant those last weeks before she died."

He looked at me sadly. "We were going to marry. We got engaged. I've never seen anyone bloom the way Alison did. We were very much in love." His voice was husky and he shook his head. "She wouldn't kill herself. Not then. Perhaps before, but not then. She was too happy. She had too much to live for."

"Suppose she used again? Suppose she let you down? Wouldn't that do it?"

"Yes. It would. But I'm prepared to swear she didn't. I was with her every moment until the day of her death. She wouldn't have had *time*. She would have to have given in to an impulse—and she was not in the right frame of mind to do that—got the drugs, taken them, killed herself, all in the space of about a couple of hours. Besides, there was no trace of drugs found in her body at the autopsy."

"Well, what's your theory?"

"You really want to know? Alison had a kid." I nodded. "Well, I think she went looking for the kid, and in some way this caused trouble. It's the only thing I can think of. You gotta theory?"

"I still think it's something to do with the drugs," I said. "Someone wanting her to do something she was not prepared to do anymore, or something she knew that they were afraid she'd talk about. What I mean is, suppose the supplier, the pusher, whoever, thought she was going to spill the beans about delivery dates, oh, I don't know, identities, name names, something they were afraid would be found out, some danger for them, something that could pin them down. Then they felt they had to get rid of her. You see, Barclay, since the attempt on my life . . . well, it *proves* that she was murdered."

He nodded. "Yeah, I see that," he said. "Yeah, you may be right."

I told him about the address book and the diary. "There was something in there—names, places that this Mr. Moto, or Sebastian Kohl, didn't want me getting into."

We talked until the light faded. Mandy brought us tea. I don't think my guest was too keen on it, and I offered him coffee instead, but he was too polite and gulped it down manfully.

"Look, if there's anything I can do . . . to help, don't hesitate," he said. He gave me his number, then left. I sat and watched the lights come on and thought about the case. There *was* something more than drugs. There was a thread that was waiting to be woven into the whole and I didn't know how to cast it on. It was on the periphery of my mind and I couldn't catch it; it kept eluding me.

That night Mandy slid into bed with me and turned her back to me with a softly whispered goodnight. I touched her shoulder and she turned and snuggled up to me, and this time the pain didn't seem to matter at all.

CHAPTER 15

The following day energy finally returned and I bathed and dressed before anyone could stop me. Mother had told me the previous day that Revel's funeral was on Saturday, and I made up my mind to talk to Talia and Jason before then. I knew instinctively that they would stay in town for the funeral, but I could not be certain what they would do after it was over. They might split to anywhere in the world, and I would have the devil of a job catching them.

I got an eleven bus up the Kings Road to Sloane Square. The street swirled with a glorious mishmash of society: mini-skirted girls sashayed along on the arms of their fellas, yuppies looked too hot in their business suits on this heavenly day, and German-crew-cut Rambos strutted along, cock-of-the-walk, people scurrying out of their way. The punks were out in full regalia, ugly as sin, gorgeously decorated; parrots in the animal kingdom; they were brightly plumed, grotesquely visaged. Smart women in neat navy, and Clarke's shoes with frill-necked shirts and velvet bands holding their hair back hurried into Peter Jones, and on the steps of the Royal Court Theatre, crowds of students in torn jeans and shirts congregated, smoking and reading, or talking earnestly.

I bought a paper from the cheery little man in the kiosk and walked to Wilton Crescent. A Filipino maid answered my bell.

"Miz Morgan not here now," she said sullenly, polishing the door brasses with her sleeve as she spoke. I could see it was a reflex action; she was in the habit of service.

"That's all right, I'll wait," I said and walked in and up the stairs to Talia's flat before the woman had time to gather her wits.

She had left the flat door open and I was sitting on the sofa intent on my paper when she returned, puffing, out of breath after the climb.

". . . not sure is okay. Don' know if Miz Talia would like . . ." She grumbled on and I acted deaf until she ran out of steam and went elsewhere in the apartment.

I didn't mind waiting and it wasn't that long before I heard the key in the lock and Talia came into the living room, a huge bunch of flowers in one hand and a Partridge carrier-bag in the other. "Oh, shit . . . you," she said, slamming the door behind her with her foot.

The Filipino woman emerged from the nether regions wailing, ". . . not my fault, Miz Morgan . . . 'e jus' came in, sat down. I din' ask 'im in. I tole him you was out, Miz Talia . . ."

"Oh, shut up, Della, and get some coffee. And please fill this with water." She handed the groceries to the maid and gave her a Chinese vase. She looked incredible. Her black hair fell to her waist, shining like burnished ebony. She wore a scarlet suit and scarlet lipstick to match it. The skirt was thigh length, the jacket collarless with self-covered buttons that fastened all the way up. She had a thick gold necklace at her throat and round gold earrings in her ears. Her long legs were encased in sheer black and her shoes were flat pumps with velvet bows. She sank into an armchair with a sigh, not looking at me at all.

Della brought the vase back, placed it on a table beside Talia, glared at me and left. Talia started arranging the flow-

131

ers. I did not speak; I wanted her to take the offensive.

"Well," she said at last, "what do you want?"

"You're a tough cookie, aren't you, Talia?" I remarked. "Your our old friend and roommate Alison is killed, murdered, and your bosom-buddy Revel ditto, and you dress up in red and arrange flowers."

She glared at me, her eyes flashing fire, but her lip trembled. "I *do* care. I'm *not* heartless. It's you who's being hysterical. They were *not* murdered. Alison committed suicide and Revel O.D.'d. You're talking rubbish."

She suddenly burst into tears, dropping a fistful of flowers on the carpet.

"I'm not being hysterical," I said, icy calm. "They *were* murdered. You can't be so stupid as to think—"

She looked up, eye makeup ruined, mascara running down her cheeks. "Oh, stop *saying* that. It's just not true."

I could see she was scared. For the first time it showed.

Della came in with a tray. She placed it on the low table and looked up at Talia suspiciously, then at me with venom. Talia got up and left the room, her face buried in tissues. A muffled "Excuse me," and she disappeared.

Della poured the coffee, glaring at me. She handed me a cup and left. In about five minutes, Talia returned and sat down, picked up her coffee and sipped it. She was very calm. Too calm. She had washed her face and it gave her a smoothed-out, childish look. Relaxed.

"What did you take?" I asked.

She looked up, eyes slightly hazy, pupils enormous. "I don't know what you mean."

I gave up that line. I would get nowhere by being antagonistic. I had thought that fear might loosen her tongue but all it had done was drive her to her anesthetic.

"It helps, does it?" I said softly, sounding as sympathetic as I could.

She nodded. "Oh, yes."

"It helped you all? Alison, Revel, Jason, too?"

"Oh, yes."

"You all liked it, yes?" I was trying to pinpoint the common denominator once and for all.

She nodded.

"We played together," she confided slurrily, "games."

"What sort of games?" I asked.

"Sex," she said, "Sex. All sorts of combinations. All sorts of positions. Me and Jason, and Alison. Revel brought his little playmate and we did things you wouldn't believe. We coated ourselves with it. 'Sensation dust' Jason called it. Jeez, the feel of it. If you've never tried it you've never lived—"

She looked at me defiantly, like a child who had confessed to stealing the cookies, admitting she had gobbled them all up but refusing to acknowledge that they made her feel sick. Then, meeting my eyes hers veered away and she put her hand to her forehead.

She smiled again. The smile was soulless. There was, I thought, despite her great beauty, something repulsive about Talia Morgan. I was trying not to be judgmental but she repelled me.

"And it took all the pain away," she said so quietly I hardly heard her.

"What pain?" I asked gently.

"The pain of the babies."

I felt a stir of intense interest. "What babies?"

"Oh, you know." She frowned and began to look suspicious. "No. You don't. Oh, I don't want to talk to you. You're trying to trick me. You're getting me to say things I don't mean."

Her movements were slow motion. She was feeling no pain, but she was slipping away somewhere, losing control of what she was telling me and I watched as she tried to hold on to herself and failed.

"Oh, yes, you do want to talk to me. You know you'll feel better if you do. Besides I know. About Alison's baby. I know. You had one, too?"

She smiled again, that vacant, empty smile.

"Yes. Mine and Jason's. Yes."

"But Revel? Revel was not the father of Alison's child, was he?"

She began to giggle helplessly and shake her head. "No, no, no, no, no. Oh no. Revel is . . ."

"Gay," I said. "Yes, I know."

"Yes, you *do* know." She nodded. "Then why ask?"

"A gay can father a child, Talia," I said.

"Well, Revel wasn't the father," she said. "Tom was."

I thought: Tom? Tom? Tom? Who the hell was Tom? Oh yes. It dawned. Abigale's Tom. Tom McNaughton. Little Abigale's Tom. "What happened to the babies?"

"*You* know." She giggled and winked.

"Yes, but I've forgotten. Tell me the story."

She settled herself like a teacher in front of a class of children. "Well, Revel said he could fix it, you see. Alison's old witch aunt threw her out. Said Alison was bad. A bad girl. We were all friends from college. Not Revel. He went to Oxford."

"Yes I know. I knew him there."

"Yes, well. He said he knew people. Alison didn't want to be saddled with a baby. She came to me asking for advice. It was too late for an abortion. She'd left it too late."

She nodded her head slowly, up and down. The sun shone through the long curtained windows onto the Aubusson carpet. There was a tapestry on the wall. It held all tones of grey and green and dun and showed a pastoral scene: hunters and deer, nymphs sporting in Italian ruins and thick under-growth.

I felt that stir of excitement I always felt when I was near to finding the truth. An expectation of explanation: a solution. It hung there on those full lips, half-open, revealing crowned teeth that were unnaturally pearl white. I was terrified of asking the wrong question, of annoying her. She was in an unpredictable state and I was afraid of shutting her up with a clumsy remark so I said nothing.

She bent to pick up the flowers, hung over the arm of the chair a moment, then gave up and sat back up again, all movements languorous. She gave me a brilliant smile but still she said nothing. She looked as if she had forgotten what we had been talking about.

"So what did Revel do?" I asked softly.

"Sent her to Mr. Moto, what else?" She raised her eyebrows and spread her hands as if it was obvious. "Look, you say you know all this but—"

"And your baby? Yours and Jason's?"

"Oh, that was deliberate. Jason crashed," she said. "Lost a fortune. He was in the city. You remember all that trouble . . . ?"

I nodded.

"Well, he didn't want to go to his mother for the money for drugs. He couldn't do that now, could he? He had to do something."

"And what did he do?" I asked.

She was about to answer when there was a loud banging on the door. The mood was broken. I cursed whoever the untimely visitor was and watched helplessly as Della scuttled out to answer it. We both looked in the direction of the door, and I felt a wave of fury shake me. So near and yet so far. I could see that Talia was trying to reorientate herself when we heard a terror-filled yell from Della and two men burst into the room.

I had hardly any time to register them before a tall black guy shouted, "Shut that bitch up," and ran across the room to where Talia sat. The other man was Bernie and he had Della, a hand over her mouth to stop her from screaming. She was struggling and it took all his energy to restrain her. She bit his hand and he let her go with alacrity. She shrieked, a piercing sound that would have wakened the dead.

"I said, shut that bitch up," the black man reiterated, holding Talia, who, in her drugged state, did not seem to grasp what was happening.

Bernie grabbed Della again but by now I was up and out of the sofa, and I chopped the side of his neck with the side of my hand and he dropped to the floor like a felled ox.

I slapped Della's cheek, which stopped her screaming and turned to see the black guy holding a gun to Talia's head. The gun shone in the sunlight. "Don't move. Don't even stir, my man, or I'll blow her away."

I believed him. "Look, put that gun away. There's no need—"

"Shut up," he said. He must have been six-six in his stocking feet. His head was shaved and he had an earring in his right ear. He had the face of an Afro carving and steady cold eyes. He was very calm.

"What are you rappin', man?" he asked.

"This is not going to get you anywhere," I said. "Let's sit and talk . . . "

"This is not a game we are playing here, Mr. Dangerfield." He enunciated every word very clearly.

"Look, put that gun away. Talia is harmless. She won't—"

"You hear that, honey? You harmless? This guy thinks he

knows. But he don', do he, angel?" He was digging the snubnose of the gun into her cheek, pushing her face out of shape. Talia looked dazed. She was obviously frightened now.

"She won't what, my man?" the black man asked me. "Talk? Man, oh man, I think she done that already. She gabs and gossips when she on a trip, don' you, Talia? Don' you, baby?" His voice was like honey.

"No, Butterfly, no. I haven't said anything. Have I, Mark?" She appealed to me. She glanced at me with pleading eyes for corroboration, but I knew it wouldn't do any good. This guy was nobody's fool. Although Talia was becoming more and more terrified, her movements and reflexes were still drugged and slow.

"She said nothing, truly. Nothing," I said, and the guy she had called Butterfly laughed showing a mouthful of ivory teeth.

"You think I some kind o' dope? You think I believe what you say man?"

I made a sudden lunge to try to get the gun and he hit Talia across the temple with it. The blow was hard and she was bleeding. She began to whimper.

Butterfly smiled again. "Don't mess wi' me, man," he said, "Don't even try."

He jerked her forward, dragging her along for she seemed limp in his grasp. I kept alert. I watched. As he passed me he moved the gun fractionally, and I could see it pointed just off-target. It was enough. I turned my body, brought my knee up hard into his groin and came down with a chop to the side of his neck. It was bloody difficult because he was so tall, but he was bending his body to keep the gun to Talia's level. He dropped like a stone and I felt a second of sheer triumphant delight, then I acted swiftly.

"Go home. Leave everything and go," I shouted at Della. Della was dithering in a state of shocked indecision. Bernie was making grunting noises on the floor and trying to push himself up on his hands, but he was having difficulty. However, he would not be immobilised for long. I grabbed Talia's arm and, without waiting to see if Della took my advice, I pulled Talia after me downstairs and out into the sunny street.

There are always cabs cruising Wilton Crescent, but, perversely, today there were none. I dragged Talia along behind me. People looked and moved away or stood and stared. I gathered speed and ran, looking over my shoulder to see if Butterfly or Bernie had surfaced and were following. I did not think those two would be out of action for long. At last I reached Knightsbridge. The traffic there was bumper to bumper but on the other side of the road going towards Hyde Park Corner it seemed to be flowing much more easily.

I saw a taxi with its light on, and, at the same time, as I glanced behind me I saw Butterfly and Bernie emerge from the flat into Wilton Crescent and look up and down the street. I did not wait to find out if they had caught sight of us but pulled Talia behind me across the street to the cab.

A couple of pretty ladies with Harrods bags had beaten us to the cab and were on the point of opening the door but I shoved them aside. "Sorry, ladies."

"Well!" Outraged faces, looking at each other and me.

"An emergency. Hospital. Quickly," I said to the driver.

I got us in, slammed the door, glimpsed the women looking mollified, said to the driver, "No. No, forget that. Landsdown Road please. Off Holland Park Avenue."

He looked at me through the rear-view mirror, withering contempt in his eyes.

"Lengths people will go to!" he said with blistering scorn.

Talia had begun to shake, and I took her hand. Her skirt was damp and I realized that she had wet her pants. The fear had got to her through the drug barrier. Drugs deaden fear, then heighten it. We reached Landsdown Road. No cars had followed us. There was no traffic on the road. I paid the driver who had been muttering to himself about the appalling lengths humanity will go to to get what they wanted, but as I paid him he caught sight of Talia staggering up the garden path. I could see him register the state of her clothes, the mess she was in and the reassuring sight of my mother standing in the doorway, and he began to wonder if perhaps he had got the wrong end of the stick. I gave him a large tip and that swung it. He looked at me, bid me good day quite cordially and drove off.

I watched a moment as he turned left into Ladbroke Grove, noting that nothing else moved in the vicinity. There was no traffic at all on the leafy street so it seemed we had not been followed.

My mother had taken charge of Talia. Stoury, who said absolutely nothing, was dispatched to make coffee.

"That girl needs a stimulant," Mother said.

There was no one in the living room when I got there. My wound ached and I felt old and bruised.

After about half an hour Mother came down and sat in her favourite armchair with a sigh. "I've put her in the spare room, Mark, and left Stoury with her."

"Is she okay?"

"Frankly, no." Mother glanced at me. "She's a mess. Funny how people like her can look okay on the surface but underneath . . . When people like Talia crumble they really crumble. No ballast."

"The drugs undermine ballast. They remove resistance."

"Yes, Mark. You're right." She looked at me seriously.

139

"You don't look too hot yourself. Why not have a brandy? I'll join you."

I went and poured a Courvoissier for her then got one for myself.

"Mother, I'm bushed," I said.

"Well, tell me what happened."

It helped telling her. It all seemed clearer. I felt I could go to Wendy Cadbury and the police and sew the whole thing up. After today's events it looked obvious to me what had happened. What was happening. Alison Alyward, Talia Morgan, Revel Blake and Jason Bestwick had all been on drugs. Poor little privileged pets had wanted to go to the limit of erotic sensation, not understanding that the bill has, eventually, to be paid. So they got heavily into the drug scene. I thought how stupid people were. They all imagined that they would be the exceptions, that they would stay on top. But it never worked out that way. Alison had got clean and that had thrown a spanner in the works. Afraid she would talk to the police in her clean and sober state and tell them about him and Butterfly and Bernie and God knows who else, Kohl had her killed. Or this Mr. Moto, whoever he might be. Then I came poking around and found their names and appointments in her diary and address book and they had told Revel to get it for them. But Revel tried blackmail and they killed him. They had managed, so far, very well. Alison's suicide, Revel, a known drug addict found O.D.'d, was to be expected. Now they were certain Talia knew too much, and it seemed to me that she was in grave danger.

And me! Jeez me. The sooner I told the police the better.

Mother and I talked it out to that point, and I got on the phone to Taylor and Rawlings.

CHAPTER 16

Rawlings listened to me in silence.

"Well, well, well, we have been busy," he said dryly when I had finished. He didn't say he'd had a hunch, he didn't say 'why the hell didn't you tell us', he didn't say, 'I knew there was something fishy about it all.' He didn't waste any time. I had to admire him.

He nodded to Taylor who flipped his walkie-talkie. I could hear in the background while Rawlings cleared up some points with me. "All units to zero Oscar . . . go to South End Road, Hampstead, N.W.3. Pick up Jason Bestwick, that's J for . . . He may be . . ."

But Jason was dead. I felt my stomach sink. This was Wendy's son. His death could be laid at my door. Taylor was unemotional. "Shot through his mouth. Self-administered probably. Papers strewn about. Left a note. Suicide. He was in deep shit financially. Had been involved in the crash. Lost a lot, owed more. All fits together."

Rawlings looked at me quizzically. "But we know it was not suicide, don't we?" I could not tell whether he was serious or not. "We can't prove a thing," he continued. "I could pick up Butterfly Prescott and Bernie Baxter now but it would be your word against theirs. *And* they would have an ironclad alibi. And they'll have a first-class mouthpiece. They'll have left no fingerprints or incriminating evidence. We'll have nothing but your word and you knew them. Jason, Alison and

Revel. You were friends with them. People will say you're biased. Bound to."

"I didn't know them," I protested. "Not really. I was at college with Revel Blake and I didn't even know he was gay, for God's sake."

Inspector Rawlings looked at me pityingly. "That doesn't matter," he said. "Makes no difference. The defense would say you were at college with one of the deceased. You frequented the places the others did . . ."

"Not really . . ."

"Were you, or were you not, at a party in Wendy Cadbury's house when Revel Blake, Jason Bestwick and Talia Morgan were present?"

I nodded. "Yes, but—"

"Having planted that impression of familiarity in the jury's mind, you'd have a hard time removing it. Look Mr. Dangerfield, I'm impartial and I keep asking myself, 'surely he knew them all?' No, Mr. Dangerfield, we have no case. Remember, innocent until *proved* guilty. In France now . . ." He sighed. "We've got our eye on that bunch and one day they'll slip up. At some point they'll boob. But to pull in those two small fry at this juncture on such minute evidence would be counterproductive. Believe me, I'd do it if I felt we had the ghost of a chance. But we haven't, and they and their lawyer, Mr. bloody Stephenson, know it." He paused and frowned. "I've never heard of a Mr. Moto. Some gag I think he must be. Now, Kohl I know. Icy bastard. Takes his orders from someone bigger, someone much, much more important than he is. We don't know who it is yet, but we'd give a lot to find out." He looked at me steadily. "I think your meddling days are over, Mr. Dangerfield. Go home."

"What about Talia Morgan? She's in danger now, surely? What can we do about her?"

"What do you expect me to do, Mr. Dangerfield? Give you men to watch over a silly girl who should know better?" He closed his eyes, then leaned over his desk towards me. "Mr. Dangerfield, we are overextended. My men are working at full stretch. I'll be frank with you, and I'm only speaking for myself, unofficially, off the record. I would not give you the men even if I had them. I would station them near the old people's home in Ladbroke Grove where a gang of moronic thugs are given to beating up the old dears and taking their pensions. A couple of quid!" He looked disgusted. "I'd put them there if I had them to spare, not looking after your spoiled little girlfriend. Or I'd deploy them near the alley in Westbourne Park Road where a rapist has been attacking nine-year-old girls and causing them grievous bodily harm. The next one he attacks, or the one after, he'll murder, I'd bet on it. No, Mr. Dangerfield, your chick with the yen for far-out sex is not very high on my list of priorities."

He tapped a biro on his desk and added, "But I'll tell you what I will do. I'll ask the bobby on the beat to check as he passes by. Okay? Drop in maybe? Your mother's house is where you say Miss Morgan is . . . ?"

I suddenly felt sick. My mother's house. The women were alone there. I had felt confident that I had not been followed. But they might have known where to look anyhow. What was to stop those two maniacs . . . ?

I rushed out of the station. I had not got my car. It was still in the car park at Hyde Park Corner. I had walked down to the police station in Ladbroke Grove. I ran back now, down Ladbroke Road, out into Landsdown Road, opened the gate, heart beating, head throbbing, put my key in the door and heard my mother's voice saying, "Mark? That you? You were quick."

Relief flooded me, then another thought made me freeze

and without going in to my mother I dialed the shop. Mandy's voice came sweet and calm, balm to my ears.

"Dangerfield Books. May I help you?"

"Mandy, it's Mark. Are you all right?"

"Of course, darling. Why? You sound funny. Are *you* all right?"

"Darling, listen. Listen to me. Go to the door and lock up. You hear me? Lock up completely. Now."

"But darling, why? We're doing fantastic business today and—"

"Mandy, just do as I ask. Now. I'll hold on."

"Well, okay, darling. If you're sure I—"

"Mandy. *Do it. Now.*"

"There's no need to—"

"Mandy!"

She put down the receiver and I waited. And waited. And waited. But she never came back, and eventually the phone went dead.

CHAPTER 17

I felt sick. I wanted to hit out, to attack, to break something. I was also filled with panic. If anything happened to her! Dear God, let her be safe.

I phoned Mr. Gupta at the little mini market next door. We sometimes left keys with each other, looked after each other's shops if needed, were mutually helpful. He said my shop was open, but no one was there. No one at all. He was sure. With sinking heart I asked him to lock it.

I couldn't look at my mother's sympathetic face.

"I'm going to talk to Talia, Mother," I said and went upstairs. I had to act. I had to do something.

Stoury was sitting beside the bed holding a basin and it seemed that Talia was in withdrawal. She shivered and shook and retched green bile and blood, paying the grisly price all addicts pay. What was going on in her mind? Her beauty was not visible now. She looked ugly and used, old and dry cracked lips and swollen eyes, nose streaming, body convulsing, fingers clicking like castanets.

"I have to talk to her, Stoury," I said.

"She's not . . . well, Mr. Mark."

"I know, Stoury, but my Mandy is in danger."

She looked at me, her little eyes becoming hard in her plain face as she looked at Talia, and back to me.

"Then do what you have to do," she said simply. She stood, patted my shoulder and left the room.

I lifted Talia up, propped the pillows behind her. She wore one of my mother's nightgowns, a lawn and lace affair. It was saturated with cold sweat and stained with vomit. Talia's dark hair stuck to her shoulders like thin black snakes and she had a huge, swollen and discoloured bruise where Butterfly had hit her.

I fed her some coffee, but she couldn't keep it down. She shuddered, her eyes flicking open.

"Jason?" she asked.

"No. It's Mark. Listen, Talia, you'll have to help. Everything is out of hand. You must help."

She threatened to slide away again, and I slapped her face sharply.

She plucked at my arm. "Jason," she said, pleading. "I need Jason now. He always helps."

"Jason is dead." I didn't mean it to come out baldly like that but I had no time to waste. "They've killed him. We are next. You've got to help."

With the selfishness and self-absorption of all addicts, she said, "Then it's too late. I don't want to live if Jason is dead."

"You selfish bitch. My girlfriend has done nothing. Think of someone other than yourself for once."

She looked at me with glazed eyes. I didn't know how much of what I said she understood.

"Look, Talia. You've got to help me. Please . . ."

"Get me some tranks," she said. I didn't at first know what she was talking about. "Some tranks," she insisted. "Your mother has some valium or librium or something?" Her teeth were chattering. "Just to quiet me down. To steady me. Please. I can't talk otherwise."

"Okay," I said.

I knew Mother had a bottle of librium in the bathroom. She took one whenever she flew to the States. It was not that she didn't like flying so much as it helped her to recover from jet lag, monitor her sleeping, she claimed. I got the container for Talia, and she took at least four or five. She drank some coffee and seemed shortly a bit better.

"It's like this all the time," she said, glancing at me defensively, almost apologetically. "I need to be monitored, need to gauge when I need what. Tranks, amphetamines, drugs. You're up, up, up, then way, way down. It's a pattern. And it will get worse, I know. But I can't stop. Alison managed to. She went to Narcotics Anonymous. They helped her through. But it frightened everybody, her stopping. She knew too much. Enough to put us all behind bars. Kohl was furious. He seemed to blame us: Jason, me, and Revel. As if we could have stopped her. No one could stop Alison when she had her mind made up."

She glanced at me, appraising me, her hands restlessly plucking the sheet. "She wasn't really one of us, you know. Not really. She did a lot of this just to keep up." She gave a little snort of derision. "We were plumbing the depths, going for the full stretch, for the sensation, y'know, for thrills. But she was doing it so's we'd include her. Y'know, the inner sanctum."

"Appears to me you got out of your depth, you four. Were not able to handle it, eh?"

She looked at me angrily. "We paid the piper," she said. "We knew we would have to."

"Did you know it'd be as bad as this?"

She turned her face to the window and looked out at the plum tree shake its leaves in the sun. She shook her head. "No." It was a whisper.

I said, "Alison is dead. Revel is dead. Jason is dead."

She gave a gasp of pain and turned her face to me. Her eyes were wide and terrified. "Ah, God, I don't think I can live without Jason."

"You'll have to, Talia."

"How did he die?"

"They say he blew his brains out."

She looked incredulous. "But he'd never . . . never. And he'd tell me . . ."

She looked out of the window again.

"They said he had terrible financial problems."

"Yes. He had. And he had to borrow, do things . . . But he'd never kill himself. That's nonsense. In the last extremity Lady Cadbury would have underwritten him no matter how much was needed. He knew that. He didn't want to ask her, but if it came to such . . . extremes, I *know* he would have." She sighed. "Jason and I had everything we needed, everything we wanted, everything our little hearts desired." This last was bitterly said. I thought that perhaps that had been the trouble.

Yet it was the silliest thing to do, it was making a commitment to degradation and pain. It was giving up freedom of choice.

"They are all dead, your friends," I said, "Revel, Alison and Jason, all dead, and you are in grave danger. You have to help me now. Please help me."

She looked at me with tired eyes. "What's the point?"

"They've got my girlfriend," I repeated, wondering how much of what I said she heard. "She never hurt anyone. She was not part of this mess. I have to find her."

"I thought you fancied me," she said. I looked at her involuntarily. She must have seen the disgust in my face, revulsion I had tried hard to conceal, too late. She gave me a look of infinite exhaustion and she turned her head away from me once more. "I'm sorry," she said in a chastened voice.

"Why has this whole thing blown up?" I asked. "Please tell

148

me what you know."

"They wanted the books. They couldn't have anyone know their connection with us. I had the books, you see, I never thought you'd find them. I used them as collateral."

"For drugs? Blackmail! Oh, you silly girl."

"No. Not so silly. It worked from the time Alison died until you came along. Anyhow, I *had* to. They were making me *do* things. Things I didn't want to do. Like pushing. I'm not into making other people use. Kohl was forcing me. Threatening me with leaks to the newspapers, the gossip columns. I never thought you'd take them. The books, I mean. I didn't think you were bright enough. When I found them gone I told Kohl and Revel. Revel took them from your flat. Kohl rang up and I told him everything. About you and Revel. I was out to lunch. I'd had a fix. It always makes me talkative. Bernie must have gone to get them from Revel and Revel must have refused. Bernie would have . . . " She paused and swallowed, then shrugged. "I don't know why they . . . killed Jason," she added.

"I think it was because things had gone too far, and they decided to get rid of all of you. And me. It still doesn't explain why they got rid of Alison in the first place . . . " I took her arm. "Look, Talia, I don't understand. There must have been more than the books, the connection, the drugs. Believe me, they're not worried about that, at least not to the extent that they'd panic. The police *know* about them. They know the connection and they can't touch them. Not at the moment. So it has to be something else."

She stared at me, dark-circled eyes wide, shaking her head. "You still don't know, do you?" she said. "I thought you did by now."

I felt my anger rise, and I was overcome by a desire to shake her. It is not nice to be accused of stupidity by someone whose life you have just saved.

"What?" I said exasperated, "What should I know?"

"It's not the *drugs*," she said contemptuously. "Kohl is not worried about *that*. It's Mr. Moto. It's the babies. It's the children."

"What are you talking about?"

"Have you ever heard of private fostering? Private adoption? Mr. Moto runs the business for . . . someone. We don't know who. If it came to light . . . well, no one would believe . . ."

She was looking out of the window again. I remembered Alison's baby. Talia's baby. The thread. It had been under my nose all the time but I hadn't seen it.

"Alison found out. About Moto's boss, I think. Bob and Abigale send people to Moto. They get handsomely paid. Charmian Anderson, she's a registered nurse, she runs two clinics. And they wait in Mangoes. They take—buy—unwanted children and find a good home for them. They have a huge waiting list. Adoption agency. Fostering agency. They get away with it. It's a multi-million pound business. Thousands change hands. All races, creeds, colours. All are welcome at the agency. And the ones not given to childless couples, 'suitably placed' as they say, are used, well, for videos. They pay well for unwanted children of all ages. They can't get enough. The demand is greater than the supply. You can't imagine how many couples are desperate for children. They act under the anti-abortion lobby. You'll never stop abortion, but when they make it difficult, Mr. Moto always has a place for a kid. He puts it to them. 'We been told we shouldn't abort,' they say. He says, 'Well, I gotta suggestion . . .' All right and tight. People are happy to transact in secret. They use the homeless kids too. The older ones. For porn. For movies. Moto runs them all. He runs children. Forget Fagin. Moto makes Fagin look like St. Francis of Assisi. Alison gave hers. I gave mine."

My head was reeling. I looked at her stupidly. "Yours?"

"Yes. Mine and Jason's. Jason didn't want it. It would have interfered with our games. I hadn't been on the pill. My periods were so irregular. So . . . I never thought I'd get pregnant. But I did and Jason flipped. Said, get rid of it. So I went to Moto."

For the first time since I had met her, Talia showed some emotion.

"I only saw her for a few minutes," she said, "a little girl. Quite perfect. Charmian was pleased." Her voice trembled. Her face looked tired. Her energy was running out, the librium's deadening effect was wearing off. She began to scratch her face and scalp, at first absently, then more frantically.

"Look, Talia, where would I find him? Mr. Moto? Where would they take Mandy?"

"I don't know where you'd find Mr. Moto. Someone in Cardboard City might know. I don't. They know there. They can get two grand for a kid there. For themselves if they're old enough."

"Does he actually give it to them?"

"Well, no. He, like, gives it to them in kind. Most of them have a forty-to-fifty pounds a day problem. Sometimes more, much more, sometimes less."

"You ever hear how much the parents pay for the kid?" I asked.

"Depends. The market varies. From five thousand pounds upwards to twenty thousand pounds. Depends."

"On what?"

"On colour, race, creed. Oh, there's a lot of prejudice here, in this racket."

"And Mandy? Where would they . . ."

"To the club. To Mangoes. They would never let her near the clinics. Never." Her irritability was rising. I could see she was becoming acutely nervous. She was suffering now that the tranquilisers were wearing off. Drugs made the whole nervous system unbearably raw.

"Okay. Rest now, Talia. Take it easy. Get some sleep."

She gave me a tired smile and we both knew there would be no healing sleep for her for a long time.

CHAPTER 18

I gave Mother a very brief account of my conversation with Talia. I left her bewildered, trying to assimilate what I had told her, and set out for the club. My main consideration was Mandy.

I tried to calm my fevered fears, reminding myself that if I got into a blind rage, as I was inclined to, I'd be no good to her. I *had* to stay cool.

My car was still in the Hyde Park car park so I decided to use the underground. The lifts were out of action at Holland Park tube station, and the ticket machine didn't work. My temper kept flaring and escalating, and I kept trying to control it. I descended the filthy spiral stairway to the platform and got the first train.

The seething mass of commuters and tourists pressed around me. Garlic-laden or wine-laden or just plain bad breath tainted the air in the carriage. Pretty girls and young hopefuls, briefcase-carrying men, sweetened the atmosphere with perfume and aftershave. I did not know how they miraculously preserved their crisp appearance.

The man beside me took his jacket off. He was sweating alcohol and he read his paper, one eye closed. The train stopped for ten minutes between Bond Street and Oxford Circus, and I suppressed feelings of claustrophobia.

People sat and stood, waiting, their patience was like balm to my anger, soothing me. Tired faces, some smiling; dreaming faces, most of them prepared to wait, resigned to the rampant inefficiency that beleaguered them. I was filled with love for their acceptance, their docility. It made me ashamed of my irritability.

I got off at Tottenham Court Road. There was a busker playing quite good jazz at the intersection between the tunnels, and a young man sat in the warmth of a corner, a notice lying beside him with the torn lid of a cardboard shoebox anchoring it. It read:

I AM HOMELESS AND HUNGRY. PLEASE HELP.

The boy had a pale face and his eyes were closed. He looked dead, but when I dropped a pound coin into the box he looked at me with eyes empty and hopeless and said, "Thank you."

I walked through the underpass. It was littered with empty beer and Coca-Cola cans, cigarette packets and clear plastic bags. At the end of the underpass there was an encampment of alcoholics. Full six-packs of Long Life and Tennants Extra sat near the ageless men who huddled filthily in sleeping bags, cardboard boxes and ancient mattresses salvaged from tips and refuse dumps. They drank, then slept, shouted incomprehensibly for a moment, fought off imaginary ants or rats or pink elephants or whatever bogeymen terrorized their addled brains, then drifted back into their haunted comas. There was a strong smell of urine, stale vomit and decay there.

I emerged from that underworld up into the bright neon lights of Tottenham Court Road. The Centre Point building towered above me diminishing all us little people who scurried below, reminding us of our smallness and insignificance. I walked down Charing Cross Road. Once again the street was littered and dustbins overflowed and black plastic bags abounded. The gutter was cluttered with rubbish.

I walked past Foyles and turned into Old Compton Street.

The Three Greyhounds on the corner was full, the crowd had spilled out onto the street. They stood in the cool night air, pints in hand, laughing inanely under the new moon. Time for them was slipping away, responsibilities receding. Thoughts of home were growing faint and unattractive, prospects of adventure in the neon-sleaze haven of Soho more and more seductive as each pint was downed and another ordered.

I passed Lovejoy's Book Bargains, past the Tandoori and Ed's Diner, past the Prince of Wales Theatre. "Anything Goes" was playing and I thought "You can say that again." Wheelers and the Soho Brasserie were crowded, choc-a-bloc with people eating and laughing and flirting. I walked, hurrying to Mandy, past Frith Street and the Family Leisure Entertainment, the pinball arcade, all lit up, machines clanking, whirring, tinging and pinging. It was full of teenaged kids, bug-eyed and solitary, each one concentrating on the whirling lights of his machine, hoping to win a fortune. Or the price of a meal. Or a fix.

I was nearly there when I realized what I had to do. My mind on the tube had been overactive, but walking down Old Compton Street I had become calmer and the squirrel thoughts ceased chasing each other around my head, and I realized that I would get nowhere unless I had a plan. I couldn't just barge into Mangoes. Then I remembered the back entrance. That would be the sensible way to go in. I was sure that if they had Mandy there, they would keep her well away from the customers.

I remembered the faces of the children I had seen there. I was suddenly profoundly aware of the reality of their situation. I shuddered. That was a whole separate part of the building, a sort of clearinghouse. So I decided I would enter the back way and to that end I set about trying to discover where it was. I turned down alleyways, into lanes. Girls in skimpy stage costume stood with their backs against the wall, smoking or smooching. Pimps argued with hookers. Drunks relieved themselves or vomited, their overindulgence erupting at one end or the other.

Eventually I found what I was looking for. The back entrance down the evil-smelling alley, dark and full of shadows.

The door was closed. I tested it. No dice. It was one of those barred doors similar to the exits in cinemas. They are easy enough to push through to get out but only lock in more firmly when pushed to enter.

I was dashed, convinced that Mandy would be in this part of the building. Seeing no way to get to her, I heard the sound of an iron door or window opening above me, and a match being struck; the sound in the stillness of someone drawing greedily on a cigarette and the odour of tobacco smoke floated down to me on the night air.

I had pressed myself against the door in an effort not to be seen. That was difficult as the lane was a series of flat walls and rear entrances with precious few angles or corners to hide in. But I need not have worried. Whoever was above me had obviously not seen me.

I hazarded an upward glance. It was Gilda. I gasped and she heard me and looked down. When she saw me she smiled and beckoned me up. She pushed the fire-escape ladder down and I grabbed the end and climbed up briskly.

She was sitting on an iron ledge, legs through the bars, swinging her bare feet to and fro.

"Hello," she said and smiled at me. Her smile was soft and intimate. I was astonished. She must know something of what was going on, yet she was as unconcerned as if we had met at the vicar's tea.

"Where is she?" I asked, standing above her. A blue neon

light shone on her face and removed all the colour. She looked like a ghost child.

"Your girlfriend? Down there." She jerked her head backwards, and I had the dubious satisfaction of finding out that my supposition was correct.

"Is she all right?" I asked. I could feel a tight knot of anxiety in my chest. I was almost afraid of her answer. She nodded.

"Christ, Gilda, what kind of a girl are you?"

She shrugged. "I'm a survivor."

"Well, bully for you."

"You don't have to be so goddamned smug," she said bitterly. "In the end, Mark, everything boils down to survival. Bread. Both kinds."

"Let me pass."

"Okay." She stood, but took my arm as I passed by her. "I don't want you to think badly of me," she said softly.

"I don't. But get out, Gilda. Before it's too late. Get out while there's still time."

"You're all the same. Spout garbage! Where do you think I'd go? Cardboard City? Be independent of Kohl and be a hooker? What do you suggest? There's nowhere for us to go, Mark. Unless you take care of me? It's a good offer. You'd be mad to turn it down." Her voice was light, but the undertone was serious. I looked at her. Her face was softly rounded, still young and unmarked, vulnerable. She was very lovely, and as I stood looking at her, my heart was filled with pity for youth too soon corrupted.

"I have to find Mandy," I said. She said nothing, just stood there like a schoolgirl in front of the headmistress, hoping for praise but not really expecting it. I touched her cheek as I passed and she looked up at me swiftly. Her eyes held a suspicion of tears and she merely glanced at me, then shrugged and turned from me and went to lean on the rail.

I went through the iron door behind her. It led to the flies. There were ramps, lights, rolled backdrops waiting to be let down on cue. There was a man up there, beer-bellied, sweating and bald. He didn't look at me; he seemed intent on the stage below him.

They were playing a Pointer Sisters number, ghetto-blaster loud. The gels turned from red to green and back again, like traffic lights, and the man stared down and scratched his belly and yawned.

I went down a flight of rickety steps and found myself in the passageway on the other side of the stage, the beaded curtains on my right, closed doors in front of me. Gilda had followed me and stood at the top of the stairs I had just descended. She stood, arms crossed, watching me.

I opened the first door. Nothing. Props again, only down here they looked new and freshly painted and I figured were probably in current use.

I opened the next door. It was the one the children had looked out of the last time I had come this way. It was dark, so dark I felt as if a black mask had been drawn over my eyes. As I became accustomed to the pitchy gloom, I realized that this, too, was a corridor and there were doors here on either side. I judged that I had gone into another building; the atmosphere, the smell was different.

The first thing that struck me was the sound. It was creepy. Eerie. A scrabbling, a scratching, a scraping. Like rats. I remembered having heard that sound somewhere before, but I couldn't place it. It wasn't until much later that I remembered it was the sound I had heard in the underpass from the Tottenham Court Road tube and in Kensington Church Street. That sound was of little restricted movements. Movements in confined spaces.

I opened the first door I came to. There was a dim light on

and I could see it was quite a comfortable room . . . cubicle, really, like a room you would have in a clinic. There was a narrow iron bed with a plain white coverlet, a bedside locker, a dressing table with mirror in some kind of balsa wood and a built-in closet. There was a bedside light on and a pretty girl, approximately twenty-three or four, sat in a Dranlon-covered easy chair reading *Hello* magazine. She was heavily pregnant. She turned at my entrance and smiled at me.

"Hi. Who're you?"

"My name is Mark Dangerfield."

"Are you the doc? They said they'd send—"

"No, no. I'm just visiting."

"Oh." She looked vague. "I thought we weren't supposed to have any visitors?"

"Look here, are you okay?" I asked. I felt awkward.

"Sure. Why not?" She looked suddenly alert, suddenly suspicious. "He's not going to change his mind? I mean, the deal's still on? I really need the money, you see . . ."

I nodded, excused myself and got out of there quick. I felt sick. My head was spinning. However, it was no use thinking about the girl's situation. Now I had to find Mandy.

She *had* to be here. She just had to. I opened the next door. A boy and a girl, both about fourteen, sat there playing cards, and the girl was biting her thumb. They both looked up as I came in. Their faces were shocking, coarse, their eyes like stones.

"Piss off, mister," the girl said. "We don't do it in here. Piss off."

The boy looked me over speculatively as if I might be a customer. "You lookin' for trade?" he said. "I don' mind. Here, anywhere." He came over to me and slipped his arm around my leg. "You buy me a Big Mac an' I'll do anythin' you wan'."

I pulled away, disentangled myself and ran out of that room. I felt dirty, yet also I felt a fool, as if they had made me lose face. I stood a moment, breathing heavily, then crossed the hall.

I opened about ten doors all into similar rooms, all with similar inhabitants. Child prostitutes, pregnant girls. In one of them was Jade. I stared at the elfin face. She stared back.

"Jade," I said.

She didn't recognize me. "The fuck you want?"

"Nothing. Nothing. You okay?" Why did I keep asking that? I think I could not believe that they were there willingly, by their own request.

Jade looked at me, remembrance dawning, suddenly hopeful.

"Kelvin send you?" she asked.

I shook my head. "No, no. Sorry." She looked crestfallen.

"I haven't seen him," she said. "Don' know where he is. You see him you tell him I'm okay."

I nodded and she smiled at me. "The bed's nice. After the cardboard," she said.

I left her there, small and alone.

I was frantic now. I pulled at doors, looked in at the in-mates, willing victims. What horrified me was that in another context those cubicles would be completely normal and cosy. They looked neat and clinically clean.

As I reached the end of the corridor I was beginning to lose hope. I heard loud voices at the entrance to the corridor down the passage but I paid no attention. Mandy, Mandy, Mandy where are you? I screamed silently.

I opened the penultimate door and saw her. She lay curled on the bed and at first I thought she was asleep. Then for a terrible moment I thought her dead. I went over and touched her. She rolled over and I realized she was drugged. I held her fiercely in my arms, folding them around her, wrapping her in them, not wanting to let her go. She lay within their circle, inert, unconscious. I squinted my eyes tight shut and relief flooded me, relief such as I had never known. I had never realized how precious she was to me, how essential.

Suddenly, as I cradled her, the high voices of children impinged on my awareness and I realized they were growing louder. They were in the corridor outside and mingled with their babble, I could discern the voice of Sebastian Kohl.

"Where? Where was he?" he asked. "Are you sure? What did he look like?" Someone had given the alarm. I thanked God I was so average that my appearance was in no way remarkable. I realized that only a miracle would save me. I looked around the room. Nothing. Under the bed? They were sure to look there. Out of a sort of reflex panic I opened the closet door and dived in. It was very small and I curled myself, my back to the side, sitting on the floor, knees bent. I pulled a blanket that lay on the floor over me and hid my head behind the terry-towel dressing gown hanging there.

I had heard Kohl say something about searching all the rooms and, "If you kids are playing me up, I'll . . ."

I didn't hear any more and nearly gave the game away when the closet door was opened suddenly, briefly, then closed. I heard someone say, "No one here," in a dull voice, and then Kohl, "Ah. Let me see. She's safe. That means it wasn't anyone . . . We'll move her tonight. It's one of those bloody girls bringing in a boyfriend or husband for a visit. I've warned them not to. Someone'll squawk if we're not fuckin' careful."

The voice died away. I stayed, suffocating, for what seemed hours in the closet, afraid to move in case someone had remained behind guarding Mandy.

Eventually I pushed the door open a crack, cautiously.

Nothing happened. No one pounced on me. I pushed it a little more. No one there. I emerged into the room, relieved. I could take my girl home. The nightmare was over. Then I saw that Mandy was not on the bed. She had disappeared.

CHAPTER 19

I opened the door and went into the passageway. I had walked its length when the door at the top opened, and the boy I had seen first in the room with the girl stuck his head out.

"I know where she is, mister," he said, grinning at me. I wanted to strangle him, taking his remark as a taunt.

"Where?" I grabbed his arm.

"Ouch! Yer hurtin' me. I won't tell you nuffin' less you let go o' me an' give me fifty." His face was weasel-like and he looked at me with hard eyes. I groped for my wallet. I was having difficulty with my breathing. I took out the note.

"Where?" I said, firmly holding it just out of his reach.

"Gimme."

"No. Not until you tell."

"Then we'll be here all night, mister. Gimme. You got no choice."

"Okay." He was right. "If you rat on me I'll tan your backside," I said.

"That'll be extra, mister," he said and rolled his eyes, then became serious. "Look, mister, I tell you 'cause I like gettin' one over on them." He stabbed the air upwards with his thumb. "They're scum. Like all pimps. Scum. Makin' out it's all legal. Above board. Drivin' flash cars. Garbage they are. But look, I got no other way of makin' out. They put her in there, mister."

He indicated another smaller door I'd missed, right opposite his own door and in an alcove. I must have thought it was the broom cupboard. I looked at the middle-aged youngster. The girl had come out and stood beside him. She was smoking.

"Good one, mister," she said in a hoarse voice. "Get one on them."

I opened the door. This room was meaner, more utilitarian, but she was there, lying on the cot. My heart skipped a beat, relief flooded and I picked her up in my arms. This time we'd have to be pried apart. I ran down the corridor, watched by the boy and girl; I pushed open the exit doors, which gave easily at my touch and I walked away carrying my precious burden in my arms. As I left, I could not resist a look back.

Gilda was standing there, on the iron balcony, leaning on the parapet. A thin spiral of blue smoke rose upwards from her cigarette. She saw me and she raised her hand and waved. I could not return her salute for my hands were full.

I was taking Mandy home.

CHAPTER 20

I knew I had to act quickly. I knew that something had to be done before Sebastian Kohl and his thugs discovered that Mandy was gone and started creating mayhem.

I took Mandy back to the Kings Road. I put her in my bed and phoned the doctor. Then I phoned Inspector Rawlings. I told him what I had found and what I had seen. He didn't say much and hung up when I had finished. Dr. Hawks jumped to the conclusion that Mandy was an addict. In spite of my assurances, he found it easier to believe that she was injecting heroin and had taken too much, than that she had been abducted and that the drug had been forcibly administered.

"Can you get her into a hospital, Doctor?" I asked.

He sighed. "Hospital beds are like gold dust, Mark," he replied. "Someone like that, comes from a good home, is warned and warned but pays no attention, experiments with drugs, aware of the consequences, well, can't say as I think they deserve preferential treatment."

"But, Doctor, I told you—"

"Yes, yes, yes, I heard." He brushed me away irritably. "But I'd still prefer to have the bed occupied by someone who really needs it; a life and death case where the person did nothing to deserve their pain."

I was relieved to hear that Mandy was not a life and death case, because until then I had not known how seriously she had been affected by the drug, but I was intensely aggravated

165

by his refusal to believe the truth.

"Kids today, all around here, the Kings Road, they won't *listen*," he grumbled. "They all imagine they are the exception. Well, they're wrong. The graveyards are full of kids who thought they were a special case."

I wondered why truth is always stranger than fiction, and when will people start to understand that?

"I don't like it when addicts come to the National Health for their fixes," he continued. "But I'll tell you what I *can* do. Only thing is, it'll cost you."

"What?"

"Get her into a treatment centre. They'd keep her overnight, or perhaps for a few days. Monitor her withdrawal. There's one just up the road from here."

The girl in the treatment centre was helpful and efficient, but she was just as skeptical as Dr. Hawks when I told her the truth. I had to leave it at that. I knew Mandy would be safe and that no one would guess where she was.

I left her then, there in a room that was a carbon copy of the one in the annex at Mangoes. I warned the staff that no one, repeat *no one,* was to be allowed to see her. They looked at me with that superior, pitying look professionals have when they know something you don't.

"We never allow our patients visitors," the night nurse said, tight-lipped. "Especially those withdrawing. Those who have just been brought in."

"I'm only insisting because her life is in danger. She has been threatened."

The nurse's eyes widened and she looked at me narrowly. "You on something, too, Mr. Dangerfield?" she asked crisply.

"No, no. Just look after her, will you?"

"Of course, Mr. Dangerfield. That's what we're here for.

That's what you are paying for."

I had to be content with that and I left her there, hating to have to do so.

The phone was ringing when I got back. It was Mother in a panic.

"Talia's gone," she said. "Stoury said she left. Just got up and went. Stoury couldn't stop her. I was out. I blame myself, Mark."

"Don't, Mother," I said wearily. Things were happening too fast. "Don't worry about it. If she decided to go, then no one could stop her. Not really."

"But you trusted me and I failed . . ."

"No, Mother, you didn't. And when you think about it, you'll realize that."

I felt too exhausted, too dispirited to say any more, so I put the phone down. I sat for an hour just thinking. Mandy's involvement had undermined my confidence. I felt justified in risking my own life, felt capable of defending myself. What I couldn't cope with was that innocent people I loved could be hurt by the forces I fought. This whole case had nothing whatsoever to do with Mandy, yet she had been sucked into it in a most frightening way. It was all wrong.

I phoned Rawlings at once.

"I've lost Talia Morgan," I said.

"I know," he said. "She has just been fished out of the canal. Throat cut. No pretence anymore. Some fishermen heard the splash at Westbourne towpath and went to investigate. There was a lot of blood staining the water. Whoever killed her, and I think you and I can guess, put her in a sack weighed down with a stone. But the blood seeped out and up to the surface of the water. Listen, Mr. Dangerfield, I think you better—" But I put the phone down on him. I did not want to be restrained now.

Now they were all dead, the beautiful people, the Fab Four. I felt deeply sad.

They had not deserved to die that way. Particularly Alison. Alison had set about changing her life and had been the innocent instrument of all this violence. I thought of her again, as I had seen her. She had that peculiar radiance so unusual, so difficult to find. She had been all things to all men. So Barclay had said. And then she had found herself. Found faith. Found love. Poor Alison. Floating, facedown, at the bottom of the river, under the willow tree. Poor lost life.

I phoned Wendy Cadbury. It was a duty I knew I had to perform. I didn't know what to say to her. I remembered our light-hearted conversation that first day when she had asked me to take this case, the casual way I had agreed, my preoccupation with my capability in solving the mystery of Alison Alyward's drowning, my crass ignorance with what I was getting involved in and, more important, its effect on those I loved. In retrospect, I was appalled at my smugness. I had grown since then.

I told Wendy about Jason. She said the police had already informed her. She was crying but seemed calm and unhysterical.

"Come over to Eaton Mews, Mark," she said.

She received me wearing a housecoat or robe-de-chambre by Christian Lacroix. She had a cigarette between her fingers. Her eyes were dry but I could see she had been weeping. She asked Bard, the butler, to bring drinks. I had a Johnnie Walker Black Label and she had a vodka.

There was a portrait on the wall behind her of Archie in uniform. He looked handsome but tentative, as if he was waiting for the viewer to answer a question. We sat on the enormous beige sofa under the crystal Russian chandelier. The room was quiet.

"I'm so sorry, Wendy," I said, sipping my drink. "Do you blame me?"

"No, Mark. I could blame myself. I, after all, asked you to meddle. But, no, I don't blame you. We—I by asking you and you, because you obeyed my orders—precipitated his death, but we mustn't blame ourselves. Jason got himself into this when he started doing drugs."

"Did you want me to investigate because of Jason as well as Alison?"

"Yes, I suppose so. I wanted you to find out about the set-up. I had some silly notion that it could be sorted out. Foolish, bloody notion. Oh, don't get me wrong. I wanted you to clarify Alison's death. But I wasn't entirely truthful about Jason. I knew he was up to his neck in it."

I told her everything. She was resigned rather than grief-stricken.

"Drug addicts die, Mark. They die young. I knew that." She looked very sad. "I was a lousy mother, Mark. When Jason was a little boy, needing me, I sent him off to school. It was partly Cadbury. I was busy keeping him, holding on to him. Men like Cadbury have a never-ending stream of nubile young bimbos after them all the time and I didn't have enough confidence to relax and trust him. And it was partly snobbery. I wanted my son to go to the *right* schools, have the *right* education." She sighed and looked out of the window. "Oh, Mark, I had my priorities all wrong. I wasn't there for Jason when he needed me and now he's dead. I'm American. I don't believe in public schools. Every instinct told me it was wrong, sending him away. His father, whom he adored, did not want to see him. At least his wife didn't. I married a cool, inhibited, member of the English aristocracy who is incapable of showing affection. Poor Jason got lost somewhere in between all of us. My daughter, too, by my first husband—tragically neglected."

She looked at me regretfully. "Oh, Mark, it's too late," she said. "What sad, sad words they are, 'too late'."

"Well, you know it all now. At least as much as I do," I said. She lowered her eyes.

I was about to leave when she stalled me. "Don't go any further, Mark," she said. There was something furtive about her manner. Her eyes, which had been so candid, kept gliding away from mine.

"What do you mean, Wendy? I can't stop now. There's all this business with the children. You don't seriously expect me to let that continue, do you?"

She seemed to find something on the wall behind me riveting, refusing to meet my gaze. "Listen, Mark. Don't you think there has been enough death? Jason and Alison. Revel. Don't you think . . ."

"I think they'll have died in vain if I don't find out what is happening and who is running this and why Alison really died. So far, I don't know that. I know that Jason and Revel died because they knew too much about the books Alison left. But I don't know why Alison died. And that's why you employed me. You don't expect me to let things drop now do you?"

She shook her head impatiently. "Well, yes, Mark. What good will it do to rake up a lot of dirt?"

"Child porn? Illicit fostering? Adoption by payment? Jeez, Wendy, I can't just turn a blind eye—"

"Oh, Mark, don't be naive. That sort of thing will always go on. It's been going on since ancient Greece, and Roman times, and it always will. Like prostitution."

"I can't believe my ears, Wendy. Don't you understand that because it has always *been* there is no excuse? We have to fight it."

"Oh, I don't *condone* it," she assured me. "You mustn't think that, Mark."

"Well, good! Good!" I said sarcastically. "Bully for you." She did not seem to notice my ironic tone; she was not really listening to me.

"It's just that . . . if you *do* succeed in, er, stopping Mr. Moto, it will not finish there, and it's stupid to think it will. It would be foolish and idealistic to imagine that. There will be someone to take that man's place within weeks. No, within days, hours even. God, Mark, do you think it's worth losing your life for such a hollow victory?"

"Yes." It was an automatic response and I hadn't realized that I was so committed until that moment. "Wendy, listen," I said, "Even if a similar operation comes into being within days, hours, as you say, don't you see it's worth it if we save only one child? If we put Mr. Moto and whoever runs him away for a while? Don't you see that? We can't give up and wiggle out of it saying it will always exist because it always existed? If Shaftesbury and Dickens, Abraham Lincoln and all the others who fought injustice thought the way you did, we would still condone slavery, and child labour, and such exploitation in all its horror. At least however shocking life still is, however cruel the human race can be, at least we have made some progress. But not by giving up."

"Well, be careful, Mark," she said. "It's just that I'm rather afraid of it, what I might have to do if you delve too far."

"What do you mean? What are you hiding from me?"

She shook her head. "Oh, nothing. Just be careful. How could I ever face your mother if anything happened to you?"

I left her there, sitting under the David Hockney portrait of herself as she used to be, as she desperately wanted still to be, and as she knew, in moments of honesty, that she never would be ever again.

171

CHAPTER 21

I walked up Buckingham Palace Road to Hyde Park Corner and, finally, got the Audi. I drove to Elgin Crescent and was surprised when Abigale McNaughton, flanked by the two solemn children, opened the door to me at once. I don't know what I had expected, but it seemed odd to me that other people's lives had continued routinely when mine had been so violently disrupted.

"Oh, hello," she said unenthusiastically. But she was not alarmed, and I wondered if she had heard the news about the deaths and what she made, if anything, of it.

"Can I come in?"

"I suppose." She sounded doubtful, and she kept looking around as if there was someone else there.

We went into the same room as before. It was sun-filled, warmly cosy. There was a nursery rhyme on cassette. It was turned up loud. Abigale lowered it but it was sung by a clear-voiced soprano and I could hear the words distinctly:

Doctor Foster went to Gloucester,
In a shower of rain,
He stepped in a puddle right up to his middle,
And never went there again.

I looked at Abigale coldly. "Okay, Abigale, you can drop that crappy act," I told her. Her eyes widened. "Tell me where I can find Mr. Moto."

She let out a little gasp and went a funny grey colour. She

172

sat down at the table. "I don't know what you—"

"Don't even say it. I *know*. I *know* your involvement with him. I know how you pass your friends along conveniently—"

"But I don't." She sounded outraged. "I didn't. Only Alison and . . ."

"And, exactly, and . . ."

I felt my arm taken from behind.

"All right, Dangerfield. Quiet now. There are children here. Out. Let's go quietly."

I jerked my elbow backwards, felt it land on soft muscles, heard the grunt, and turned to see my apprehender slump over the back of the chair, moaning softly.

"You're Tom?" I stated. The cassette was now playing.

Ladybird, ladybird, fly away home,
Your house is on fire and your children all gone.

I thought, "Children all gone . . ." They both looked at the radio. Abigale turned it off. Tom nodded. "Yes. Please. Get out of my house."

"I'll be only too glad to, Tom. I have no desire to hurt you. I have really no desire to *talk* to you even, but sadly I must."

"What do you mean?"

"I mean you disgust me. You have your excuses, though, looking here," I indicated the children with a flick of my eyelids. "I cannot imagine how you can square it with yourselves, how you can live knowing what you are doing."

"You don't understand," he began.

"Why do people always say that? I understand only too well. It's greed. Greed, Mr. McNaughton."

"No. In our case . . . it's necessity . . . it's different."

"It always is. Your case . . . crap. But as I said, I have not come here to talk about your foul behaviour." He blinked. He had a weak face, fleshy and self-indulgent, and he looked at me with uneasy eyes. Abigale was aflutter with nervous agitation. Her hands flew here and there, opened a packet of biscuits, pulled at buttons on her blouse, tugged her hair, pulled at her lip. They were both consumed with defensive righteousness and all they wanted to do was explain their culpability away.

"We have to do as he says. When we first agreed . . ." Abigale began.

Tom continued and they spoke in turns as if they had rehearsed this many times, perhaps told each other, over and over, justifying, always justifying.

"Agreed because Alison was pregnant . . . "

". . . and didn't want the baby . . . "

"Couldn't really afford it . . ."

"She's such a ninny. She didn't even know she was pregnant . . . " This was Abigale.

"Aunt Sally hadn't fully informed her about the facts of life, it appears so . . ." Tom said, sounding contemptuous. I remembered he was the father. "We heard about Mr. Moto from Revel. He sometimes supplied Revel with . . . er . . . boys."

"And we told Alison . . ."

"She was *so* relieved . . ."

"Why didn't Revel tell Alison?" I asked.

"Oh, that was in Cottesloe, before she came here."

"I see."

"Mr. Moto *guarantees* superb homes for unwanted children." Abigale looked fondly at her two standing silently at the table, eating biscuits. "Not all children can be as lucky as ours," she said piously.

"How much does he pay?" I asked.

"Ten percent of the total, plus expenses," she said crisply, then realized how it sounded.

"But we don't do it for the money," Tom assured me.

"No. No." Abigale agreed.

"What do you do it for then?"

I couldn't believe it when she said, "Well, you see, we offer a service, a much-needed service. As long as the adoption laws in this country are harsh, people will suffer from not having the babies they want. We provide that service. And if the service didn't exist, then all those poor babies would be in an orphanage. This way they are *guaranteed* a good home."

I was speechless. I shook my head. They sat around the table, father, mother, children, in the sunlit room. A normal family. Expecting medals. Abigale and Tom looked relieved. They had needed to convince someone of the purity of their motives and now they sat thinking of how good it sounded.

"The laws are there to protect children," I said.

"Those children are lost." Abigale said. "Without Mr. Moto they would be in an orphanage."

"So you said. I just want to know where I can find him?"

"Oh, we can't tell you that." Tom sounded prim, as if I had asked for the secret of the Masonic handshake.

"I think you had better," I said conversationally. "There have been at least four murders to date and my girlfriend was drugged and is now in a clinic." They both turned pale.

"What nonsense," Abigale said. "You're talking rubbish. This has nothing to do with us."

"It had nothing to do with her," I insisted. They were becoming distinctly uneasy.

"In any event we don't *know* where he lives," Tom said. "Or is. He phones us. Asks us if we have any . . ." He cleared his throat.

"Customers?" I asked.

He nodded and looked at me straight in the eye for the first time. "We really don't know. If I had an urgent message I wouldn't know how to get in touch with him. Honestly."

I had to believe him. Short of tackling him physically here in front of the children, there was nothing more I could do. Besides, he seemed to be telling the truth and it seemed unlikely that Mr. Moto would have lasted so long if he had been free with where he could be reached.

"Who runs Mr. Moto?" I asked. "Do you know?"

There was no doubting their genuine puzzlement.

"What are you talking about?" Abigale asked, looking alarmed. "You mean . . . he's not the boss . . ."

I shook my head. I had the satisfaction of seeing that I had frightened them. I had upset their idea of the *status quo.* I could read Tom McNaughton like a book. It was okay to deal with Mr. Moto, a Soho *habitué,* a gangster. And they knew where they were with him. They were anonymous as long as he was. But if there was someone pulling his wires, then that was different. That spelt insecurity, the unknown, the unpredictable. It had started up an acute anxiety. They could never rest again.

I left the McNaughtons very alarmed indeed, and they hardly noticed my exit. I left the flat in Elgin Crescent with relief.

CHAPTER 22

In the afternoon I went to see Mandy. I had more difficulty explaining to the day staff in the clinic that she was not an addict. They treated my explanation that she had been shot full of heroin by some people with derision. Their faces said that they had heard a lot of bizarre excuses in their time and they were not going to believe the nonsense I was talking. But they were too polite to come right out and say it.

Then my mother showed up. She backed me up to the hilt. She stood there in her tweeds, her cashmere sweater, her Hermes scarf, her halo of silver-grey hair, her matched pearls and she oozed Olde English reliability and trustworthiness and they believed her instantly.

Mandy was still groggy. "It was a nightmare, Mark. I never want to go through that, again." Two men, she said, one tall, cool and black, the other built like an ox, had been at the door just as she was about to close up. She had thought I was being neurotic until she saw them standing there, and then in a split second she had realized what I was trying to protect her from.

"But it was too late, Mark. They held something over my nose, then hustled me into a car. Wouldn't you think someone would have asked them what they were doing?"

I shook my head.

"Not nowadays," Mother said, "They used to. People were helpful. But not anymore. Poor Mandy."

"I don't remember anything more until I woke up here. I

was frightened at first, then the nurse told me you had brought me in. She seemed to disapprove of me and treated me quite harshly. But they're all right now. Oh darling, what's happening?"

"Mandy, there's no way to make this easy. Talia has been murdered."

"Oh Mark, no. Oh, poor Talia. She was silly, but she didn't deserve to die."

Mandy looked shocked. She looked tired and strained as well. Her natural healthy appearance had undergone a change, and she was pale as a lily and my heart went out to her.

"Mandy, I want you to stay here until this is over. A day or two at most. The security here is first class. They didn't want to let *me* in until Mother came. You'll be safe here. I couldn't live with myself if anything happened to you, my darling."

"I'll come and see you often, Mandy," Mother said, holding her hand. "Mark is right. There's no point in you taking chances. In any event, you need a long rest. You've been through quite an ordeal. But you must have no visitors except myself and Mark."

Mandy agreed. I think she was quite relieved. I don't think she felt up to any more excitement.

I kissed her. Her small white face on the pillow touched my heart and caused me renewed anger against the men who had put her here. The sooner I got this awful business sorted out the better. I kissed her again and left her in Mother's tender care.

It seemed to me that there was only one person who could help me now, and that was Kelvin. If Jade was in the building behind Mangoes, about to give birth, then he must know Mr. Moto. He *had* to, he was my last chance. There was, of

178

course, Gilda. Gilda who always knew a little more than she said.

I drove to Church Street, parked the car in the same place as I had that night when we had dined at Clark's. It seemed so long ago now, and in reality it was not more than ten days.

Kelvin saw me coming and ran. He took to his heels like a hare and hot-footed it down to the High Street. He left his pathetic little corner, stacked with his pitiable possessions behind him, untenanted, and ran.

I went down the alley beside the Carmelite Church and lurked. It was the only way to describe what I was doing. I skulked in the shadows blending with the night. I was becoming good at that sort of thing.

I guessed he would return. He would be convinced I had followed him when he ran and I lost him, and, as I had hoped, after about an hour he came back.

I grabbed his arm from behind. He gave a grunt but did not protest too much.

"Okay, okay, man, what is it?" He sounded resigned.

"I want some information, that's all. Can I let you go?"

"Sure, man," he turned. "Oh, it's you."

"You knew it was me. That's why you ran."

"Not necessarily, man. Still, you the guy with the five. 'Spec me to be sooo grateful? I s'pose you're lookin'—"

"I'm not looking for anything, pal. Don't jump to conclusions. You took my cash, remember?"

"So? Wouldn't you, you was me?"

I shrugged. "Maybe you needed it mor'n I did."

"Maybe?" He laughed. "Only maybe? What you think, my man? Eh?" His black face split in an engaging grin.

"Okay, I said I'm not after you for that. I told you I needed information."

"Information costs."

"Okay. Where can we go?"

"You buyin', man?" I nodded. "There's a McDonald's in the High Street. It's the Ritz of the vagrants. They'll let me in, I with you. I could do with the nosh."

He gave me a cheeky grin, perking up at the thought of the food. He was shivering and I resisted the temptation to give him my jacket. The styled linen garment would have looked incongruous over his torn jeans and his black Marylon heavy metal T-shirt and I knew it would do little to keep him warm. Besides, the shivering did not come because the weather was inclement. It was a manifestation of inner turmoil: hunger, drug withdrawal, nervous tension.

He loped along beside me, glancing at me now and then with speculative eyes. I was pretty sure he was planning to rob me again. If he could.

"You got something wrong with your foot?" I asked.

He looked down. He was wearing sneakers. His toes were coming through the shoes.

"Naw, man," he said. "It's difficult to walk. Hard to keep these things on, man, but I got to cover my feet. But see, I got peripheral neuritis. They told me in the hospital. So I gotta keep these shoes on, man, and it's not easy."

"You better have that attended to," I said. One of the things I dislike was the way my thoughts came out. Since all this happened I knew I sounded like a twit. I found it hard to articulate my real feelings.

Kelvin was laughing at me. The sound was derisive and mocking. "Get it tended to? Hear the guy! 'Ark at the man! Cor!" He turned to me. "I told you. We get nuthin' without an address." He banged his fist in his palm. "Nuthin'. Listen, man, the first thing the receptionist asks anywhere, any practise, any hospital, is your address. No address, no treatment. Got it?" He gave a snort. "Unless I go private." He grinned at me. "Like, man, do I look like I could go private?" He shrugged. "I don' blame the docs. It's bureaucracy. It's not their fault. Docs treat me all the time, outa kindness. But it's forms, forms, forms—"

"So what do you do?" I asked. "For the neuritis?"

"I wait, man. I wait. I go to casualty an' I wait. Sometimes all day. Least it's warm. Depressing, but warm. I haveta use different hospitals. They always busy. When an' *if* they let me see the doc, (I'm not, strictly speakin', *casualty,* see?) well, when an' *if,* he's usually so tired, so exhausted he can hardly keep his eyes open. I'd be at the end of the queue, see. An' the docs, they work fourteen, fifteen hours a day. They're tired, man. They give me pills. I sometimes take them. I sometimes sell 'em, get real dope, get nose candy. That makes me feel a whole lot better."

"The . . . er . . . nose candy won't help you forever." There I went again!

"You think I don' know that?" He looked at me with withering contempt. "Jeez man, in our situation you can't plan *nuthin'.* Naw! No sayin', tomorrow this, that or the other. Naw! Tomorrow you may be dead, man. You get through today, best you can, leave tomorrow out, man. O.U.T. Otherwise you scramble." He made a circle with his forefinger against his temple and smiled.

We were in front of the big M. I always hated McDonald's facades. The horrible neon. The great childish M in yellow, the red glitz, the ghastly little cartons and polystyrene beakers, the deplorable encouragement to eat on the trot, fast basic food from synthetic containers and plastic cutlery. I could not fathom anyone other than children and tramps actually wanting to go to this fast-food depot to eat, sitting on uncomfortable stools in garish lighting.

However, tonight I was glad it was there. I took my companion by the elbow and steered him inside.

"God, I hate these fast-food places," I said involuntarily.

"They're the Savoy, man, to us," Kelvin said, rubbing his hands together.

I bought him a Big Mac, French fries and a giant Coca-Cola. I watched him eat. He was swift and greedy. I wondered when he had eaten last. After a second Big Mac, Kelvin, still eating as if a famine were scheduled for the next day, cocked an eye in my direction. "Okay. Talk, man. What you wanna know? Nuthin' for nuthin', eh? I gotta sing for my supper, eh? Ask. What you wanna know?"

I felt ashamed, but he was right. There was no way I would be here buying him supper if I had not needed to find out about Mr. Moto.

"Mr. Moto," I said.

He choked on his Big Mac. I thought for a moment he was going to leave. He hesitated, one foot off the foot rail, one buttock off the seat, then smiled, showing his ivory teeth. "I owe you one," he said and gave a surreptitious glance around the ghastly neon-lit interior of the place.

"Looking for the F.B.I.?" I joked.

"Are you outa your tree, man?" His voice squeaked and he looked at me with wonder. "This no jokin' matter. You don' understand. You can't play games with Moto. No. I promise you that."

An overtired child began to scream. I tried to enjoy the milky liquid in the polystyrene beaker that had been sold to me as coffee. The masquerade didn't work, and I put it down on the Formica ledge in front of me.

"I'm not playing games, Kelvin."

He looked at me cockily. "Jeez . . . he remembered my name!" he said rolling his eyes in mock astonishment.

"Uh-uh. Listen. This Moto is responsible for the deaths

of four of my friends."

"No!" Kelvin didn't bat an eyelid. "No," he said with certainty. "No, he isn't. Only deaths Moto responsible for, man, is kids who get done in by the over-enthusiastic pedophiles. The porno team. Kids who can't take it. Suicide themselves. Kids who get beat up by the pedophiles who don't know their own strength. An' that's not direct. Not murder in the first degree. Have a hard time pinnin' that on him, man. No, Moto got nuthin' to do with murder. That's Kohl and Bernie and Butterfly. That's who does that sort of thing. Keep outa their way. They lethal, man."

"Yea, but I'm looking for Moto and the man who gives the orders. Who runs him and Bernie and Kohl and Butterfly?"

"Ah, well, see, no one knows that. Some smart dude, like way up. Like up so high *no* one, I mean *no* one, can touch."

"Well, Kelvin . . ."

"Can I have a piece of pie?"

"Sure." I gave him a fiver and he loped up to the permanently smiling eighteen-year-old at the counter, got his pie and returned.

"I'm going to find that guy, Kelvin. I'm going to stop him. But first I want Moto."

"Well, I wish you luck. An' I'll come to your funeral." Kelvin laughed, his mouth full of the pastry. He had pocketed the change saying, "Fair game."

"Why laugh, Kelvin?"

"You do-gooders sure are all the same," he said wryly. "Come in. Catch people. Put them away. So what? It's the system is wrong, man, never mind 'bout them. Stopping Mr. Big, Moto, Kohl an' Bernie an' Butterfly'll do no good. Don't you see? They'll be replaced. There'll be another lot along to work the likes of us, pounce on us, exploit us. Opportunity's too good to miss. Likes of us supply likes of you with your special tastes, see? Your peculiar needs. The next lot may not be as generous. Jade gets a grand if the baby is okay." For the first time he looked on the defensive.

"The baby'll be an addict, Kelvin. You know that."

"Yea, I suppose. Like it seemed a good opportunity. Y'know. I suppose it was too much to hope for."

"Whatever she's on . . ."

"Heroin, man. Not crack, heroin."

"Is that better?" I asked.

"Sure. Heroin sedates. Crack, man, hypes you till you off the walls. Leaves permanent damage."

"Well, the baby'll be an addict . . ."

"People won't know that till it's too late," he said. "Can't send damaged goods back to Mr. Moto. Can't find him. No one can. An' in those circumstances, you sure can't sue."

"How much of that grand will be paid to you in drugs?" I asked. "How much will you actually get to keep?"

"Aw shut up, man. Your sort piss me off. Crusading! As long as there are people like us there'll be people like Mr. Moto. Y'know?" Kelvin paused and looked reflective. "You should see him. Cock o' the walk. Little man struts, y'know? Gold cufflinks, gold watch, gold chains. Diamond on pinkie. Cashmere coats. Loves to throw his weight around. School bully. But in our world there's no authority to stop him. That's what you do-gooders don't understand. Your rules don' apply here. You can't do nuthin'. It's the survival of the fittest time and, boy, is Mr. Moto fit!"

"You're a bright lad, Kelvin. Observant. Eloquent. How come you're in this fix?"

"Don't patronize me, mister. Listen, I got my university entrance, Leeds. I did like the good guys tell us. Kept my nose clean. In Brixton. An' it was not cool to do that, man. Oh no. Not there. Gotta hate the filth. Gotta break the rules to prove you a man. But I din'. However, my home fall apart. Old man ran off with the Indian girl from the supermarket. Mam takes to the juice. My sister goes on the game. Landlord repossesses. Bailiff throws us out. On the street, man, just like that. The neighbours are not sorry to see us go. Say pride comes before a fall an' all that shit. So. There I am. No address, so as I tol' you, nuthin'. You don't listen good, mister. I tol' you no address . . ."

"Yes. I get the picture."

"No address, you can't fill in forms. They tear them up. Don't listen to what they say. It's all lies. It's cast iron. Don't you read the newspapers? I fell through the net, man."

He shook his head, looking at me as if I was a half-wit. "Come on. I'll take you where you'll find someone who knows where Mr. Moto is. You aimin' to get blown away? You persist, you will be a dead man soon." He shrugged, wiped his mouth with the back of his hand and put the paper napkin in his pocket.

We went downstairs to the toilets. He pushed open the door to the ladies. I tried to stop him but he was in and out like lightning. "Toilet roll," he said, his hands full of white tissue. "Men's never have it." I looked blank. "For my shoes," he said again as if I was an idiot. "Jeez man, you born yesterday?" He looked at me, but there was a certain affection in his derision. We went into the street where the populace, hell-bent on enjoying themselves, pushed past us on the way to the tube.

CHAPTER 23

We got the tube from High Street Kensington to Charing Cross. There was a half-hour delay on the Circle Line, a nasal voice told us. We were also informed that the Northern Line was not running at all and that the Victoria Line was delayed owing to a fire-check at Warren Street.

People were sweating in the train. So were the walls. There was a suppressed fury in the crowd. Raw irritation just below the surface waiting to erupt. Kelvin was unconcerned.

"Man, like this is utopia," he said. "Ridin' the underground. Great." People left him alone. Shrank from him as if he had leprosy.

"We moved on, man," he told me. "If I was alone I would be moved on." He twinkled at me. "You get everythin' wrong, man, don't you? You think because we're vagrants we morons, huh? Vagrancy Act 1824. Sleeping abroad. Have to be arrested. Only there's no room for us in the jails.'Sides, we like jails. Jail is a great alternative. Her Majesty is more hospitable than Mrs. Thatcher. More hospitable than London Transport. Provides soap an' a shower. Provides food an' drink."

"I'm sure if I took you to the DHSS and spoke to them for you they'd give you an allowance. Until you got on your feet," I said.

He burst out laughing. People pulled away from him adding possible madness to his obviously down-and-out appearance.

"Listen to you, man. Allowance! It 'ud be a wasted effort, I'm tellin' you. 'Sides I'm seventeen. No benefit till yo' eighteen. And got an address." He whistled through his teeth, "Address, address, address," to the "Here we go, here we go, here we go," refrain.

We got out of the train at Charing Cross.

Nothing had prepared me for what Kelvin showed me that night in Cardboard City. We walked past at least a couple of thousand people, each separate, each in their own hellhole, dug in, clothed in rags, sheltered by black plastic and cardboard, wrapped in newspapers, pinned together in scraps and tatters, dumped and degraded, forgotten, sexless, humiliated, deprived of human dignity or pride, condemned and despised by society, left to forage in dustbins for food, scavenge in garbage for sustenance, crawl into a nook at night, a hole, a burrow, creep under a bench, into a doorway, neglected, loveless. Many were mentally retarded, disturbed, thrown out of homes and hospitals which were at the worst, institutions, at best, a place to lay their heads, a safe harbour, a bed-and-board refuge. Now these helpless wandered witless in a hostile and alien world, cold, hungry, perplexed. Many of the people were alcoholic, sick, addicted, people who needed help, not contempt. What normal person would drink meths or cleaning fluid cocktails or shoot up a many-punctured arm with heroin for a short respite from a physical hell? What normal person would risk dreaming of creepy crawlies, have rat-infested hallucinations, and continue to poison themselves? The very word, addict, meant couldn't survive without. What choice had these people got? Then there were the unfortunates; the evicted, the men whose marriages had broken up and who couldn't afford another home, the kids thrown out by unsympathetic parents or those who ran away to the bright lights of the big city.

They dragged themselves to Cardboard City and existed as best they could. They had their own language, their own morality, their own rules and regulations. There were children there, but not for long. You aged fast here and tricks were sometimes the only way to earn a coin.

Sex was often used simply to keep warm for ten minutes. There was no sense of time here and night and darkness were blessed, for once evening sputtered out you pulled your newspapers and bits and pieces around you, you arranged your nest, you burrowed in, you stacked your boxes, you dug your billet. You had kept a pill, a slug of whatever potent mixture you had been able to buy/steal/concoct. You chased your dragon into oblivion. You hoped it would last and you knew it would not. The best you could hope for was to forget, for a while, in sleep.

Not real sleep. Not the sweet sleep you had known once in airy rooms with mattresses and pillows and soft bedclothes smelling of comfort. But a drugged sleep, a sleep induced by paralysing the brain and nervous system, stunning it into numbness. Then, for a while, a little while, you did not feel the damp, the cold, the pain, the discomfort, the fear, and tomorrow was a long way off.

Some of them were chirpy, could manage a lewd retort. They held onto that tiny spark of human dignity that others had let slip away under the continual drip, drip, drip of charity accepted gratefully, of saying a "thank you, sir, madam, thank you," of having to tip the cap, of having to beg for basic necessities.

I reeled away from the place, appalled by the smells of urine and vomit, of unwashed humanity and stale breath, of madness and fear. I reeled away from the sights of prematurely aged faces, grooved with despair and dirt, old/young faces, cynical and full of self-loathing, of ruined teeth and rheumy eyes, unfocused in the half-light, of cracked and dried lips and dripping noses, of pitiful glimpses of bodies: a withered leg, nails caked in filth, hair matted and alive with insect life, arms punctured, mottled and crustaceous. I reeled away from the sound of obscenity, hoarse broken voices, snores and retching, screams, and grunts and more terrifying than all the rest the muttered prayers to a God who could hardly be said to be listening.

Kelvin enjoyed himself hugely at my expense. His attitude shrieked a triumphant "what do you think now?" But he said nothing. He showed me over the place, from Charing Cross, the Strand to Waterloo like an estate agent sure he would astonish.

He asked this one and that where we could find Mr. Moto, but no one could help. They were either too far-gone in drink or drugs or astray in their minds that they did not understand what we were asking them. Some were frightened by the name. Some shook their heads and avoided answering. Some were totally indifferent or too intent on their own plight.

"Mister, spare a couple o' bob? For a cuppa?"

"Mister, give us the price of a pint?"

The night had warmed up, no big deal, so I took off my linen jacket and gave it to a young chap sitting cross-legged in one corner. He grabbed it from me and I was glad he did not thank me.

There was an old guy under an arch, masturbating.

"God sake's, you got no shame?" Kelvin squealed at him. The old guy looked embarrassed, his face beaded with sweat.

"Means ten minutes warm," he muttered. "Ten minutes rest."

"Some of the old guys do it 'stead of booze or a fix," Kelvin said shrugging. "You know where we find Moto? Where he hang out now?" he asked. The old codger shook his head and disappeared back under what looked like a pile of rubble.

Kelvin asked everyone we saw who acknowledged us. "You know where we find Mr. Moto?" and the answer was always the same. He asked coarse-faced women and men with blasted faces, vacant-eyed youths of both sexes and the answer was always the same.

We went to Heaven, the gays' nirvana where I was propositioned. They seemed to know Kelvin well. The music blasted the eardrums, the lights swirled, the noise of human fever-excitement reaching a cacophony of intensity. No. No one knew where Moto was tonight.

I was confused by the exchange of affection, the hand clasps, the hugs in this place. I felt stupidly *gauche*. I was convinced that men and woman had absolute rights to their own sexuality no matter what that sexuality entailed, except for the corruption of minors, rape, or other violent impositions. Where love was freely given and freely received, what right had I to impose rules? I believed in tolerance. I believed that as long as you were not harming anyone then what damage could it do? And certainly over the last period I had seen enough heterosexual deviation to feel that we had no right to sit in moral judgment. But at this moment, surrounded by exuberant gays, I was at a loss to know how to conduct myself and felt I suddenly understood Mandy better. This is how she must feel when she found herself in all-male company and they teased her and taunted her about her femininity.

"Do you?" I asked Kelvin stupidly as we left, having got no further with our quest.

He shrugged. "Depends on how much I get," he said. "A poke's a poke and I have to eat. Depends."

This other world that had grown alongside my world was

teaching me lessons I would rather not learn.

Kelvin stood beside me on the lonely street. There were few people about now. Street lamps cast an orange glow on the pavements and I could hear the bundle in the corner snoring.

"Sorry, man. I don' everything. Ain't nobody knows where Moto is." Kelvin looked at me apologetically. He looked sorry for me. He hit my arm with his fist. It was an affectionate gesture. "Sorry man," he repeated.

"Thanks, Kelvin. You did all you could," I said. I handed him a fifty, all I had. I felt bad, really bad, inadequate and ashamed under his ironic gaze.

"I ain't got no pride, man, that's what worrying you," he said. "Been knocked outa me long ago. Thanks."

He gave my arm another bang. I could not even manage that. I just stood there, awkwardly.

"Sorry I can't help," he said. He was shaking now, his thin body giving little involuntary convulsions every now and then. "You better go," he said. "This no place for you alone, man. An' I need—"

"It's okay," I said. "I've still got Gilda."

"Hey, man, watch out for her. You never know with Gilda." And suddenly he was gone, swallowed up in the night, disappearing into Charing Cross Station. I felt tired and dispirited. I could see Kelvin's point. Catching Mr. Moto and the Big Man would not solve much. This kind of community poverty always spawned the predators, the exploiters. But it might redress the balance a little and that was better than nothing. It was with relief that I shook the dust of that terrible place off my feet.

CHAPTER 24

Gilda was the only one who could help me now.

I went home to the Kings Road. There were two thugs outside in a yellow fifties Cadillac trying hard to look as if they were part of the scenery. They stood out like Kelvin would at a yuppie party. I hoped they would try something. I would have welcomed the opportunity of working off my rage. But they simply sat there, trying not to look conspicuous. They pretended not to see me, which was ridiculous as I was the only moving object in the road.

I let myself in, went upstairs and stripped. I put everything I had been wearing, including my trousers, into the basket. I felt like casting them into a fire.

I showered, staying under the hot spray for a long time. My wound was throbbing. I sent up a prayer of gratitude to whatever deity had bestowed such advantages upon me. What had I ever done to deserve such abundance? I thought of the wretched dregs of humanity I had just left. There but for the grace of God, I thought, put on my pajamas and crawled into bed. It was three a.m. and I fell asleep instantly.

The nightmares began about four o'clock in the morning when my initial exhaustion had been slept off. I was one of them, down there in Cardboard City. I lived amid the plastic and the wet boxes, wrapped in newspaper and I bedded against dark, greasy stones. There were ants crawling all over me. Kohl and Bernie had Talia. Bernie held her arms and

Butterfly cut her throat with a smile on his handsome face. There was blood everywhere. It spurted over me, drenching me, and I awakened with a start to find myself dripping with sweat.

I got up and made some coffee. I showered again, pulled on a tracksuit and went for a jog in the early-morning silence of the Kings Road. The two goons were asleep in the Cadillac. How ostentatious could they get? I asked myself. One sat in the back, mouth open; the other was slumped sideways over the wheel. His eyes had tiers of bags under them and he looked as if he lived in the Caddy. Maybe he did.

There was a little circle of trash around the car; the familiar blue plastic McDonald's containers, empty Marlboro packets, a couple of Wrigley wrappers, some crumpled tissues.

They did not stir as I stared in at them so I left them and trotted up to Sloane Square. When I returned they were startled to see me. I must have given them a shock. They had not seen me come out and here I was returning. They opened and shut their mouths in amazement. They looked rough and both had stubbly chins, which on them, unlike Don Johnson, looked awful. I gave them a cheeky wave and left them looking idiotic in the yellow car surrounded by the debris of junk food and fags. I ran upstairs, showered again and crashed.

When I came to, the sun was high over the street and life hustled once more. People swarmed outside, horns tooted, ghetto blasters competed with the canned music from the leather-gear boutique next door to Mr. Gupta's grocery.

There was one thing I wanted to do more than anything else, and that was see Mandy, but I was nervous of leading the gorillas to her. I didn't want them creeping into the clinic like some TV thriller and hurting her just to get back at me. I knew I'd have to shake those guys if I wanted to get anywhere today.

I realized that I was ravenously hungry. I got myself some cereal, chopped a banana in, added a fistful of sultanas and raisins and consumed it while I scrambled some free-range eggs.

I sat down in the sun-filled kitchen, and while I had my breakfast I stared out the back at the roofs and speculated.

I phoned Rawlings. I told him where I was at (or rather wasn't at) in my investigation, and I put down the phone before he could give me a lecture or tell me he knew already. I phoned mother but she wasn't home and then I remembered this was her beauty parlour day, so I phoned the Body Shop where I knew she would be having aromatherapy.

Mother was furious at being, as she phrased it, plucked from her blissful inertia to answer my call. I told her about the two stooges, about what I had seen the night before and why I might not be able to see Mandy today. She became conciliatory and concerned.

"Mother, if I led them to her I'd die . . ."

"There's no need for that, Mark," Mother said crisply. "One day will not matter to you. I'll take care of Mandy. You are quite right not to put her at risk. You leave her to me. And good luck. But be careful. Now I'm going back to these wonderful healing hands and herbal oils. See you later."

My flat did not have a rear exit. I never had any reason for thinking about going that way until now. The shop and my apartment above it were slap bang wall to wall against the house at back of the shop and the apartment had been extended and extended further and further, and it almost met the back of the house in the street behind. My exit, via the kitchen window, was watched with keen interest by several people who happened to be near their windows at the time.

With typical British reluctance to interfere, they stared out at me as I manoeuvered my way across the rooftops. They gazed, mildly speculative looks on their faces, determined not to get involved and made no move to enquire what the hell I was up to. There I was crawling about outside and I could have just murdered someone, been a burglar or a thief who had robbed a bank, or stolen a fistful of gems from the jewellers up the road. I could have been a vandal or a kidnap victim (just spent three weeks/months in someone's cellar and was making an exhausting escape). But no one offered to help or tried to hinder me, or even lent out the window and tried to find out why, exactly, I was there.

A man with a pipe was reading a newspaper in his shirt-sleeves. He looked mildly interested to see me hanging by my fingernails from the kitchen ledge. I nearly fell as he watched, but he simply shook the paper and returned to his perusal of it. My six-foot drop onto the flat roof, which I nearly missed, was watched by a girl who was typing in a window across the way. She peered over her glasses at me for a moment, then recommenced banging the machine again. A fat woman was doing a Jane Fonda workout. She stopped and gazed attentively until I crawled over its ledge and onto the van parked there. I saw the tip of her head disappear and reappear as she went back to her exercises. "Burn it. Burn it off." I slid over the roof of the van onto the ground and took off towards the Fulham Road, giving a cheery wave as I left. Did anyone see? I doubted it.

I grabbed a bus, which took me to Knightsbridge very slowly. It took an hour crawling beside the pavement in a car-to-car jam. People stared out of stalled busses; van and lorry drivers gazed down on the Volkswagens, Fords, Audis and Minis. Jag and Porsche owners tapped irritably on their wheels, incapable of containing their impatience, and pedestrians weaved around and about the traffic as if it was a not-very-difficult obstacle course. Some of the drivers cursed them, blew horns, some nodded in time to music they heard and no one else could. Some had open windows and played their cassettes at full volume.

I decided that this was not going to get me anywhere. Much as I hated the underground, it would not delay me as much as the bus, so I got off at Knightsbridge, took the Piccadilly line to Tottenham Court Road; the jolly old Centre Point revisited.

The fountain shot into the air blowing grey spray in a plume across the street, spattering cars and making dark-haired girls with shiny red lips and blondes with soft pink cheeks, shriek with startled delight as the fine mist of water caught them in its vortex. Without exception they clung onto their men as they squealed and looked for protection with submissive expectation. So much for Women's Lib.

I looked at my watch. Nearly noon. Where had the morning fled? The answer to that was: sitting in the traffic.

I walked down Old Compton Street. A black girl, lovely as Diana Ross and clothed in a Jersey leopard-skin print mini-dress came up from a strip joint, screaming obscenities at a little guy in a check suit who looked as if he had stuck his head in a vat of Vaseline. A busker was blowing a trumpet with gusto and the kids playing pinny in the arcade were puffing cigarettes and staring at the machines with the intensity of gamblers.

I reached Mangoes. I went down the back alley, something I seemed to be making a habit of. There was no one there; the place was deserted. I sat on the fire escape and waited.

It was all solved. There was nothing more for me to find out, nothing more for me to do. Except to nail these guys. The police knew, though they had no hard proof, that

Sebastian Kohl had killed all those useless and beautiful people.

But I wanted Mr. Moto. He ran children. He was involved with illegal adoption, fostering, child pornography, child prostitution and child video-porn and I hated him. But he was untouchable. When I asked Rawlings if he couldn't raid the place, here, in Soho, he said that they already had, once or twice, and it was amazing how quickly everyone disappeared. Beds were still warm but there hadn't been sight or sign of patients or children. The place had not exactly smelled of roses, but there had been no sign of overt immorality.

"The women *want* it, you see. They are there of their own accord. Either they are in a mess and this is the only way out, or they are here to make money. The kids are afraid. They are told that terrible things will happen to them if the police find them. Have you ever come across a kid who can't hide? A lot of them have been lured off the streets. Moto gives them a reasonably comfortable billet, food, drink, cassettes, TV. Drugs, if they need them or want them, or can be persuaded to take them. They think they're in heaven, those kids. Except for the sex. That's the snag, the price they pay. And the drugs help to blot that unpleasant bit out."

"Do you know where they are kept? The kids?"

"It changes too frequently for us to pin them down. I only wish we could. God, I wish we could catch him at it. Catch his G'vnor. Find out who the bastard is. If you run him to earth just let me know. But be careful. If cornered he'll bite."

It was one o'clock when Gilda came out onto the fire escape. I almost didn't recognize her. She had a whole new image. She was wearing a couple of inches of rah-rah skirt in pale blue denim. Her thighs were slim and brown and bare. The skirt was decorated with silver studs and she wore about three T-shirts all torn in different places and over them a man's huge pale blue denim shirt, which came down, below her hemline. The shirt was encrusted with silver studs and bobs and motifs and logos and flaps and badges. It was very artistic. Her neck was laden with chains and the cheap silver rings on every finger had stained her skin black. She wore armfuls of tacky Indian bracelets and a chain around her ankle. She had five little studs in both ears and her hair fanned out around her in a mass of pale platinum waves. She looked enchanting.

I was surprisingly glad to see her. Apparently she was not nearly so pleased to see me.

"Bugger off," she said briskly. She removed chewing gum from her mouth and stuck it under the iron rail she lent against.

"Oh, come now, Gilda. Is that the way to greet an old friend?"

"Christ, you're a cramp, y'know that? You have caused a lotta grief, mister."

"Good," I said.

"Oh yeah? Well. An' suppose you fuck it all up? Stop them, what then? You thought of that? You ever think of where they go, smartass? If you get your way an' stop them? Huh? You know somethin' you're not goin' to believe? Most of the families Moto sends those kids to give them the best. They want those kids desperately. So where'll they go if you stop that?"

"So everyone keeps asking me," I said. "Oh come on, Gilda. What about the kids he runs? What about the porn?"

"They'd do that anyway an' for less, an' no perks like a bed an' food an' such. Most of them are on the run. They're runaways. They'd do it in the street up against a wall for a piece of gum."

It was what Rawlings had said, what Kelvin had said, what

Abigale and Tom had said.

"Doesn't make it right," I said stubbornly, beginning to understand how the Nazis came to believe Hitler. Say something often enough and people will start to believe it. "Men like Moto shouldn't be allowed to get fat off the likes of little children," I said, "and nothing you can say makes that right."

She was silent, turning a stubborn chin away from me, staring at the patch of blue sky that showed around the grey mass of Centre Point.

"There must be another way," she said at last. "Where it's like that up there." She pointed to the rationed Madonna-blue strip overhead. "Like space. Fields maybe."

"There is, Gilda. There is."

"Well. We gotta live. Don't we? It's either hustle or go down in this day and age."

"Gilda, where can I find Mr. Moto? You're the only one who can help me now. You've gotta help. You're my last chance."

She shook her head. "I can't. Daren't."

"No need to be afraid. You can come with me. I'll take you away."

"Like, as my boyfriend?"

"No, Gilda. You're too small."

"I'm big in bed."

"What?"

"You heard. I like you. If you take me away I'll be good to you."

"No, Gilda. Not like that. You see, I've got someone."

"You mean that plain-looking girl they had in the back?"

"Yes. No. To me, Gilda, she's beautiful. She's my girl-friend." I felt stupid saying it but it was true and I would not fill her with lies and promises I could not keep.

"Yea, I figured. What makes you think I want to leave

here? What alternative are you offering? Back to school? Can you see me? A job in a hairdresser or a supermarket?" She hung over the rail, her hair falling about her shoulders like a spun-silver cloud. "A job in your bookshop." I looked up sharply. "Think I didn't know?" She laughed. "You hadn't thought it through, had you?" She was right. I hadn't. "It's okay here," she continued, "I got money. I got my ticket to heaven, my gold dust. Kohl doesn't try to stop me, y'know. He doesn't keep me prisoner. He wouldn't even notice if I did go. Wouldn't miss me. No. This is the life I know. I'm comfortable here. So don't you come preaching here, trying to be superior. Making me feel bad for living as I do when there's no other way. Not really. You know that, so why don't you face up to it?"

"Gilda, where is Mr. Moto? Look, four of my friends are dead. You must see . . ." Why should she see, I asked myself as I spoke. She was right. I had no authority to criticize. I had no alternative to offer.

I expected her to dismiss me, tell me to go to hell when she said, "He's at Cramner Mews. Off Praed Street. St. Ignatius Clinic, if you must know." She sounded angry as she spoke.

"Who is the Big Man?" Her skin lost its colour. She stared at me a moment incredulously. "You're mad, y'know that? You're off the wall." Then she laughed. "Look in the Tower of London," she said, then added angrily, "Now piss off and leave me alone. You make me sick, y'hear?" and she pushed open the door behind her and disappeared.

CHAPTER 25

I did not have a clue what she meant. I puzzled over it as I made my way down to Covent Garden and out onto the Strand. The vagrants were there, even in broad daylight. I could not help noticing them now that they had impinged themselves on my consciousness. So many kids. A middle-aged man with bleary eyes accosted me in the Strand. His clothes had once been the best. On impulse I asked him why he was there, begging. I thought he might object to my question, but he shrugged.

"Wife threw me out," he said "She got the house and the kids." He shrugged. "It's just the way the chips fall." He seemed philosophical. "Can't blame her. She needed the house for the children. I got a bed-sit. In Earls Court, but the fight went out of me. Coming back there every night. It humiliated me. People asked where I lived. One room in Earls Court at my age! I ask you." He looked at me with self-loathing. "I lost my drive, then lost my job, then lost even the room. Now I'm on the Golden Mile." He laughed. "Bullring through to here." We were standing outside Thomas Cooks. The shop window displayed advertisements for exotic holidays in far-off glamour spots. I could see an advertisement for a week in Goa at a knockdown price.

The man had followed my gaze. "I used to have holidays," he said. "Can't remember when. It's so long ago. A lifetime. Now can I have a couple o' bob?"

I gave him a few pound coins. He thanked me civilly and left me.

I hurried over the street and into the Savoy. I had a steak lunch in the Grill Room. I felt guilty as hell when I finished. The poverty and want I had seen and felt around me these last days seemed to have created in me an acute hunger, an unnatural greed. It was as if I, too, was threatened, and the day would come when I would not be able to satisfy my appetite.

I am not usually preoccupied with food, and normally, after a breakfast such as I had eaten, I would not be hungry until evening, yet here I was scoffing sirloin steak and onions, apple crumble and cream in the middle of the day and not even enjoying it. I felt as if I simply must fill a great hole within me. I felt slightly sick when I had finished.

I phoned Rawlings from the Savoy. I told him where Mr. Moto was purported to be.

"Do you want to get bumped off?" he asked acidly.

"No. I do not," I replied. "But you can sneak some men there and if I get in trouble, maybe you can come in and help, who knows what you might find. If I shout loud enough."

"Can I stop you?" he asked.

"Not a chance in hell," I said.

"Okay, then, can we wire you?"

"Sure," I said. "Only too happy to do your work for you." That was unfair and I knew it. The letter of the law today makes an arrest that will stand up in court a very complicated business.

"Look," he said. "Come down here and we'll tape you up. If we go in they'll be stum. We'll get nothing out of them and they'll walk. If you're sure?"

"I'm sure. But I won't go *there*. You'll have to come here. It would be crazy in case they're following me."

I was taped in the gent's lavatory in the Savoy. None of us saw the funny side.

"You realize the risk you're taking?" Rawlings asked. I nodded. "I have to ask you," he said.

"Don't make them suspicious," Taylor said.

"As long as you keep in the background." I smiled. "I'd hate them to kill me because they spotted you." As I said it I realized that I was, in fact, risking my life. I had a moment of pure panic, then I shrugged. What would be would be. "Keep your distance," I said. Rawlings nodded. Taylor smiled. "If the chief could see us now," he said. "Remember this is unofficial. If you fail we know nothing."

I left the Savoy alone. I got a number fifteen bus outside the Savoy Taylor's Guild in the Strand. It took me to Praed Street. The sun shone as we passed Trafalgar Square. London, seen from here, looked very beautiful.

I got out opposite St. Mary's Hospital and had a look around. The street is tawdry, dotted with For Sale signs like broken teeth. I stood looking at an adult bookshop, turned around the corner and walked down toward Sussex Gardens.

I soon found the entrance to Cramner Mews. There were two stone pillars at the entrance. It was shaded by thick bushes and ivy, which trailed over an archway. It was dark in there in spite of the sun and it was an entrance that the casual passerby would not notice.

I walked down the left side, the side nearest the house. If anyone was looking they would not see me. The bushes rose into trees and almost met overhead. As I drew nearer I could see the corner of the house, then the front door. It had a brass plate, which said:

ST. IGNATIUS PRIVATE CLINIC.

Instead of going to the front door, some impulse sent me around the corner of the house, keeping in the shade of the bushes. As I was getting my bearings I heard a car door slam and the crunch of feet on the gravel.

I peered streetwards and saw the yellow Cadillac parked outside at the curb.

"You fuckin' shut up and don't even try to say a word or you're dead." It was Sebastian Kohl's voice, deadly and full of suppressed fury.

"You're probably dead anyway, lettin' that girl get away," he added and I knew he meant Mandy.

I peered through the bushes. Sebastian was close enough to touch. He wore a pale grey silk suit that matched his restless eyes, eyes that darted hither and thither like an eagle's.

I stayed as still as I could without breathing as he looked around. At one point he seemed to be staring straight at me, but he had not seen me. Bernie stood on one side of him and Butterfly the other. Butterfly wore pink leather and Bernie wore tartan pants. They were the mean-tempered bears to Kohl's serpent. They would have looked funny if I had not known what they were capable of.

I kept motionless, afraid that I might shake the shrubs and signal my presence. However they remained in ignorance and went to the door and rang the bell. I could hear it peeling in the depths of the building. The door opened, I could not see who by, but the voice was female.

"Can I help you?"

"We're here to see Mr. Moto. We got an appointment." Sebastian's voice. "Oh, yes. Please come in. He's in the . . ." The rest was lost as the door closed.

I had two choices. I could skulk outside, risk being caught trying to enter through a window, or I could grasp the nettle and follow the example of Sebastian and his mates. I decided on the latter. Before I rang the bell I looked about me for any sign of Rawlings or Taylor but nothing stirred. They obviously had not arrived yet. I hoped to God they would not leave it too long, getting someone there. I felt far from brave and I did not want to find myself one man against that pack of ruthless men. Unofficial, he had said. I hoped there would not be an emergency that took them elsewhere. I decided to quit worrying and get on with it.

I rang the bell. The girl who opened the door was a delightfully pretty creature. I thought that she probably did not know anything about the real purpose of the clinic. She greeted me with the same cordiality she had accorded Sebastian and company. Private practises always elicited extreme graciousness. I replied as Sebastian had, "I'm here to see Mr. Moto. My friends went ahead. I was locking the car."

"Oh, your car will be quite safe, sir," she said and waved her hand towards the red-carpeted stairs.

I climbed up to the first floor with a confidence I did not feel. The place was comfortably appointed. It looked like your average private clinic: deep-pile carpet, undertaker flower arrangements on stands at every corner, out-of-date magazines arranged with precision, an anticeptic-white decor and a discreetly sepulchral atmosphere.

I stood on a broad landing, listening. I quickly realized that the voices were issuing from the closed double doors at the end of the corridor. There was nowhere to hide on the landing, so I went into the room to the right of the double doors.

It was a room almost identical to the one Mandy was resting in at this very moment in the clinic off the Kings Road: cot-bed, bedside table, balsa wood closet, all pristine white. There were Dranlon curtains on the window and I closed them, plunging the room into darkness.

I knelt on the bed and put my ear to the wall. As I thought, the partition was thin, the conversation in the next-door room audible.

"You realize, Moto, that this farce cannot be allowed to continue." The voice was familiar but not immediately recognizable. I wished I could see.

"No, Lord Ravenscroft, I know."

Ravenscroft! That was it. The last piece of the jigsaw fell into place. Christ, Ravenscroft? Look in the Tower of London, Gilda had said. I couldn't believe it. I thought of Davina Ravenscroft. I shook my head. Then I realized that I was missing what they were saying. I hoped the sensitive little mike would pick it up and felt fairly sure it wouldn't. A voice I thought to be Moto's (I knew the others) was saying, ". . . kill him. He knows 'ee's being followed. Gives Bernie the slip every time."

He had a curiously feminine voice, Asian mixed with Cockney. "Ain't my fault, G'vnor. He's slippery." This was Bernie sounding nervous and servile.

"You subhuman gits." It was the ice-cold tones of Sebastian Kohl. "You couldn't act like intelligent men if you tried. You got no brains either of you. Farts you both are . . . "

"Hey, hey, man, go easy," Butterfly said. "Cool it, man, don't go over the top . . ."

"It's no use fighting among yourselves," Lord Ravenscroft put in a calm, boardroom voice. "It's what we can do about it we're here to discuss . . . "

"Dangerfield will have to be rubbed. By me. I don't trust no one else," Sebastian said, his voice chilling in its lack of emotion. I felt my flesh creep. It was me they were talking about.

"You'll have to, Kohl," Moto said. "Unless we put out a contract. We can't 'ave 'im messin' about in our lives any longer. 'E's gettin' closer an' closer an' our Lordship 'ere can't afford a breath of scandal, now, can you?"

"I'll be happy to oblige," Sebastian said. "I'll enjoy it. Bastard's been messin' with Gilda."

"Did she tell him anything?" Ravenscroft asked.

"I took care of it," Sebastian said, and I didn't like the way he said it. "Anyhow, she didn't know nuthin' to tell. I belted her a few. Threw a scare into her. She'll keep out of his way from now on."

I could feel nausea in the pit of my stomach.

"I tried to warn him," Ravenscroft said. He sounded sad. "Damned amateurs. Getting in the way. Well, Kohl, I'll leave Mr. Dangerfield in your hands."

There was a moment's silence.

"Is everything else all right?" Ravenscroft asked after a pause.

"Everything is just fine, sir. We have thirty mothers here. Charmian in Belsize Park has another thirty. So that's at least one hundred thousand. And the Americans are offering more. The Mayfair house is takin' in a fortune. Kids are happy. Nice home there. Warm beds. Nice food. No problem. The boys with Butterfly are cool . . . eh, my man?" There was a "humph" from Butterfly. "And Sebastian is slippin' out that gold dust on oiled wheels. It slides into the community, no problem, and the money slides right back. Just like you want."

I heard no more. What I felt was a gun in my back and the cold voice of Sebastian Kohl in my ear.

"How convenient, Mr. Dangerfield. How very convenient."

I was strong-armed out of the room through the open double doors and into the next-door room. Kohl pushed me violently and I skidded on the highly polished floor and ended on my knees in front of Ravenscroft. There was a long boardroom table and I hit my head on the edge. Butterfly stood on one side of Ravenscroft and Bernie the other. On the periphery of my eyeline, and sitting, there seemed to be a huge hulk emanating an appalling aura of evil. It had to be Moto.

Kohl grabbed a fistful of my hair and yanked it back then jabbed my head repeatedly against the corner of the table. I felt blood in my eyes, tasted blood on my lips, felt the pain sear through my brain and the patina of evil from the mountainous man above me was palpable. I could see him through the mist of my own blood, coloured crimson. A huge man. A Wellsian figure. Kelvin hadn't mentioned that. I could see the gold on his fingers. His lips were thick and he looked at me with small eyes glinting with hate. My head dropped on his fat knee. I tried to lift it, but my neck felt weak. He put fat fingers under my chin and lifted my face. He smiled at me, then rose to his feet and I could not see him anymore.

"Not here, Kohl," Ravenscroft said mildly. He looked down at me with distaste.

"Search him, Kohl."

They found the bug. They did not seem to be worried by it.

"We'll go the other way," Ravenscroft said calmly. "It's a pity you did not take my advice, Mr. Dangerfield." He added, "People usually benefit from my advice. My, my, my, fancy being wired." Kohl had wrenched off my jacket and pulled the tape from under my shirt. He kicked me and hit me frequently as he did this. His face was a grimace of fury and he hit me again with the barrel of the gun. I let out a yell. I couldn't help it. The plaster tore my skin off, and the beating I was taking was reducing me to pulp.

"I'm enjoying this," Kohl said. "You're going to die slow, mister."

Ravenscroft repeated, "Not here, Kohl."

I had been afraid that Kohl was going to pull the trigger there and then, and I would be dead before anyone could do anything. As it was things were happening too fast.

"We'll go now," Ravenscroft said smiling. "The back way. No one knows there is a back way from the Mews, Mr. Dangerfield. So even if your friendly coppers are outside, we'll be long gone. If they've taped any of this conversation, we'll deny it's us. Whole thing was a setup. My lawyer'll make mincemeat of those stupid boys in blue."

I bet he could! I felt sour and in pain, frightened and fairly hopeless. I thought of Mandy—her soft, round breasts, her shining hair. I forgot my recent criticism of London, its filth, its poverty and I remembered only the beauty. It was, in that moment, the most beautiful place on earth and my life was the most precious gift.

"Okay. We go."

Ravenscroft left. I looked back. Moto still sat, half in shadow, like a squatting toad. His eyes glittered in the gloom and he smiled at me. Bernie jerked my head and pushed me. Kohl kept hitting me. Butterfly kicked me casually every now and then, but there was no personal animosity in his violence to me. Unlike Kohl, it did not turn him on. I wondered what did. Probably hitting women.

We did not go through the double doors behind us. Ravenscroft turned and opened a concealed door in the book-lined wall. We followed. Kohl and Butterfly dragged me along. I heard the door click closed behind Bernie. The police would never find me now.

The corridor we went down was, contrary to my expectation, brightly lit and carpeted. We had entered the back of another building and this one housed children. I could hear them. It was like school, that steady high roar that amplified cacophony of excited shrieks and yells. We could hear laugh-

ter, argument, singing, an innocent and happy sound anywhere but here. Here they were in a human hell, whatever it
looked like and however comfortable it was.

I did not see anyone. A child was crying somewhere but
there was nothing anguished about it.

The very normality of their voices brought home the trag-
edy to me as nothing else could.

My knees were giving at every step; my eyes were closing
in pain. I was battered and bleeding. We had walked down
another long passage into what appeared to be a garage.
"There will be no one in the courtyard. There never is," Lord
Ravenscroft remarked casually. I felt sure he was right. We
had turned to the right, then left again and I doubted if we
were now anywhere near Cramner Mews. Lord Ravenscroft
kept well away from me.

"But just to be sure," he added, "Bernie. Go outside and
check the car. We'll follow."

Bernie opened the door and went out. It was a narrow side
door.

Kohl gave me another kick. It brought me to my knees
again.

"Take him to the canal," Ravenscroft said, *sotto voce.*
"Best place. Private. No interference."

Kohl looked at me, wolf-like teeth bared, pale eyes glazed.
"You're a bloody mess. You're not going to spoil my car." He
kneed me in the kidneys. "You know what we do? Put you in a
sack. Like your friend. Have a little fun with you, eh, Butterfly?" Butterfly looked at me, bored. "Then we dump you wi'
the pollution-free fishes. That canal is sure not going to come
up to EEC standards tomorrow? Eh?"

"Can we come out, Bernie?" Ravenscroft called.

"Yes." Bernie sounded far away. I heard a car door bang. I
was filled with panic. I couldn't make a break for it. There

was no place to run and I had no more strength. I stumbled to my feet. I could hardly stand. I thought of Clint Eastwood and how, no matter how badly he was beaten up he could always manage the *coup-de-grace*. I knew I couldn't. I was whacked. But I'd try. Jeez I'd try. I'd skip that promised bit of fun at the canal and go out in a blaze of glory. If they shot me it might at least bring the police down on them.

I staggered to the door and blinked painfully in the sunlight. Shapes swam into focus and I couldn't believe my eyes. I stopped myself from crying. I was so sure it was all over for me, but as we emerged into the courtyard I saw a semi-circle of police. About seven of them. Ravenscroft's face was white, and he stood demanding a lawyer while they handcuffed him. Kohl was struggling demonically, receiving some rough treatment as he fought. A little of his own medicine. Butterfly was plea bargaining already, promising to testify in return for immunity, grassing while they read him his rights. Bernie was resigned, he appeared to be used to the routine. All of them were handcuffed. I saw it with my own eyes. Except Mr. Moto. Mr. Moto was not there.

Rawlings grinned at me. There was affection and concern in his eyes. "Come on. Let's get you fixed up," he said. "There's an ambulance on its way."

"How'd you know?" I asked thickly. "About the back entrance?" I could hardly speak; my lip was swelling up bigger every minute.

"Oh, as usual," he said. "Help from the public."

I heard Kohl scream a string of four letter words. He had seen her at the same moment I did: Gilda. Face cut almost as badly as mine. Eye swelling. She would have a shiner tomorrow.

She stood beside Rawlings, looking small and vulnerable. She also looked angry. She completely ignored Kohl.

"You bastard," she said to me. "Look what you got me into. All that moralizing! Fuckin' nuisance you are." She was half-sobbing.

I leaned over and kissed her, then slid to the ground, my knees rubber. She took my head on her lap.

"Your girlfriend ever gets fed up, I'm there," she said. I remember that moment, worrying about her pale blue shirt and the blood I was scattering about everywhere. She kissed my lips and her kiss was infinitely sweet, innocent and tender. I touched her cheek and felt her tears. Then I heard the ambulance siren.

I let go then. The job had been done. It had had a very unexpectedly satisfying conclusion. The bad guys were put away. Mandy was safe. Mother would be waiting with some tea. Some small victory had been won and small victories led to bigger triumphs. The fight for justice for all was a long, slow, uphill struggle. The strong had to learn to help the weak and not with charity but with the restoration of basic human rights. And, I told myself, as I felt Gilda's kiss on my brow and the wonderful paramedics lifted me up into the ambulance, bloody, beaten-up but hopeful, that there are more good guys in the world than bad ones. Then I lost consciousness.

CHAPTER 26

It was not that easy and my euphoria did not last. When Rawlings came to see me in the hospital the next day he looked dejected and he had an uneasy air about him. "How are you?" he asked, not meeting my eye.

"I feel as if I've been kicked by a horse," I said, but he did not laugh, did not even smile.

"I seem to keep ending up here," I said. "It's funny because the only time in my life that I've been in the hospital is since this case started. I've never even had my tonsils out, yet in the past weeks I've ended up here twice."

"Well, if you get involved in activities out of your league," he said, "what do you expect? These people don't pussyfoot around. They're deadly."

"And they're all behind bars," I stated. He was silent a moment and in that moment I tried to persuade myself that he would reassure me. But he did not. When he shook his head I was filled with a sick dread. I took a deep breath and tried to calm myself.

"Kohl and Bernie and Butterfly have taken the rap," he said. "But Ravenscroft walked. And Moto cannot be found."

"What? I don't believe you? Ah Christ, no."

"It was sickening, Mark. Ravenscroft's lawyer had to be honeyed by the Super, and persuaded not to sue us for false arrest or file a complaint against us for harassment." It was the first time I had seen the dour Rawlings angry. His usually philosophical acceptance had been shaken and he was furious.

"Coercion, entrapment, wrongful arrest." He ticked them off on his fingers. "He accused us on quite a few counts. He admitted he had been in the clinic, said he could prove it was all above board. I'm sure he could do that, Mark. Unfortunately. The kids were not there. They had vanished into thin air. The women made statements that would make you blush. Dewey-eyed, they professed to be pregnant mothers awaiting the birth of their babies, privately because they had lost faith in the National Health Service.'The National Health is so impersonal and oversubscribed these days,' one actually said, 'That's why I came here.' I think she must have been an out-of-work actress, she was so convincing. What it amounted to was that St. Ignatius is an expensive, but perfectly legitimate clinic. All above board. Came out whiter than white. We're the ones who are looking bad. Christ, Mark, what can we do? It's the system."

I wondered where I had heard that before, then I remembered: Kelvin. I visualized his tough, disillusioned face, and knew he would chuckle at the situation.

"So that's the way it is," Rawlings was saying.

"But the tape?" I protested. "I heard him. You heard him."

"Heresay. The tape was not to be found."

"But you heard."

"It would be my word against Ravenscroft's." He shook his head, "Sorry, Mark. Not a chance. Ravenscroft simply walked away with that superior smile on his face."

"And Gilda? Surely her word counts for something."

He shook his head. "I'm sorry, Mark, but no. No one believed her in the police station, for Christ's sake. Said who'd believe an addict's word and what was in it for her. No, Mark.

My advice: leave it. It's a no-win situation. He's too powerful. The powerful are invulnerable." He rose. "Now, I must get on. There are villains out there, you know." He was smiling. "Take care."

Gilda came to see me. She was wearing a pair of pale washed-denim sawn-off shorts. The jagged edge moved against the tanned thigh like a caress and she was aware of it. It didn't do my blood pressure any good at all. She had a little top that left her midriff bare.

She sat beside me, smiled into my eyes and said, "Hi."

"Hi." I was glad to see her. I liked her and although I hated to admit it, I fancied her. She touched my hair, pushed it back from my forehead. "All covered in bruises," she murmured.

"You too," I said, touching her cheek which was swollen and purple.

"Oh, Mark."

This would never do, I thought. I raised myself up in the bed and broke the mood. "Well, what's the news?" I asked brightly.

"Oh, Mark," she said reproachfully, hesitated, then said, "There's something I gotta tell you." she paused, screwed up her face. "The day Alison died . . . I saw her."

"Gilda! Why didn't you tell me this before?"

She shrugged. "Wouldn't have done any good. Remember," she smiled impishly at me, "my loyalties were divided."

"Where did you hear that phrase?"

She blushed and plucked at the sheet. "No, honest. You must remember. Kohl is my father. Whatever he did, he *is* my father."

She stared at me with large eyes troubled and full of conflicting emotions.

"Never mind, Gilda. Just tell me what you know."

"Well, Alison came to the club. No one comes in the

morning," she looked at me sideways, "as you know. No one's there except me and Kohl and Bernie or Butterfly. I was sitting in that window where you first saw me, and suddenly I heard voices. They came from my father's office, which as you know is next door. I can't tell you exactly what they said, but I heard Kohl use the name Alison a few times and I heard her askin' about a baby. I reckoned it was her baby and I got the idea she was trying to find it. The voices rose. They were making a terrible din. I went to hear what they were saying, hear what all the excitement was about and I heard the girl Alison, with the posh voice say, 'If you don't find him I'm going to talk, Sebastian. You hear?' Then something about finding the baby, then something like 'You have no hold on me anymore.' Then she flounced out. She didn't even look at me and any fool would have known I was eavesdropping." She shook her head. "Jeez, she was beautiful. The most beautiful woman I ever saw."

That was why Alison was killed. She had got herself clean and sober. She had fallen in love. Her life lay spread before her, a promise of fulfillment and happiness such as she had never dreamed was within her grasp. And she wanted her baby back. They could not produce it. I felt fairly sure few records were kept in those clinics. What she threatened to expose had nothing to do with drugs. It was the baby racket and Lord Ravenscroft, and that could not be allowed, so Alison had to die. I was prepared to bet that they had not known about the books. Talia took them and used them, but they did not fear Talia. She was an addict. But when I got them and Revel took them from me and admitted to them that I had had them, they got extremely worried. Gilda finished the story for me.

Again it was morning and from her description it was Ravenscroft who paid Kohl a visit. "He was in an' out so fast it 'ud make your head spin," she said. "Cautious. A handsome man. Like Alison. Good-looking, upper class. I was curious . . ."

"Your curiosity will get you into trouble someday, Gilda," I said.

"I love it when you get cross with me," she said and pouted when I laughed. "Anyhow, you're glad enough of it! Well, I listened and this big shot said that Jason Bestwick and Talia Morgan had to go. He said Alison would have told them an' they had to be got rid of." That was how it had happened. It was all that simple.

Gilda smiled at me. "Can I see you again?" she asked.

"I don't think my girlfriend would like it," I said. "You'd make her jealous. You're far too pretty." She tossed the silver-gold web of hair provocatively, pleased.

"She needn't know," she said, looking at me under her dark lashes with a siren glance that would have made Joan Crawford envious.

"You know I wouldn't do that," I said. I felt prim and silly saying it and expected her to ridicule me.

But there were tears in her eyes and she said, "I envy her, you know, I really do. Do you think, someday, I might find someone who loves me like you love her?"

"I'm sure of it, Gilda."

"Problem is I probably won't love them," she said with disillusioning acumen.

"What are you going to do now?" I asked her. "You can't stay on at Mangoes, can you?"

"Well, a friend of Butterfly's is goin' to run it until Kohl gets out. He says I can do . . ." She stopped and looked at me. "But I don't think you wanna know about that."

"Gilda, you can't stay there."

Her face flamed. "And what will I do?" she asked me angrily. "Where will I go? Down Cardboard City 'cause I'm so moral an' I might get contaminated by a strip joint? Huh? Down where I'd become a real addict an' a hooker in twenty-four hours? Huh? You do-gooders are all the same! You tell us what we mustn't do, but when we ask you, well, what do we do, you got no answer. Listen Mark. I can keep myself for this guy that's goin to come along, an' I will. No one would dare touch me, not Sebastian Kohl's daughter."

"Except Sebastian Kohl," I said.

"Well, he doesn't do it much. Anyhow, that's what I'll do. I made my mind up," she said stubbornly. "See, Mark, I don't expect you to understand, but I love Mangoes. It's my home. It's all I've ever known. It's my place, my territory. The smell. The stage. The girls. They're ever so nice to me. An' I dream there. I got my space. And I'm safe." She smiled at me again, her lovely, heartbreaking smile. "I'll wait for that fella. I just hope he finds his way okay to Soho."

She kissed me and left.

CHAPTER 27

I checked out of the hospital. There was no vital damage done and thirty-six hours of enforced hospitalization was thirty-six hours too much. I was simply a mass of bruises, cuts, aches and pains from the beating up, and I was much too angry to remain cooped up, agonizing about the justice system. Analysing my difficulties and resentments would get me nowhere. I was chaffing under the knowledge that there really was nothing I could do.

I went home and found Mandy waiting for me.

"I knew you wouldn't last long there," she said. She was a sight for my eyes to feast on and I held her close, burying my face in her hair.

"I can't bear to see another black plastic bag, my darling," I whispered. "I cannot look at the debris around me or sit bumper-to-bumper in another traffic jam or travel on an outmoded, sleazy and inefficient train in the underground. We, you and I, my darling, are going to shut up shop and go to Marbella and have a little break. We deserve it. How's about that."

She snuggled close and I could feel her heart beat against mine. "Yes, please," she said. "Oh, yes."

"Let's feast our eyes on blue sea, white houses, bougainvillea and breathe in the clean, clear air. It'll heal me and I'm bruised, my love. Not just physically, but mentally."

"I know, my darling." She looked up. "But you know

something?" I looked at her quizzically. "The problem, Mark," she said seriously, "is, you have turned this into a crusade and forgotten that you were hired by Lady Cadbury to enquire into the death of Alison Alyward. That you have done, so it's over now."

"What I find difficult, Mandy, is that bastards like Ravenscroft get off scot free. Just walk away. It infuriates me."

"It's the system," she said and I ground my teeth.

"If anyone else says that . . ."

"Well, it's true."

"Then it should be changed."

"Leave it, Mark," she said, echoing Rawlings. "You can only get hurt and to no avail. We can't pin down the powerful ones."

"No one should be above the law."

"In this country, Mark, the rich are very, very innocent until it is proved beyond any reasonable doubt that they are guilty. Short of actually *watching* Lord Ravenscroft kill someone, or, if he was discovered overseeing a dope shipment with the drugs actually in his hands, there is unfortunately little chance of nailing him. Best just accept it. The rich and powerful get away with it."

"What about the poor, Mandy? Are *they* protected so carefully until proved guilty?" I asked. She shook her head.

"They take their chances. It depends on luck, on colour, on the climate that day, whether the police need to make an arrest, set an example, and sometimes, eventually, how you are dressed, or, worst of all, how you talk." She shrugged. "It's sad, but it's a fact of life."

There were some messages on my machine. One was Wendy.

"I think you did the job well, Mark," she said. "Can you come along to see me and we'll wind things up?"

"I must do that," I said to Mandy.

"Tomorrow," Mandy insisted firmly. "Not today. You're whacked."

She made love to me that night, tenderly, careful of my wounds. She made me forget for a while the horror I had discovered beneath the polished veneer of life as I had known it. She eased my pain with her generous love, her womanliness. Like mother earth she took me to her warm, full bosom and soothed my hurt and healed my bruised spirit.

We slept entangled about each other and when I awakened I felt much better spiritually and mentally. But physically I was a wreck. Every joint ached. Every move I made was agonizing.

Mandy had cooked breakfast. We ate in the kitchen and I felt as if I had been away for a long time. The sun shone outside and I wondered if the typist was still typing, whether the man with the pipe was still reading his paper, and the fat woman still doing her calisthenics. I wondered if they remembered the man on the roof.

I looked across at Mandy. It seemed suddenly very important to me that she was there. I thought I would never take her for granted again. I was on my second cup of coffee when the phone rang. It was Wendy.

"Mark?"

"Yes, Wendy. I got your message. I was just going to phone you. I know—"

"Oh, Mark, I want to see you."

"Yes. Of course."

"Can you come here today? For lunch? Please."

"Of course, Wendy."

"One o'clock?"

"One o'clock."

I showered and Mandy helped me to dress. I was incredibly clumsy, restricted in my mobility. Mandy decided I mustn't drive and I agreed.

Mother phoned. She was shaken by what I told her. "Ravenscroft?" she gasped. "Ravenscroft? A pillar of society. Dear God. But I told you Mark, didn't I? That I thought he was dodgy? Listen, Mark," she added, "I want to hear all about it. In detail. I want you and Mandy to come over for supper tonight."

"I'm having lunch with Wendy, so that would suit fine. Mandy?" Mandy nodded. Mother said, "She's there?" Mandy put her hand over her mouth and rolled her eyes. "Tell her I was very cross with her. She left that clinic and never told me. I was worried sick." Mandy was making faces. She grabbed the phone from me.

"Oh, I'm sorry, darling Alice. Truly I am. I just had to get out. The place was filled with very sick people and I thought I'd go mad if they kept treating me as if I was an addict. Forgive me? Please?"

"Of course I forgive you, dear. See you about seven for drinks. Save all the news till then. Bye."

"Bye, Mother," I called into the phone and Mandy replaced the receiver. I phoned Rawlings to ask if there was anything new. He sounded perky and bright.

"Yes. As a matter of fact there is, Mark. Moto has been found dead."

"What?" I could hardly believe my ears and though I knew it was wrong, I allowed myself to feel a surge of jubilation and triumph.

"Yes. Oddest thing. We got a call from a clinic in Belsize Park. From some woman named Charmian. He was covered in blood. Sat in his chair, not even slumped over. God, the man was a mountain. Face was horrified. He was covered in stab wounds. You wouldn't believe it, Mark. He must have been stabbed twenty times at least. Whoever did it hated that guy."

"The instrument?"

"One of the knives from the clinic. Obsidian, or something. From the medical equipment. The one in his neck killed him. I don't think the knife, which was there, wicked looking thing, could have got through or penetrated his layers of fat, but the stab in the neck did it."

"Rawlings, I won't tell you a lie, I'm delighted."

"Don't blame you one little bit, Mark," Rawlings said.

"Any suspects? Whoever it was I hope he or she gets the same treatment as Ravenscroft."

"No. No one yet. We're not searching too hard. You okay?" he asked. "They told me at the hospital you'd checked out. You sure you're all right?"

"Yea, Rawlings, I'm fine."

"Well, Mark. That's it. It's a wrap. Been nice knowing you."

"Ditto. See you around."

I put the phone down feeling much better. At least some of the evil men had got what they deserved.

Mandy said she was opening the shop. I got my favourite Thomas Cook rep and made travel arrangements for the following week, then I sat watching the crowd swirl past below in the Kings Road. Nothing had changed, yet nothing would ever be the same for me again. I would never again be able to take my good fortune for granted.

I made Mandy an eleven o'clock coffee and brought it to her. I had to put a great deal of effort into the smallest movement yet the action gave me great pleasure. She kissed me gently and I returned upstairs to rest. Even that little exercise had exhausted me. I wondered how Philip Marlowe had managed it, especially the lovemaking. I forgot he was fiction.

CHAPTER 28

I ordered a taxi and asked him to drop me at the Carmelite Church in High Street Kensington. I hoped Kelvin would be there. He was. I realized I had never seen him in daylight before. He looked very sick, his skin an unhealthy grey-tinged spotty surface, his eyes bloodshot and dull. He crouched over his knees, huddled in his corner, rocking to and fro, not looking at anyone.

I moved over to him like an old man. It would take a long time to mend completely. I wondered why Kelvin always returned to the same spot. What instinct drew him back to the same doorway? Were we all territorial?

"Kelvin," I said. He glanced at me briefly.

"Oh. It's you."

I squatted on my hunkers beside him. He seemed to have lost all his vitality.

"What is it, Kelvin?" I asked.

"Jade's dead," he said dully.

"Oh, Kelvin, I'm sorry." It seemed so inadequate. Jade, that little moon-faced *gamine*.

"It's to be expected, man," he said. "Ex-pec-ted." He kept rocking, backwards and forwards, backwards and forwards.

"I'm sorry, Kelvin." What else could I say? "Can I do anything for you?"

"No, man. Nice of you to offer, but no, my man, ain't nobody can bring my woman back." He was shut up in his own grief.

"How, Kelvin? How'd she die?"

"Mr. Moto killed her same's he took a gun, shot her."

"Moto's dead, Kelvin."

He nodded. "Yea."

"How'd you know?" I asked. I knew with sudden certainty how Moto died.

"Jade's baby died. Was born dead. He let her rest, four, five hours, then asked her to leave." He looked at me with dumb, anguished eyes, "Ask her to go like that. She exhausted, man. Then they tell her, no expenses. No money. Not one single penny she gets. No compensation at all. Wouldn't even give her expenses. Threw her out. Jeez, man, can you believe?"

I could. These people were not charitable institutions.

"So, she packs her few things. She got so little. Made me break my heart, man." There were tears in his eyes and he didn't try to hide them. "She hears Moto's voice down the corridor. He runnin' away. Talk about goin' to Cannes. Someplace in France. She goes next door, gets a knife, six-inch, seven-inch blade. She waits till whoever is with Moto goes, then she goes into his room." Kelvin took hold of my arm. "Man, oh, man, the next bit's sweet. She say he look startled. Then she tell him she going to kill him. He gets so scared he wets his pants. Jeez! I'd love to have been there, see him. Then he begs. Promises her the moon, the stars. Trouble is, she don't believe him. She stabs him. Over and over she tells me. Again and again. And he screams. And no one comes. No one at all. And she throws the knife on the floor and picks up her little case and leaves. She comes here. To me. She sits down there." He indicated the pavement beside him. "Last night. She is exhausted. She asked me not to leave her. She lays her head in my lap. She is very quiet, man." He spread his hands helplessly. "Then she just goes.

Just like she fell asleep."

He was rocking faster now, his head in his hand. We sat in silence for a while. People passing by gave me funny looks and hurried on, as if we were contagious.

At last I said, "Fancy some grub? A Big Mac?"

He shook his head. I could hear him sniff. "No, man. Don't feel like no fuel. I'd throw up an' that'd be a waste," he said. "Listen, man, you get goin'. Next thing the police'll be asking if I'm propositioning you." He grinned feebly, then took my hand. "I'm not good to be with right now," he said. "You piss off, you be better man. I don't feel nuthin'. Not at the moment. I don't *feel*, see. You go, man." I stood up. He was right. There was nothing I could do for him. He squinted up at me. "You okay. You know that?" he said. "Now piss off." And he buried his head in his hands again and began his rocking, backwards and forwards.

I left him there, an isolated figure of despair, the unheeding crowd swirling around him. I hailed a black cab, which took me to Wendy's. I arrived at ten minutes to one.

She looked calm and prettier than I had ever seen her and I was surprised. "You look well, Wendy," I said.

"Good of you to say so, Mark. What'll you drink?"

"Scotch, please. With ice."

She poured the drinks, her back to me. She wore a white silk shirt under a black wool Chanel suit with gold chains and buttons. She gave me my drink and fetched hers.

"I'm surprised you look so well," I said. "After all you've been through."

She came over to the sofa and draped herself on it. Her skin was smooth and she looked rested. Her eyes were clear and she had lost her nervy manner.

"That's because I *know*," she said. "I know what happened to Alison. And Jason. So I can rest." She smiled at me.

"Thanks to you. But you must sum up and tell me all the details. Tell me everything."

I told her. We had lunch. In that quiet elegant room, the mahogany shining, the linen crisp, the silver gleaming and the crystal sparkling, it was hard to visualize anything but the gracious, the beautiful, the nonviolent. We had watercress soup, steak and salad. And lastly, a huge silver and crystal bowl of fruit. I talked all through and she did not interrupt me once. I talked about Kelvin and Jade, Kohl and Butterfly and Bernie, about Gilda and Mr. Moto. I talked about Cardboard City and things that had little to do with why Alison Alyward was killed.

"Alison was murdered, Wendy, because she wanted her child back. It had nothing to do with the drugs. Those guys had their drug racket all sewn up and they weren't worried what she'd say or who she'd tell. Now, I'm not so sure. But-terfly, Bernie and Kohl are out of action, at least that's something. But her child was a different thing altogether. They could not find it and she threatened to expose Ravenscroft. They couldn't and so she had to be shut up. What's driving me crazy is that Ravenscroft is responsible for her death yet he can wriggle out of any responsibility."

"So he got away with it," she said. Her face was very pale. She was silent for a long time and I thought that she had stopped listening.

"Wendy? Are you all right?"

She seemed to gather up her thoughts and she sighed. "Yes. Yes, Mark. You did a good job."

"But Wendy, I unearthed so much . . . Remember Ravenscroft that night I met him? What was it he said? Something about people who turned over stones being sure to uncover nasty things? He was right."

"Yes. I know you feel affronted that the villain of the piece walked off scot-free. But Mark . . . that's life."

"It's so unfair." I paused and we were both silent awhile. "Wendy, why did you want me to investigate Alison's death? Was it because of Jason? Or was it . . ."

She looked, at me with clear eyes. "Alison was my daughter, Mark."

I stared at her.

"That was why I had to know," she added.

"But how? I don't understand."

"I don't blame you. It's complicated. James Alyward was my first husband. Alison was our only child. She stayed with him when I ran off with Paul Bestwick, that egocentric poet that I married, Jason's father. I sent Alison to Sally."

"Mrs. Everton?"

She nodded. "Yes. I sent her to Sally when James died, killed in that car crash."

"Mrs. Everton is your sister?"

"My half-sister. I'd left Paul by now, or rather, he'd left me and I was very cut up about James' death. It seemed like a judgment, y'know. So I pissed off to Italy and went mad for a while. Everyone was doing it then, it was quite the thing, collecting foreign aristocrats. I married an Italian count. But it was over in months." She looked at me sadly. "I sound awful, I know. When we broke up, well, truthfully, Mark, I was once again dumped! I'm afraid I shocked him terribly. I returned to England, determined to marry money and sense and make a respectable home for my children." She looked at me again. "It's funny, Mark, how intentions are never enough. I married Archie and was so busy keeping up, that I simply left the children where they were. Sally told me in no uncertain terms to keep away from Alison, that I would upset the child dreadfully if I disturbed her, that she thought I was dead. She felt I was an unreliable mother, and

God knows, who could blame her?"

"But she's English. Your sister Sally, she's—"

"My half-sister. Yes, she's English. My father was English. She was his first child. Her mother died and Pa went to New York where he met and married my mother. Sally never approved of me, or of my mother, and I'm afraid that eventually she did not approve of Alison. We were all very alike, in looks as well as temperament."

"But you were . . ."

"Oh, yes. We were sisters, really. Well, Alison stayed where she was. But eventually she came to town."

"Did she find out? That you were her mother?"

"Oh, yes. Very recently. I told her. She was so happy. She didn't blame me. I think it must have been the fact that she had a child she couldn't keep that made her so understanding. But she didn't want it known that I was her mother. She liked to hold herself apart. There would be too much pressure on her if it became public, she said. I was winning her confidence though, getting to know her. She was learning to love me. There were all the similarities, you see. I think that our coming together may have made her decide to try to find her child. I don't know."

"I see."

"I know you do. That's what I like about you Mark. I always know you understand." She drew a deep breath. "I asked her to forgive me. She just held onto me and said there was nothing to forgive. That she had done exactly the same thing. History repeating itself, you see. I did not know what she was talking about then. I'm glad you found out for me—"

"That was after she got sober."

"Yes. I think I had something to do with that, I hope so. But it was wonderful to watch how she bloomed."

I remembered Barclay Norman and what he had said.

"Then, then she was dead," Wendy said. Her voice caught in a little sob.

"Why didn't you tell me all this when you asked me to investigate her drowning?"

"I don't know. I felt ashamed. I didn't want you to think ill of me. I didn't want our past to become public knowledge. I wanted to protect Archie. A hundred reasons and none of them valid. Now," she shrugged, "it doesn't matter."

"What do you mean?"

"Nothing."

She stirred her coffee. "Are you coming to the funeral tomorrow?" she asked.

"Revel's? I thought it was over. That I missed it."

"Jason's. It's tomorrow. Please come. I want you there for a reason."

"To sign off? Case over?"

"Yes. In a way. Dear Mark. Thank you."

"What for?"

"Everything. Finding the enemy, even if there's nothing you can do about it. Finding out the truth, even if I didn't help you."

We sat for a while longer; quiet together. Then I left her there, silent and pensive, staring out at the trees.

CHAPTER 29

Mother was supportive as usual. "We'll get him, Mark, don't you fret," she said vengefully. "We'll kill him with neglect. I'll ostracize him! I'll tell everyone his true character. I'll expose him for what he is. Decent people the length and breath of the land will cut him off."

"Mother, you sound like Georgette Heyer," I said. "Decent people won't even *hear* you. They'd never believe it of him. Decent people don't cut off important and influential men. Decent people don't accept wild stories like that, and people like you can bankrupt themselves defending charges of defamation of character."

"But darling, if I tell everyone—"

"They'll say it's your fertile imagination, Mother dearest, and they'll *never* believe you."

"But I could do a certain amount of damage . . ."

"It wouldn't hurt him, Alice," Mandy said. "A few people cutting him wouldn't bother him in the least. And if it did, by some extraordinary chance, become fashionable to cold-shoulder him, he'd simply sail his yacht to the south of France or spend a year cruising, or go to Anguilla until the clouds blow over. People like Lord Ravenscroft survive no matter what and they do it in luxury."

Mother was downcast. She was bursting with righteous indignation. It infuriated her that Ravenscroft got off so easily.

We mulled over the facts of the case until late that night. I took Mandy home and she put me to bed. I was very tired and we fell asleep in each other's arms.

The next day the sun woke us up. The glorious weather continued unbroken. We were neither of us looking forward to Jason's funeral but Mandy wanted to come with me, so we closed the shop, dressed in our sober black. Perspiring in the heat, we picked Mother up and drove to the chapel where Jason was to be cremated. The West London Crematorium is not the most seductive of places. The funeral chapel was a cold and bare sort of place, very modern, and I suppressed the wish for a little Baroque, or Gothic, to break up the hard, square lines. There was a cross in balsa wood, unadorned and little else to indicate that this was a chapel for last rites to suit most denominations.

We were a little early. A lot of people arrived after us. We had chosen seats near the aisle about ten rows back. We did not wish to assume an importance we did not deserve. People came in wearing subdued expressions and dark clothes. They spoke in hushed tones and settled themselves in pews around us.

I could see the curtains where the coffin would roll on oiled wheels into the cremation furnace. They were decently closed at the moment. I did not like to think what happened behind those little purple curtains and I was trying to groove my mind into other channels when there was a small stir at the back of the chapel. I turned to see.

Wendy, very slim and elegant in a black linen dress and jacket, had arrived on the arm of Archie Cadbury. She wore black patent shoes and carried a matching bag. A wide-brimmed hat covered her hair and a sheer veil was draped over her face so that I could not see her expression. But she advanced up the aisle, following the coffin, her shoulders squared, her head held high and I admired her at that moment more than I had ever before. The party reached the front pew and knelt. The coffin was placed in the mouth of the purple-curtained cave.

Mother suddenly grabbed my arm so tightly that it hurt. I jumped. "Mother, wha—" I began, and she jerked her head backwards. I looked over her shoulder, not believing the evidence of my eyes.

Lord and Lady Ravenscroft had arrived and were making their way into the second-row seats.

"Oh, my God, Mark, I don't believe this," Mother said and sat down abruptly. I didn't reply. I stared at the tall, handsome man, his profile clear-cut and strong, his silver hair giving him a distinguished air. No amount of condemnation would shake people's confidence in this specimen of reassuring urbanity.

He must have felt my gaze on him for he turned and gave me a little nod. His eyes were ironic. Mandy gasped. Davina bowed to me, her expression blank. I wondered how much she knew, how doped she was.

I looked to see if Wendy had noticed his presence. I could see her profile, pale under her veil. But she was looking ahead, at her son's coffin, and she did not turn.

The service started. It was conducted with all speed in a very perfunctory manner. The advantage of belonging to a particular church or sect was, I thought, that one's final farewell would be conducted in a familiar place by a cleric who had known one and with a ritual that one had loved and understood. Here the minister spent all day speeding strangers into eternity, dispatching them quickly and efficiently on their final journey. But the dead don't care, do they?

The service went fast. Within moments the coffin was moving with dignified stately measure on the canisters through the open curtains. There was a buzzing sound as it commenced to travel down that black tunnel and into the fire.

It had not completely disappeared when Wendy suddenly

left her seat. She stepped into the centre aisle, turned and stood with her back to the altar and the sight of her son slowly moving into the roaring furnace.

People looked puzzled. The priest looked shocked. He was muttering something about green fields and pastures new and he paused, mouth open and stared at her back. I thought that she had found the sight of her son's last exit too much for her, that she was overcome with grief, that she was about to run away, flee from her sorrow and loss.

But she was smiling. She lifted her veil back over her face with her left hand. She then opened her bag and took out a gun. It looked like a toy, small, shining, black. Typically Wendy, I remembered thinking, it matched her outfit perfectly.

"I want to see your face when I kill you," she said. Her voice echoed in the half-empty place.

She was looking at Ravenscroft. At first he, like us, did not understand what was happening. Then his face lost its confidence. It became a putty-grey. His eyes darted around the chapel as if desperately trying to find a way out. He began to move sideways when Wendy's shot winged him. He stopped, stunned, staring at her in disbelief.

I made a move towards the aisle to try to stop Wendy, take the gun away. Mother and Mandy grabbed me and Wendy said coolly, without looking at me, "Don't try anything, Mark. You'll only get hurt and you won't stop me. Not a chance."

She never took her eyes off Ravenscroft. He was sweating now. There was a dark stain on his shoulder that could only have been blood.

Everyone was staring, transfixed, not able to understand what it was all about, not wanting to get involved. A few people at the back sneaked away, but most of the congregation stood motionless and stared. Incredulity lasts minutes and immobilises people. Some still had their attention on the slowly disappearing coffin. Others stared at the gun in amazement.

Wendy fired the gun again. Ravenscroft grabbed his shoulder and took his hand away. It was scarlet. He screamed, "No!"

"Yes," Wendy's voice was cold and firm. "Oh, yes."

Ravenscroft didn't ask why she was doing this. He knew and he was terrified.

She held the gun steadily, pointing at him and he grabbed Davina and pulled her body in front of his, using her as a shield.

"That's not going to help," Wendy said and winged his ear. The bullet left a trail of blood pouring down his cheek. It ricocheted across the chapel, pinging as it hit a wall. People flinched and crouched back. Ravenscroft slackened his grip on Davina's arms. His wife gave him a look of withering contempt, gently shook her head and moved away from him. I could see him realize how tacky it made him look. Not that that would have stopped him if he thought it would work and she would take the bullet for him. He could see that it wouldn't work. Wendy knew what she was doing; she would not be panicked into a mistake.

Ravenscroft took a few steps toward Wendy. She backed a pace, tense, wary. "Don't move," she snapped.

Ravenscroft spread his hands, palms out. "Wendy," he said placatingly. "Wendy. Let's talk about this. You're upset. Jason's death . . ."

"You killed him. Shut up. Murderer." Her cool voice was now tinged with rage.

"Whoever told you that was lying." Ravenscroft glanced at me, his eyes full of honest-seeming pain. He deserved an award! I had never seen anyone so sincere. If I had not known I would have been sure that Wendy had made a terrible mistake.

"Wendy. Wendy. You're in a state. Listen to reason. We'll talk. We'll discuss whatever is troubling you. I'm your friend, Wendy . . ."

He had been moving imperceptibly towards her and she had retreated and she took a backwards step up onto the altar. The coffin had disappeared. So had the minister. It was only a few moments since Wendy had pulled the gun, yet it seemed hours. I was exhausted, my wounds throbbing. Mother was gripping me fiercely and Mandy held my hand, squeezing it between her own which were wet with sweat.

"Don't do it, Wendy. He's not worth it," I pleaded.

"Don't move any nearer," Wendy said, calm again, ignoring me. "You have murdered four people that I knew and loved. You have corrupted many others. You are scum. You do not deserve to live."

It was not right. This was not right. I called out, "Wendy, don't. You cannot be judge and jury. Stop."

Again I began to move forward, trying to shake off Mother and Mandy. Ravenscroft moved forward, too. He was gaining confidence. He thought he could talk himself out of this. He had always done so, so why not now? Hands out he took another step towards her.

Wendy pulled the trigger. This time she aimed dead centre; hand steady, she emptied the gun into Ravenscroft. He sank to his knees, incredulity on his face. He stretched out his hands again, like a penitent, pleading at the altar, then blood trickled out of his mouth and he pitched forward in slow motion until he lay prone on his face beneath the cross. And Wendy laughed. But she had not once mentioned Alison's name.

CHAPTER 30

A week later Mandy and I sat in the kitchen eating breakfast. Our suitcases surrounded us and Mandy had checked tickets and passports a dozen times. They lay on the table beside us.

I would always remember that April in '89 and the case of the drowning of Alison Alyward investigated in the blazing sun, the unseasonal heat of London and my discovery of the dark side of life in the city. I did not think I had acquitted myself very well, but I had done what I was paid to do and in the process discovered that London has dirty underwear.

The press had a field day. The names were glitzy: Lord Ravenscroft, Lady Wendy Cadbury, Talia Morgan, Jason Bestwick (son of the murderess), Revel Blake. My name cropped up once or twice in very small print but to my great relief the media left me alone. The competition was too great and I was too unimportant for them to bother with. Small potatoes. Sebastian Kohl, Bernie and Butterfly were refused bail. And no one as much as mentioned Alison Alyward.

Barclay Norman came to see me. We talked and I told him everything I had found out. He accepted the facts with a resignation that surprised me. "She won't be forgotten," he said and I believed him.

I had to force myself to stay away from Mangoes. A couple of times I was filled with an almost irresistible urge to go and see Gilda, but I knew that way lay trouble. I tried to find Kelvin but I had no luck. He had left his doorway in Church

Street and I could not face exploring Cardboard City again.

Wendy's lawyer came to see me. He seemed to feel that Wendy would get off on a plea of temporary insanity. "There's not a court in the land that would be harsh with her. After all, Jason was her son and that man had him killed," he said.

I had told Barclay Norman about Davina Ravenscroft and he had gone to see her. The prognosis was good; Davina was attending meetings and group therapy and seemed to improve apace since her husband died.

"It's all over, darling," Mandy said.

"Is it?" I asked dubiously. "The worst part, the illegal fostering, the plight of the homeless, the drug dealing, the exploitation of the weak still goes on."

"But you have done a small something to stop it and that is more than most."

We spent three weeks in Marbella. The sun and clear air; the bright beauty of the place soothed my bruised spirit and dispelled my depression. I returned to London clear-eyed and more optimistic.

We went to Wendy's trial. I was needed to give evidence. It was strange because all the issues became blurred. All the people who could have told what really happened were dead, and those who were still alive had reasons of their own to stick to the facts of the case; whether Wendy was in full possession of her faculties when she shot Ravenscroft or not. The jury said she was unhinged and had, for some crazy reason, blamed Lord Ravenscroft for the death of her son. That's what came out and the verdict was guilty while of unsound mind and Wendy was committed to a rehabilitation centre for therapy until she could be adjudged normal and released.

No one blamed her. There was a good deal of sympathy for her in the press. But the suggestion that Lord Ravenscroft was in any way culpable was swiftly ridiculed both in court and in the press. Wendy's lawyers decided it was not a valid avenue to pursue. She told me they felt she might lose the sympathy of the court if they tried to discredit so well thought of a man.

People don't like to find out that their judgment has been laughably wrong.

Some little weasel of a journalist reported an amazing interview with Davina Ravenscroft in which she stated that her husband liked little boys, but none of the other papers picked the story up and it died.

Davina Ravenscroft was seen out and about, clear-eyed and happy, obviously drug-free, on the arm of Dag Nitro, the nineteen-year-old lead singer with the top-of-the-charts group, Trixie Treat.

Mandy went back to her study and I took charge of the shop again. Mother began another book.

Archie stuck by Wendy. I had a letter from her in which she said that they had grown very close, ". . . it's taken me a long time, Mark, to relax and just be myself. I wasted so much time speeding down the fast lane, trying to keep up. I tried so hard to be someone else, to change my appearance, my manners, my intrinsic American self instead of just being me. I spent my life trying to keep up and I missed so much. There was never enough time. Now it's all I've got and it brings me closer and closer to my husband. Now I realize how little I valued him, how priceless he is. He has been so supportive and guess what?—I have fallen in love with him. I have stopped worrying about aging and seem now to be able to accept myself as I am, as Archie sees me and values me. I believe now I am in the right place at the right time doing my best. What more is there?

"I want to thank you, dear Mark, for doing all you did for

me, for not condemning, not judging and being very brave.

"One criticism, and I hope you don't take this amiss. Don't waste time. Appreciate that lovely girlfriend of yours. I wasted too much time with Archie and I regret it deeply. And regret is a terrible emotion . . . "

That night I asked Mandy to move in with me. She wound soft arms around me, put her cheek against mine, and accepted.